TRASH TALK

"I finished reading that rubbish you gave me last night. It was poorly written, cartoonish, and perverted. You don't honestly expect people to buy something so stupid, do you?" Portia sneered.

"Mean-spirited witch!" Jackie blasted her. "Didn't your mother teach you that if you can't say something nice, don't say it at all? I want my book back."

"Sorry. I performed a good deed before I left the hotel this morning: I threw it in the wastebasket to spare the next poor schmuck from having to read it."

"You threw my book in the trash?"

Portia shrugged. "It's exactly where it belongs."

Jackie puffed up with so much hot air that she looked like an inflatable sex toy. "Even with my author's discount, that book set me back fifteen bucks! Do I look like I'm made of money? You are *so* going to regret doing that."

"Don't you dare threaten me!"

"It's not a threat." Jackie's eyes narrowed to vengeful slits. "It's a promise."

Turn the page to read critical raves for Maddy Hunter's bestselling *Passport to Peril* mysteries . . .

G'DAY TO DIE

"Pun-filled adventures. . . . Nonstop wisecracks. . . . A satisfying heroine-in-peril twist ending that should please those in search of a good cozy."

—*Publishers Weekly*

HULA DONE IT?

"Hunter's mysteries . . . make for some enjoyable holiday reading."

—*Wisconsin State Journal*

"The attraction of this series is the humor . . . that is somehow sustained over 300 hilarious pages."

—*Ellery Queen Mystery Magazine*

"Hunter's Passport to Peril series is pure fun."

—*Romantic Times Book Reviews*

"Another great whodunit . . . a great example of reading entertainment."

—roundtablereviews.com

PASTA IMPERFECT

"Bitingly funny."

—*Deadly Pleasures*

"Laugh-out-loud funny . . . [with] delightful characters."

—*RT Bookclub Magazine*

TOP O' THE MOURNIN'

"Hilarious and delightful. . . . I can't wait for the next trip!"

—*The Old Book Barn Gazette*

"A delightful cozy that is low on gore but rich in plot and characterizations."

—Thebestreviews.com

Also by Maddy Hunter

G'DAY TO DIE
HULA DONE IT?
PASTA IMPERFECT
TOP O' THE MOURNIN'
ALPINE FOR YOU

Available from Pocket Books

maddy
HUNTER

A *Passport to Peril* mystery

Norway to Hide

POCKET BOOKS
New York   London   Toronto   Sydney

Pocket Books
A Division of Simon & Schuster, Inc.
1230 Avenue of the Americas
New York, NY 10020

This book is a work of fiction. Names, characters, places and incidents either are products of the author's imagination or are used fictitiously. Any resemblance to actual events or locales or persons, living or dead, is entirely coincidental.

First Pocket Books paperback edition November 2007

POCKET and colophon are registered trademarks of Simon & Schuster, Inc.

For information regarding special discounts for bulk purchases, please contact Simon & Schuster Special Sales at 1-800-456-6798 or business@simonandschuster.com.

Design by Min Choi
Art by Jeff Fitz Maurice

Manufactured in the United States of America

10 9 8 7 6 5 4 3 2 1

ISBN-13: 978-1-4165-2380-2
ISBN-10:   1-4165-2380-4

In Memory of Rita Wlodarczyk.
A grand lady and a true original.
You are missed.

—mmh

Acknowledgments

My Scandinavian adventure was another of those proverbial "trips of a lifetime" that was made more memorable by the group of strangers who quickly became family for two weeks. I offer special thanks to the following people:

Tom and Ellen Simmonds, for keeping us constantly entertained and laughing.

Dan and Patti Krueger, for voluntarily hanging out with me so much.

Dave and Jan Bastin, for their friendship and thought-provoking conversations. I'm particularly grateful to Dave for sharing his photographic expertise and for sending me his great travel DVDs. I might never have to take another trip!

Sharon Gasser, Elaine Snyder, and Marge Bourne—the other three members of the Fearsome Foursome—who made the trip so much fun. I could never ask for more delightful traveling companions. I love you guys!

Thanks also to Irene Goodman and Micki Nuding, who don't accompany me on my trips, but who make sure that my adventures end up on the bookstore shelf.

Lastly, thanks to my wonderful fans who have taken the time to contact me through my website to tell me how much they enjoy traveling with Emily, Nana, and the gang. Each one of your emails puts a smile on my face. You know who you are, and you're the best!

CHAPTER 1

"Hi, everyone. I'm Jackie Thum; I live in Binghamton, New York, and I'm a published author!"

We were seated at tables in our Helsinki hotel's overflow dining room, rising one at a time to introduce ourselves to the other tour guests who were part of our seventeen-day Midnight Sun Adventure. An open bar had loosened tongues and encouraged some guests to provide every detail of their lives from the day they'd left the womb, but Jackie hadn't wasted time with that. She'd skipped over her annulled marriage to me and subsequent gender reassignment surgery to focus on the most important thing in her life right now: her new career as a romance novelist.

"Here's my baby." She held up a hardback novel with a bubble gum pink jacket, clutching it with fingernails painted the same color. "It's only been out for two weeks, so I don't imagine any of you have bought it yet, but if you'd like to read it, I packed a few extra copies that I'd be happy to hand out."

The room exploded with applause that elevated Jackie to instantaneous celebrity status. *Oh, God.* I hung my head. She'd be impossible to live with for the next two weeks.

"I've never met a real author," a big-boned lady wearing too much sparkly face powder called out when the applause died down.

Jackie flung her mane of shiny chestnut hair over her shoulder and smiled with the white-toothed poise of a former Miss Texas. "I'll let you in on a little secret: we authors paint our toenails one at a time, just like everyone else."

"What's your book about?" asked a bejeweled woman who'd introduced herself as Portia Van Cleef from Florida.

"That's so sweet of you to ask!" All six feet of Jackie tittered with excitement. "I'll read you the inside cover flap. '*Pretty Little Secrets* is the passionate story of Emma Anderson, an aspiring actress whose lust for fame is only surpassed by her lust for a man whose secrets—' "

"Excuse me, Ms. Thum," our tour director interrupted. Annika Mattsson was a tall, multilingual Swede who reminded me of Olive Oyl with a Dutch boy haircut. "Since dinner is scheduled to be served in a few minutes, perhaps you could arrange to discuss your book later? We still have a few introductions left."

"Oh." Jackie regarded the guests at our table who still hadn't introduced themselves and downsized her smile into a pout. "Sure. I was just trying to accommodate my public." She crushed her novel against her cleavage and sat down next to me, trying not to look crestfallen that her limelight had been dimmed so quickly.

"Who's next?" asked Annika.

I stood up. "*Terve,*" I said, smiling at the thirty faces in the room.

"What'd she say?" asked eighty-nine-year-old Osmond Chelsvig as he fumbled with his double hearing aids.

"Somebody take that drink away from her," demanded Bernice Zwerg in her ex-smoker's voice. "She's tanked."

"*Tehr-veh,*" I repeated phonetically. "That's Finnish for 'hello.' I'm Emily Andrew, and I'm the official escort for the twelve Iowa seniors who've already introduced themselves." They waved enthusiastically as I gestured toward their table.

"Someone actually pays you to escort people who are already on a guided tour?" asked a bearded man with Harry Potter glasses. "What would you call that? Double dipping or overkill?"

"She doesn't do that much," Bernice insisted. "It's a pretty cushy job."

Bernice, with her dowager's hump, wire whisk hair, and crummy attitude, was both a Senior Olympics grand champion and an ever-present thorn in everyone's side.

"I live in Windsor City, Iowa," I continued, "and I'm recently engaged to a former Swiss police inspector who—"

"How many books have you sold so far?" called out a suntanned man who'd introduced himself as Reno O'Brien from sunny Florida.

Jackie sprang to life again. "Publishers are so secretive about those numbers, but I have a call in to my editor, so I'll let you know as soon as she gets back to me. I wouldn't be surprised if she had good news about the *New York Times* bestseller list!"

More clapping. Hooting. A shrill wolf whistle.

She patted my arm apologetically. "Sorry, Emily. What were you saying?"

"I've been planning our wedding for the last few months and I have everything done except for picking up the invitations and addres—"

"How much money did they pay you to write that book?" asked another Floridian with a buzz cut and a voice that started in his boots. "I could write a book if they'd pay me enough."

Jackie wagged a finger at him. "Now, now, it's not polite to ask a person how much money they make."

"Why not?" asked Bernice.

"We're planning a September wedding," I said, raising my voice, "and—"

"*September Bride*," Portia Van Cleef cooed. "Does anyone remember that TV show? It starred Spring Byington."

"That wasn't as good as *Pete and Gladys*," said Lucille Rassmuson, who'd joined Windsor City WeightWatchers five months ago and had already lost a whopping three pounds. "It was like *I Love Lucy* without the Cuban accent."

"You're wrong about the name of that show," Bernice challenged Portia. "It was *December Bride*. I oughta know 'cause my boy watched it every noontime when he came home from school to eat lunch."

A hush fell over the room. All eyes turned to Portia, who skewered Bernice with a look frigid enough to cause frostbite. "Did you just say something?"

"You bet. You got your months mixed up."

Portia's gold bracelets rattled as she adjusted the sleeves of her kaftan with the nonchalance of the very rich. "Does anyone else recall the correct name of the program?"

"I remember it being called *September Bride*," said Reno O'Brien.

"Me, too," said the man in the Harry Potter glasses.

"Does this mean Emily is going to have to switch her wedding date to December?" asked Margi Swanson, who was a part-time nurse and full-time optimist.

"I don't give a rat's ass what the show was called," said the man with the buzz cut. He caught Jackie's eye. "So how much money are we talking about? Fifty grand? A hundred? They pay *you*, right? You don't have to fork out money to print them yourself and sell them out of the trunk of your car?"

"Would you finish readin' what the book's about?" asked my grandmother, whose name tag read Marion

Sippel, Iowa. Nana was four-feet-ten, had an eighth-grade education, and, despite her confusion with double-negatives, was the smartest person I knew. "Sounds like one a them potboilers. My Legion a Mary book club is lookin' for a summer sizzler that's heavy on romance and light on naughty words."

"I'd love to!" said Jackie, popping out of her chair and pausing breathlessly. "But only if it's okay with Emily."

Before Jack Potter had become Jackie Thum, he'd been the ultra-extrovert, the attention magnet, the guy who always made everything about himself. His breast size, hormones, and plumbing might have changed over the last few years, but two things had remained the same—his enormous feet and his sense of self-importance.

It was comforting to know that some things never changed.

"Knock yourself out," I said as I sat down. I mean, what else did I have left to say, other than I was thirty years old, enjoyed a long-standing love affair with Victoria's Secret, and stumbled across dead bodies on every trip I took? I was hoping this tour would be different, but in case it wasn't, I'd brought along sympathy cards. If I was a jinx, I wanted to be remembered as a thoughtful jinx.

Jackie opened her book again, only to be interrupted when a hotel staffer rushed into the room, announcing something to Annika in frantic Finnish.

"The kitchen is about to send out our salads," Annika translated, "so we need to move into the main dining room immediately. We can finish our introductions at our orientation meeting tomorrow morning. Please take your glasses with you. You don't want to waste good wine."

My group was first out the door to claim the good seats by the windows and restrooms, but the remaining guests crowded around Jackie like hogs at the feed trough.

"When are you handing out your books?" asked the man with the Harry Potter glasses. "I'd like to read one."

"Ditto for me," said the large-boned woman with the face powder.

"So would I," said Portia Van Cleef. "In fact, I recommend that your novel be our next Hamlets book-pick-of-the-month so all of us can read it. Good idea, people?"

Every head in the room bobbed enthusiastically.

Portia smiled at Jackie. "Our book club was in existence long before these new TV book clubs, but our monthly selections obviously never received the hype of the media-driven picks. If we'd been given a little airtime, we could have made millionaires out of midlist authors, too."

Jackie splayed her hand across her bulging chest. "Oh, my goodness. That would be so awesome, but I have to warn you, my book reads nothing like *Hamlet*. It's a good old-fashioned romance, with a smattering of suspense, humor, fantasy, horror, paranormal, police procedural, and action-adventure. I wanted to include a little something for everyone." She offered her book to Portia. "Here, you can have the first copy, and after dinner, I'll come down to the lounge and hand out the rest. I just wish I'd brought more!"

"Not to worry," said Portia. "I'm a renowned speed reader, so I should be able to finish this in one sitting and give it to someone else tomorrow."

"*Anteeksi*," said Annika from the doorway. "Excuse me, but you must take your seats in the dining room."

"I'm sitting beside Portia," said Reno O'Brien as he sidled up to her.

"I get her other side," barked the man with the buzz cut.

"Me and Jimbob wanna sit across from her," said the woman with the face powder. Jimbob was a tall skeleton of a man with hunched shoulders and a head like a Q-tip.

Portia smiled benevolently at her devotees. "You're too kind, spoiling me with all this undeserved attention. But I'm not the luminary of the day. Jackie is, so you should be heaping your attention on *her*." She grasped Jackie's hand as if they'd been siblings being reunited after spending decades apart. "Jackie, dear, would you be so kind as to allow all of us to accompany you to the dining room? Then you can tell us all about your wonderful novel."

"This is so flattering. How can I say no?" Jackie wrapped her arms around Portia in a bubbly bear hug and lifted her off the floor.

Kick-ass upper-body strength is one of the perks of being a six-foot transsexual. That, and a sliding vocal range that allows you to sing both soprano and bass in your church choir.

Portia jangled like a human wind chime as Jackie set her back on her feet. "Sorry," Jackie enthused as she plumped Portia's kaftan and straightened the necklaces dripping from her throat. "I must tell you, I *love* your hair. My husband is a master cutter and hair colorist, and he'd absolutely adore what you've done. I bet I even know the color. That combination of corn-silk and platinum—society blond, right?"

Portia blinked her astonishment. "How could you possibly know that?"

"Writer's block. It's a long story." She seized Portia's arm and escorted her out the door, chased by guests who looked determined not to be excluded from the newly formed "in" crowd.

"Jimbob and me still hosey the chairs across from you!" shouted the woman with the iridescent makeup.

"That's Joleen Barnum," said the lady across the table from me. She pushed back her chair and winced as she stood up. "Durned stiff joints. She and Jimbob are the Hamlets' most recent residents. Poor things are having a hard time fitting in, but they won't have to worry about it much longer."

"Nosiree, they sure won't," said the man sitting beside her.

"I'm Lauretta Klick." She poked her finger at her name tag. "And this here's my husband, Curtis."

"Pleasure to meet you," he said, offering me a polite nod.

The Klicks were seventy-something, munchkin-short, and wore outfits that made them look like a set of salt and pepper shakers with bad haircuts.

"I guess we'll be seeing a lot of each other in the next two weeks," I said cheerily.

"Probably not as much as you think," Curtis allowed, exchanging a meaningful look with Lauretta.

I hated meaningful looks. They *really* made me feel out of the loop. I regarded Lauretta's name tag more closely. "You're from Florida, too? Everyone except my group lives in Florida. Do you all know each other?"

"We certainly do," said Lauretta. "We're one big, happy family. Isn't that right, Curtis?"

"That's gospel, Lauretta."

She took her husband's hand and hobbled toward the door. "We have the Hamlets travel agency to thank for making all the arrangements."

"They're full service now," said Curtis. "We wrote out a check and they took care of everything else. The Hamlets really know how to treat their residents. Nothing but first-class service."

"What are the Hamlets, exactly?" I asked as we exited into the main dining room.

The Klicks stopped short. "You've never heard of the Hamlets?" they asked in astonished unison.

Lauretta puffed up like a fresh-baked popover. "It's only the most desirable gated community for retirees in the whole country—the biggest, the friendliest, the best laid out."

"They advertise on the golf network all the time," insisted Curtis. "How could you miss it?"

Lauretta patted his hand. "Curtis, honey, could be they don't get that channel in Iowa."

"Actually, Iowans are notorious for retiring to the Arizona desert," I said. "They'll take sand over salt water any day."

Curtis gaped. "How could anyone not want to live near the ocean?"

"It's a regional thing," I explained. "Iowans live longer when they aren't asked to guess if the tide is coming in or going out."

"That's a cryin' shame," said Lauretta, "because everyone wants to live in the Hamlets. Portia says the waiting list is so long, it could circle the globe twice. Just goes to show you that people know quality when they see it. Once you clear security and pass through the gate, you never have to set foot outside the community again."

"That's gospel," Curtis agreed. "We have our own medical clinics, shops, banks, churches—"

"—funeral homes," said Lauretta. "Two brand-new ones with flower stands suspended from the ceiling and viewing rooms in the round. Feels like you've stepped inside the starship *Enterprise*."

"We publish a newspaper that's better than the *New York Times,* and it's delivered to your mailbox for pennies on the dollar," continued Curtis. "We've got our own internal governing body, twelve executive golf courses, daily sports activities and competitions—"

"—dancing competitions, track and field events, competitive eating, pickle ball, golf cart races," Lauretta recited breathlessly. "Plus we have lots of special-interest groups: bridge club, gin rummy club, Scrabble club, Boggle club. You name it, we've got it. I bet you can't guess what residents call our community."

Only one term came to mind. "Summer camp?"

"Wrong!" hooted Curtis. "They call it utopia, because it's the closest thing to being in heaven."

"Don't let him fool you," Lauretta confided. "It *is* heaven. If I'd known retirement was going to be so much fun, I'd have skipped all those decades after high school graduation and gone directly to old age."

I smiled at their enthusiasm. "Your first day in Finland, and it sounds as if you're anxious to head home already."

The Klicks exchanged another meaningful look. "Oh, we won't be going back," Lauretta said matter-of-factly.

"Are you extending your tour?" I asked. "My group thought about the post-tour trip to St. Petersburg, but they were worried about their prescriptions running out before they got home. They probably don't have a Pills Etcetera in Russia."

"What Lauretta means to say is that we won't be going back at all," said Curtis. "No one will."

I regarded them in confusion. "Excuse me?"

"I don't want to alarm you, dear," said Lauretta, "but in a few short days, we'll all be dead."

CHAPTER 2

"*What?*"

"See there, Lauretta? You've gone and scared the girl." Curtis gave me a sympathetic look. "She's a tad more melodramatic than she used to be. Comes from all those years of watching Dan Rather on the evening news. What she means to say is, in a few days, life as we know it will be very different."

"Amen," said Lauretta.

"It's nothing to worry about," Curtis soothed. "We'll probably hear a violent clap of thunder and see a brilliant light in the sky."

"Earthquakes, tidal waves. Maybe a few flash fires," Lauretta added. "It should be over fairly quickly."

I glanced nervously between them. *Uff-da.* Were they saying what I thought they were saying? "Are you telling me we're about to experience a catastrophic climatic event?"

"The signs are all there," said Curtis.

"All a body's gotta do is read them," Lauretta agreed. "It's gonna be cataclysmic. Too bad about your wedding, dear, but think how much you'll save on postage by not having to mail out all those invitations."

"There she goes again," said Curtis.

"Who *are* you guys?" I demanded. "Meteorologists?"

"Heck, no," Curtis said, laughing. "We're Protestants."

Annika clapped her hands, motioning us to take our seats. "Come, come. The salad is already served."

She directed the Klicks to chairs at the end of Jackie and Portia's table and me to an empty spot opposite two septuagenarians who'd introduced themselves as April and June Peabody. I smiled at the platinum-haired sisters with their bronze complexions and expensive silk shells—not because a prediction of global disaster made me happy but because section thirteen of my escort's manual states that the truly professional tour escort will never allow personal crises to interfere with her duties as an ambassador of goodwill and cheer.

I ignored the swill of acid in my stomach as I sat down. Who'd written this stupid escort's manual anyway?

"Can you believe it's eight o'clock at night?" I asked, noting the sunshine that still washed the upper stories of the stone buildings across the street. "Back home it'd be getting pretty dusky by now, but look how light it is outside. Isn't that amazing?"

"Why do you suppose that is?" asked June.

"Daylight savings time," said April. "It's a big deal over here."

Hmm. Just because they were unaware that the sun didn't dip below the horizon in various parts of Scandinavia at this time of year didn't mean they weren't up to speed with current events. "By any chance, have either of you heard any obscure reports on the cable news networks about bad weather that might be headed our way?"

"We don't get cable," said June.

"Waste of Daddy's money," said April. "He'd turn over in his grave if he thought we were squandering his fortune to watch reruns of *Family Feud* on the Game Show Network." She removed her watch with the diamond wristband and set it beside her salad plate.

"He'd approve of the lovely home we bought in the Hamlets," June conceded, "but Daddy always did like real estate. At the time he died, he owned homes in each of the forty-eight contiguous states." She realigned her silverware with Martha Stewart precision. "He never forgave himself for flubbing up the Alaska and Hawaii deals. He so wanted to own fifty."

"Forty-eight houses? He sure put the average snowbird to shame. Did you actually live in all of them?"

"They weren't private homes," April explained as she poured dressing over her salad. "They were family-run businesses. June just likes to impress people."

"They were homes," argued June, grabbing her fork.

"What kind of business did your father run?"

"He was in the service industry," said June.

"He was an undertaker," said April. "He owned a slew of mortuaries."

"Funeral homes," June corrected emphatically. "Daddy never called them 'mortuaries.' He said that was way too impersonal. 'Mortuary' doesn't evoke the warm fuzzy feeling that 'home' or 'parlor' evoke. Daddy knew all the right angles about how to market a service that everyone was going to need but would rather ignore."

April shook her head and looked heavenward. "Are you ready?" she sniped, glancing at June.

"Ready," said June, at which point they hunched over their plates, forks in hand, eyes riveted on their salad greens.

April pressed a pin on her watch. "Go!" she yelled.

Salad dressing flew as they shoveled endive and romaine into their mouths like crazed rabbits. *What the?*—Russian dressing dripped down April's chin. Chicory disappeared inside June's mouth like a twig through a wood chipper. They forked down cherry tomatoes and green peppers, and when April's plate was empty, she hit another pin on her watch.

"Oi whun," she said around a mouthful of iceberg lettuce.

I looked at June for a translation.

"She said, she won. But I would have smoked her if my cherry tomato had been smaller."

I smiled stiffly as I regarded the salad dressing

splattered across their dry-clean-only silk shells. "Let me guess. Competitive eating group?"

April swallowed triumphantly. "What gave it away?"

"Do you get the Weather Channel in Switzerland?" I asked Etienne two hours later.

"Not on my television, *bella*. I can only pick up local stations. Why? Are you having bad weather in Helsinki?"

"The weather's beautiful right now. Eighty-five and sunny, and that's pretty good considering it's ten o'clock at night." I pulled back the curtain of my hotel room window to peek at the still bright sky. "I was wondering about a few days from now. Have you heard news reports about severe thunderstorms headed our way?"

"I'm afraid our Lucerne stations aren't overly concerned about rain showers in Finland."

"How about a catastrophic meteor strike that could end life as we know it? Any rumors about that?" The phone line seemed to go dead. "Etienne?"

I heard a long-suffering sigh. "Who are the other people on your tour, Emily? Astronomers?"

"Protestants, but they really sound as if they know what they're talking about."

The door rattled open and Jackie exploded into the room, flinging herself onto the bed with an anguished groan. "Why me?" she whined into her pillow. "I'm not a bad person. I like animals and small children. *Why* is this happening to me? It's not fair. I haven't even seen my name on the bestseller list yet." She dissolved into the kind of loud, slobbery tears that can ruin even the most reliable waterproof mascara.

Uh-oh. Had one of the guests said something mean to her at dinner? "Etienne, can I call you back tomorrow? I have a situation here."

"So I hear. My best to your ex-husband. Tell her I preordered her book online and it arrived yesterday, so I'm anxious to dive in. Love you."

I rang off and joined Jackie on the bed, where I massaged her back sympathetically. "Hey, kiddo, what's wrong?" The only other time I'd seen Jack cry this hard was at a Metropolitan Museum exhibition of millinery worn by Queen Elizabeth II during her reign. It was such an assault to his fashion sense that he needed counseling afterward to help him deal with debilitating nightmares. "You want to talk about it?"

"Noooo," she blubbered. "What's to talk about? The world's about to end and I'm in freaking Finland with no idea if my book even made it onto BookScan!"

"Ah-ha. You've been talking to the Klicks."

"I haven't said boo to the Klicks. They did all the talking." She rolled onto her side, eye shadow and blush smeared across her face like fingerpaints. "Shouldn't someone have told us the end is here? Would it have been so difficult for the major networks to run a segment on *20/20* or *60 Minutes*? Those reporters love disaster stories. But nooo. The biggest disaster of all time, and what's the media talking about? Some Washington politician boinking a coed half his age. Like that's news."

"Etienne says he hasn't heard any warnings about catastrophic weather."

Confusion filled her eyes. "Weather? Hel-looo? I'm not talking about weather; I'm talking about Judgment Day. The Second Coming. Apocalypse now. The Rapture. It's here, Emily. We're all going to die!" She threw her arms around me, burying her head in my lap and sobbing. "This is the worst day of my life! I'll never see my book go back to press for a second printing. I'll never be nominated for a book award. I'll never be asked to write the screen adaption for the miniseries. It's so unfair! Why me? Why now?"

I patted her head, as if she were a favorite puppy. "C'mon, Jack, people have been making predictions about the end of the world since time began. Did you stop to think the Klicks might be wrong?"

"People who are *this* happy about an upcoming event are never wrong. They even bought an expensive video camera with all sorts of special features to record the highlights."

"They're planning to film the end of the world?"

"Why do you think they're in Scandinavia? They want to take advantage of the twenty-four-hour sunlight so they won't have to use their infrared function. The instruction manual is in Chinese, so they don't have a clue how to use it." This prompted a fresh onslaught of tears. "I'm so miserable, Emily. I just want to die. And the thing is, *I won't have long to wait!*"

When Jackie was distraught, there was only one way to snap her out of it. "Your hair looks so great,"

I enthused as I twirled a section around my finger. "Killer shine. What's that from? Salon product or hormones?"

"Can the flattery," she wailed. "It won't work this time."

Uh-oh. This was like trying to revive a heart attack victim without defibrillator paddles. The situation was more serious than I thought, which meant I needed to initiate Plan B.

"Listen, Jack, I went to Mass last Sunday, and no one said a thing about the end of the world. Now, I ask you: if Father Todd thought Judgment Day was going to arrive before the new fall TV lineup, don't you think he might have mentioned it in his homily? Or at least posted a few lines in the weekly bulletin?"

"How should I know? I'm not Catholic; I'm a lapsed Episcopalian." She clutched my arm. "Oh, God, Emily, do you know what that means?"

"You don't have access to a Sunday bulletin?"

"It means when you and Mrs. S. are being beamed up to the penthouse on the top floor, I'll be on the express elevator to sub-level ten with all the rest of the lapsed folk. Take a good look at my hair, because in a few days, it'll all be singed off!" She let out a tearful howl that could have won her the lead role in a bad werewolf flick.

So much for Plan B.

I grabbed a tissue off the nightstand and forced it into her hand. "Jack, if you keep crying like this, your eyes are going to swell shut and you won't be able to apply eye liner tomorrow."

Her head popped up with jack-in-the-box quickness. "Really?"

"Really."

"What about mascara?"

"You can forget that, too."

"But I have a new color called Sugar Plum that I want to try out. It's full of all these cute little silver sparkles." Sighing dramatically, she blew her nose into the tissue and unwrapped herself from around me. "Could I have another tissue, please?"

I handed her the whole packet. After more nose blowing, she sat up. "Are you telling me the truth about you Catholics not having any recent insider information about . . . you know . . . the end?"

I raised my hand as if I were in a witness box. "I'm telling you the truth."

"So you think the Klicks could be wrong?" she asked hopefully.

"I think predictions like that are based on individual interpretation, and interpretations can vary. So if you were to ask me, I'd say there's a huge possibility that their timing is off."

"Really?" She wrapped her arms around me again and squeezed, practically collapsing my lungs. "I'm *so* glad to hear you say that! There's no one I trust more than you, Emily, so if you say it's not going to happen, it simply won't happen! I have your word on it, right?"

"You bet." If I was wrong, what could she do? Sue me?

"Thank God that's resolved. I have so many other

issues screaming for my attention right now that I don't have time to work in an apocalypse." She checked her watch. "Let's see, it's seven hours earlier in New York, which would make it—what? Three in the afternoon? Perfect." She dug her mobile phone out of her purse and punched in a string of numbers. "Wait'll you hear all the fun stuff that happened at dinner, Emily. Those Hamlets people are a stitch. Who'd you sit with?"

"Competitive eaters. They finished their entrees in a two-minute dead heat and spent the rest of the meal accusing each other of cheating. On the upside, they're both watching their calories, so I got their desserts. If they gain another ounce, they'll get bumped up to a higher weight class with Dick 'The Disposal' Duffy, and no one has ever beaten Dick."

Jackie broke into a wide grin as her party came on the line. "Hello, Mona? This is Jackie Thum calling from Helsinki. How are things at Hightower Books? Poor dear. I know you're overworked. So, can you tell me how many books I've sold today? Uh-huh. Well, people keep asking, 'How's the book selling?' so I thought—" She paused. "You gave me my own publicist. Shouldn't you give me my own data entry person, so I can report accurate sales numbers whenever someone asks? I thought that would be one of the perks of working with an A-list publisher like Hightower."

Thinking this conversation could take a while, I walked over to my suitcase and pulled out the wedding brochures I'd brought along for show and tell.

"Mona, do you know how stupid I sound when I tell people I don't know how many books I've sold?

Authors have a right to know these things. What? Of course I'll consult my royalty statement . . . when it arrives six months from now! What am I supposed to do in the meantime? Can you at least let me access your sales computer so I can find the numbers for myself? I brought my laptop with me."

I sat down opposite Jack, feeling all tingly as I flipped through the glossy pages in my wedding packet. This wedding was going to be so spectacular.

"All right, you have my number. Talk to the powers that be and get back to me. Now, tell me the good news. How many bestseller lists am I on?"

Her face stiffened as if it had been spray starched.

"Really? I don't want to tell you your business, Mona, but it might *help* if you knew how many freaking books I've sold so you can pass the word on to the *New York Times* and *USA Today*. Excuse me for a moment, would you?"

She contorted her mouth into a silent scream and beat the phone against the bedcovers before returning it to her ear. "Last item of business. There's a retirement community called the Hamlets on the Gulf coast of Florida, and I've been invited by the board president to do a book signing next month. She'd like to order five thousand books, so I'd appreciate it if you could start the ball rolling on your end. Yes, five thousand books, and she assures me she'll sell every last one. I just met her and believe me, she's a force to be reckoned with. Let me give you the name and number of the bookstore you need to contact to coordinate everything."

"Five thousand books?" I marveled when she hung up. "Wow, that should land you on some sort of list."

"It certainly should, which leads me to a prediction of my own. Stephen King may be the king of horror, but Jackie Thum is about to become the queen of romance." She snapped her fingers. "Damn. I forgot to ask what kind of advertising they're doing in the print media. Hightower is being extremely stingy with their advertising budget, Emily. Between you and me, I've noticed publishers aren't really interested in splashing your photo all over the place unless you're blond and morbidly anorexic." Catching a reflection of herself in the dresser mirror, she stared critically. "What do you think I'd look like as a blond?"

Oh, God. "Hey, I have some good news for you. Etienne ordered your book and he says he's dying to jump into it."

"That was so nice of him!" She clapped her hands in a patty-cake gesture. "Emily, would you mind asking him to write a review on Amazon when he finishes? Just a line or two saying how much he enjoyed it."

"I can ask him, but what if he says he's not into writing reviews?"

"Forget the review, just tell him to give me five stars. That's all that matters anyway."

I held up an eight-by-ten photo. "What do you think?"

"Ohhhh." She cupped her hands over her mouth, her eyes growing dewy. "Your wedding gown?"

"Yup. The latest offering by Windsor City's very own wedding dress designer. He opened an elegant little shop next to Skaartvedt's Roto-Rooter and Used Books on Main Street, and he designs and custom tailors all the gowns himself at rock-bottom prices. He's giving Bunny's Bridal Palace a real run for its money." I handed her the photo and was touched when she blinked away more tears.

"It's you, Emily. Strapless is so in. The beading is absolutely luscious. And look at that train. How long is it?"

"Twelve feet."

"Twelve feet. Imagine." She splayed her hand on her chest and sighed. "I didn't have a train on my gown, but it was every girl's dream: layer upon layer of pink organza. I looked like a controlled explosion in a cotton candy factory." She handed the photo back and asked coyly, "Is there something you'd like to ask me, Emily?"

"Yeah. I'm going to wear my hair up, so what do you think will look better—drop pearls or studs?"

She sniffed delicately. "Wrong question. Try again."

I flashed another eight-by-ten. "This is the restaurant where we're having the reception. Ashgrove. It's on the outskirts of town, brand new and very posh. Nana says it's one of those places where they won't let you inside unless you're wearing a necktie and your best control-top panty hose. So the question is, which do you think guests would prefer—the prime rib or the filet mignon?"

"What about vegetarians?"

"Iowa exports all its vegetarians to California or New York, so we basically don't have any."

"Hel-loo? *I'm* a vegetarian."

"Are you still doing that?"

She fluttered her hand. "Intermittently."

"So what do you think?"

"Still not the right question."

I narrowed my gaze. "How about you *tell* me the right question."

"You have to guess."

"NO!"

She fisted her hands on her hips and glowered. "I don't remember your being this clueless when we were married, Emily. I'm waiting for you to ask me to be your matron of honor!"

"You are?" *Uh-oh.* "Um . . . there's a good reason why I haven't asked you, Jack."

"I bet."

Where were the earthquakes and flash fires when you really needed them? "I—uh, I already have a matron of honor. Maid of honor, actually."

She clutched her chest as if the front closure on her Miracle bra had popped open and her breasts were in gravitational free fall. "You what?" she choked. "Go ahead. Twist the dagger a little deeper into my heart, why don't you? I thought I was your best friend. Aren't brides supposed to ask their best friends to stand up for them?"

"They are," I hedged, treading lightly, "and you mean a lot to me, Jack, but Sharon and I have history."

"We have history."

"Yeah, but Sharon and I go all the way back to preschool. We memorized the alphabet together. We rode tricycles together. We acted in our first high school play together."

"We had *sex* together!"

"That doesn't count. We were married."

"Sex trumps the alphabet and tricycles. Ask anyone."

"It doesn't. You can't ask me to boot Sharon out of my wedding so you can take her place! That would be too tacky for words. Besides, she already has her dress."

"I could wear her dress."

"It's a size two."

"I could stop eating. I could do it, Emily. It would only be for a few months. Pleeease?"

I hung my head in frustration. "Jack, it's going to be a very small wedding. A maid of honor and no bridesmaids."

She pretended fascination with her tissue package before sticking her bottom lip out in a dejected pout. "So what color is Sharon's dress?"

"Black. Since the Swiss are partial to black, we thought we'd do a black-and-white wedding."

Her head shot up. "Black? I can't wear black. It turns my skin the most hideous shade of green." Pout sliding into a smile, she stood up and straightened her miniskirt. "Aren't you lucky you found someone to stand in for me? I would have looked like the Grinch in all your wedding photos. Would you look at the time? Eh! I've gotta run."

She rushed to the luggage stand by the window. "Portia and her friends are probably waiting for me in the lobby. They're the most enthusiastic people, Emily. They're all fighting over who gets to host me when I fly down for my book signing. I've already decided that when Tom and I retire, we're moving to the Hamlets. Everyone is so happy. Must be all that Florida sunshine. Or maybe all the pulp in the fresh-squeezed orange juice. That's gotta keep everyone regular."

She unzipped her suitcase and pondered the contents. "I might need help carrying these things to the lobby. Would the person who didn't ask me to be the matron of honor at her wedding like to volunteer?"

Might as well get used to it now. I was never going to live this down. "Whatever!" I dragged my jet-lagged body across the room, doing a double take when I looked inside her suitcase. "This is what you call a few extra copies?"

She gnawed her lip self-consciously. "Okay, I might have gotten a little carried away."

"A little carried away? Five books are a few extra copies. Six books, tops. How many have you crammed in here?"

"Seventy-five?"

"Were you planning to hand them out on street corners?"

She grabbed my arm in excitement. "Emily! That's a great idea!"

I rolled my eyes before regarding her and her suitcase with sudden suspicion. "Where are your clothes?"

"Uhh, I know what I can do." She zipped her suitcase back up and muscled it to the floor. "I'll wheel the books down. That way I won't have to bother you."

"Did you pack your clothes in your carry-on luggage?"

"Don't wait up for me," she advised as she maneuvered her pullman toward the door. "The Hamlets folks might want autographs and a short bio."

Why was I getting such a bad feeling about this?

Chasing behind her, I jerked open the closet door. "Hold it, Jack! The only clothes hanging up in here are mine. Where's your leather bustier? Your white dress with the shoulder flounces? Your animal-print jeans?"

She turned slowly, her gaze withering. "I remember this attitude of yours from when we were married. You can be so . . . so—"

"You didn't bring any clothes, did you?"

"I didn't have to—you always pack enough to dress half of Africa. I thought we could share."

"Jack!"

"Isn't that what best friends do?"

"Not on trips abroad!"

"What else could I do? I had to pack my books! Global marketing, Emily. If I don't hand-sell my book, who's going to? I've never even heard from the publicist Hightower assigned me. I had to make a choice between clothing or career, and I chose career. And if you were in my shoes, I bet you'd make the same choice."

I looked down at her shoes, my eyes widening with astonishment. "Are those Jimmy Choos?"

"Catalog knockoffs. Aren't they adorable? They had your size, Emily. You want to borrow my catalog?"

I slid the closet door shut. "Did you at least bring your own underwear?"

"Duh? Your bras were too snug for me when I was a guy. Can you imagine how impossible they'd be now that I have breasts?"

She gave me a little finger wave and headed out the door. I retrieved a sympathy card from my travel documents and addressed the envelope to Jackie's husband in New York. I wanted to remain a step ahead of the game, because if I found too many split seams, torn hems, or popped buttons in my brand-new and perfectly color-coordinated wardrobe, somebody on this trip *was* going to die.

And I knew who it would be.

CHAPTER 3

"Here's the final tally," Osmond Chelsvig announced the next morning, reading from his spiral notepad. "I got four votes saying it looks like the organ pipes at Holy Redeemer Church."

At the conclusion of our three-hour city tour, Annika had dropped us off at the Kauppatori Market Square—a bustling fish and vegetable market set up on the cobbled stones of the inner harbor, with a view of massive government buildings painted the most unlikely shades of sky blue and lemon sorbet. Dining was alfresco, so my group had commandeered several umbrellaed tables and pushed them together, hoping to shield themselves from UV rays, and their prospective lunches from scavenging seagulls.

"I got four more saying it looks like the organ pipes at Good Shepherd Lutheran."

We'd visited Sibelius Park earlier, awed by the twenty-four-ton sculpture built in honor of Finland's most famous classical composer, Jean Sibelius. It was a massive abstraction of welded steel and vertical pipes and had prompted serious discussion about what other images it brought to mind.

"What song did Annika say this Sibelius fella wrote?" Bernice called out.

"It isn't a song," Tilly Hovick informed her, sounding like the anthropology professor she'd once been. "It's a symphonic poem: *Finlandia*."

"Never heard of it," said Bernice. "Which chart is it on? Country or pop?"

"I got two votes saying it looks like the tail pipes Clarence Peavey chained together and stuck out in his cabbage patch to scare the crows."

In the harbor, a tour boat pulled away from the quay, filling the air with diesel fumes that completely overpowered the smell of fresh fish, salt air, and bodies baking in the ninety-three-degree heat. The unexpected spike in the temperature was unbearable. Even the cobblestones were steaming.

"One person says it looks like a phone booth that got run through a shredder, and the final vote says, 'Who cares what it looks like? It's the dumbest-looking thing I've ever seen.'" Osmond repocketed his notepad. "That'd be Bernice."

"How do you know it's me?" Bernice objected. "How do you know it wasn't George? Or Marion?"

"I recognized your handwriting."

"Can I have your attention?" I asked, standing

up so everyone could see me. "I don't think any of us expected it to be this hot, so be sure to pick up extra bottles of water and stay hydrated. After lunch, you might like to take a boat tour of the harbor. That would cool you off. Or you could sit under a shady tree and listen to a concert in Esplanade park." I pointed west. "Just beyond the tram tracks. Or you could shop in the stores along the boulevard, which might be air-conditioned. I've marked on your maps where the hotel is, so you shouldn't have any problem finding it. Any questions?"

Alice Tjarks raised her hand. "Is a waitress going to come to the table, or is this self-serve?"

"Self-serve all the way," I said. "Wander around the food stalls, grab yourself some reindeer sausage or bear pâté, and bring it back here to eat."

Twelve sets of eyes regarded me uncomfortably.

"What?" I teased. "Not tempted by the bear pâté? How about grilled liver with mashed potatoes and bacon? I hear that's a Finnish specialty: reindeer liver, elk liver. Finns love red meat."

Twelve sets of feet remained eerily still, which prompted a horrible thought. "You haven't gone vegetarian on me, have you? You don't want to do that. Not in Finland. You'll be heading down the path to starvation."

"If we leave, someone might take our tables," Dick Teig finally spoke up.

Grunts of assent. Heads bobbing.

"C'mon, guys, this isn't a problem," I cried. "Six of you can save chairs while the other six get their food, then you can switch. You do it every week for the lunch buffet at the casino."

More uncomfortable looks. Discreet scratching. No stampeding.

"What!"

"That'll give the six people who get their food first an unfair advantage," complained Dick Stolee.

"They can scarf down their meals and be out of here before any of us," said Lucille Rassmuson. "It's not fair to give some such a big head start."

"Smells like favoritism to me," said Grace Stolee.

I stared at them in exasperation. "You can't promise to wait for each other?"

"We could all promise," Helen Teig fussed, "but a lot of good it would do." She arched a crookedly drawn eyebrow. "If you know what I mean."

All eyes riveted on Bernice.

Bernice blew everyone off with a flick of her hand. "If you keep ragging on me like this, I'm going to report you to Mr. Erickson and have you all banned from the next trip. I can do it, too. Erickson and I have gotten pret-ty chummy since his wife left him. He's like putty in my hands, so you better be nice to me." She flashed a smug smile. "Bernice and the bank president. Sounds like a movie starring Sandra Dee, doesn't it?"

"That's really low of you to take advantage of a man with cataracts," Dick Teig scolded.

"If you're putting out for him, I hope you're taking precautions," advised Margi. "Olle Erickson certainly doesn't want to father any unplanned children at his age."

Alice raised her hand. "Excuse me, Emily, but how are we going to decide who gets their food first?"

"Secret ballot," said Osmond. "We always decide things by secret ballot."

"How is it secret if you tell everyone how we voted?" Bernice sniped. "We need a show of hands. How many of you good Christian people are willing to remain in this heavenly shade and save seats while the rest of us risk heat exhaustion and potential death to find sausages made out of Donder and Blitzen?"

No one moved except George Farkas, Nana's one-legged boyfriend, who inched his hand shyly into the air.

Nana grabbed his sleeve and yanked it down. "Don't pay him no mind. He was havin' a muscle spasm."

"Listen here, Marion," Osmond cautioned, "tampering with a fella's vote is a federal offense."

I groaned inwardly. By the time they decided who would go and who would stay, their tongues would be dragging on the ground from dehydration and I'd be spending the rest of the day in the local emergency room instead of exploring Finland's most famous clothing store.

"George has volunteered to save our chairs," announced Bernice. "Anyone want to stay behind with him?"

"I didn't volunteer," protested George. "I only wanted to ask—"

"How many people say George volunteered?" asked Osmond.

Oh, for Pete's sake. "Leave!" I shooed them away. "All of you! Go! Get your food. I'll save your chairs."

The usual stampede ensued, complete with bumping, elbowing, and cutting in front of each other. I shook my head as they disappeared into the crowd. You had to hand it to them. They really knew how to make a dignified exit.

Jackie caught up to me as I tipped chairs forward against our tables to indicate the area was taken. She was wearing her own miniskirt and stilettoes, but she'd sweet-talked me out of my favorite pink V-neck cashmere sweater, so she was looking like Dolly Parton in the heat.

"Are you allowed to save seats in Finland?" she asked as she pressed a tall Styrofoam cup to her cheek.

"I've just refereed the election from hell, so don't mess with my head," I warned. "Seat saving is universal."

"Are you sure?"

"Of course I'm sure. Ask Tilly. It's probably a cultural thing."

After setting one of the chairs aright, she sat down beneath the umbrella and wagged a plastic spoon at me. "You better watch out, Emily. You could be breaking some obscure Finnish law that prohibits the rearrangement of ugly patio furniture in public fish markets or something."

"Where do you come up with this stuff?" I dug my Finnish/English dictionary out of my shoulder bag and scrutinized the "Useful Phrases" section. "Here you go. Remember this phrase for future reference: *Olen kasvissyoja.*"

"Get out! Is that how you say 'These seats are taken'?"

"No, it's how you say 'I'm a vegetarian.' I'm not finding any useful phrases about how to tell people you're saving seats." I eyed her Styrofoam cup. "What'd you buy?"

She tilted the cup toward me so I could see its creamy pink contents. "Some kind of fruit smoothie. It was either this or a grilled concoction made of Rudolph's internal organs. Like that was going to happen." She shoved a spoonful into her mouth before pressing the cup to her cheek once again. "I should have bought a cold drink, but the line was really long and I needed shade. Are you as hot as I am?" She blew a puff of air up into her face. "I feel like I'm going to internally combust."

She looked like it, too. "I don't want to alarm you, Jack, but your chest and throat are covered with bright red splotches. Has that ever happened before?"

She looked down at her chest, panic setting in immediately. "Oh, God, do you think it's menopause?"

"At thirty-one? Who goes through menopause at thirty-one?"

"It happens. Believe me, I'm extremely well informed about all the crappy things that are going to happen to us when we go through 'the change.'"

"Well, you're one up on me."

She fanned her face with both hands. "I've read all the brochures, Emily. It's definitely menopause. I'm having my first hot flash."

I studied the splotches more intently. "Maybe it's

an allergic reaction, or a heat rash. Cashmere probably wasn't your best choice with the temperature at nine hundred degrees."

"But the color is so luscious." She smoothed her fingers over the fabric, sniffing daintily. "I'm so bummed. Menopause wasn't supposed to happen for another twenty years. I envisioned the two of us battling night sweats, weight gain, and osteoporosis at the same time, like sorority sisters. I can't go through this alone. What am I going to do?"

"Buy yourself a cold drink. Maybe you're dehydrated."

"You *can't* be suggesting that I stand in that insanely long beverage line in the scorching sun. I'll melt, Emily. I will literally—melt."

Considering how miserable she looked, she probably wasn't exaggerating. "Okay, tell you what. When the gang comes back, I'll brave the UV rays and buy a drink for you."

"That's so sweet!" She lowered her voice to a breathless basso. "But I'll be suffering kidney failure by then. Can you go now?"

"Can't, I'm saving seats."

"I'll save the seats."

"Oh, sure. How many times did I have to sit elsewhere in a movie theater because you gave up my seat when I went to the ladies' room?"

"Emily, will you just *go*? I'm dying! I'll save the freaking seats. It's not rocket science."

I gave her a hard look. "What's your plan if someone gives you trouble?"

"I'll stand up!"

That could work. She was seven feet tall in her stilettoes.

I pushed through the crowd and located the Coca-Cola vendor between stalls of fresh green beans and plump red tomatoes. There were at least a dozen people ahead of me, so I became a sponge as I waited, listening to exchanges in incomprehensible foreign tongues and observing the spectacular good looks of the market goers. Based on my brief observation, I concluded that your typical Helsinkian was tall, blond, blue-eyed, perfectly proportioned, and jaw-droppingly gorgeous. If I were to guess Finland's largest export, I'd have to say cellulite.

"Look who I've found," said a voice from behind me. "It's the girl with the cushy job. Emily Andrew, right?"

I turned around, smiling at the man with the beard and Harry Potter glasses. "You have a good memory."

"August Manning." He shook my hand. "My friends call me Gus to my face. Who knows what they call me behind my back."

He had a head full of thick salt-and-pepper hair and a calmness in his eyes that invited strangers to divulge their most intimate secrets. His beard was scruffy, his stomach paunchy, and his trousers baggy, but August Manning seemed not to notice or care. "Quite a setup they have here," he said as he looked around. "We should have something like this in the Hamlets. We could do it early every Saturday morning in the town square. Vendors selling farm fresh fruits and vegetables. The only problem would be getting them through the main gate. They'd need security clearance, and that could be a major hassle."

"Is the whole complex enclosed?"

"Damn right. We have our own zip code and seventy-five thousand of the happiest retirees on the Gulf Coast. And the only way you're getting through those gates is with a fingerprint ID. The builders spared no expense on security measures."

"You have seventy-five thousand residents? Must be a pretty big fence."

"You got that right. It's fifteen feet high and made of white marble imported from Italy. We call it the Pearly Gates."

Iowans weren't big on gates, except on hog farms. "So . . . what are you trying to keep out?"

He blinked a couple of times as if he'd heard me incorrectly. "I'm sorry, say again?"

I spoke more slowly. "What are you trying to keep out?"

"Would you believe no one has ever asked me that before? Huh. I thought it was fairly obvious." He looked beyond me and motioned enthusiastically. "Vern! Reno! Get over here. Got a question for you."

I recognized both men from the Meet and Greet. Reno O'Brien was the suntanned Floridian who'd wanted to know the exact number of books Jackie had sold in the last two weeks. He was a snappy dresser who looked as if he spent half his time in the gym and the other half at an expensive spa being oiled, massaged, and exfoliated. He walked like John Travolta in

Saturday Night Fever and appeared to have twice as much ego. His friends probably called him Slick.

Gus greeted him with a controlled high five. "I assume you remember Emily from the Meet and Greet?"

Reno winked flirtatiously. "I can't imagine anyone forgetting Emily. She's the best-looking thing on this trip. Too bad she's taken." He tapped his name tag. "Reno O'Brien, in case you didn't catch the name last night."

"And this is Vern Grundy," said Gus, thwacking the gut of the man with the buzz cut who'd grilled Jackie about how much money she made. "The Hamlets' only three-star general." Vern looked to be seventy-something and coping with two bad knees that added a slight limp to his gait. He was fleshy without being fat, had no smile lines on his face, and looked as if his idea of a great night out would be jumping into his Hummer and invading a neighboring state.

"Pleased to meet you, ma'am." Vern nodded politely. "What's your question, Manning?"

"Emily here has a question. What are we trying to keep out of the Hamlets?"

"Solicitors," barked Vern. "We're showing those jeezers they can't knock on Hamlet doors trying to peddle everything from politics to religion. No Avon lady. No petition-toting environmental activists. No doe-eyed Girl Scouts sending us into cardiac arrest with their thin mint cookies."

Wait a minute. I'd been a Girl Scout. "You're not *required* to buy thin mints," I spoke up. "They have some nice low-fat selections now."

"Blah." He waved off the suggestion. "I'd rather eat my wallet."

"It's a wonderful benefit, not having to open your door to strangers," Gus asserted. "Living in a gated community is like having virus protection for your computer. It filters out potentially destructive unknowns and keeps your computer happy, healthy, and connected to only recognized web networks. You have anything to add, Reno?"

"Yeah, this is all news to me. I thought the wall was there to keep out alligators."

"Damn fool," grumbled Vern.

"Hey, no one's been eaten. I thought it was working pretty well." Reno gave me another playful wink. "Can I buy you a drink, Emily? Coke? Beer? If you're waiting for these two misers to offer, you'll have a long wait. They're still carrying the first dollars they ever earned."

I'd have to introduce them to the Dicks. They'd have a lot in common. "Thanks, but I need to grab a Coke for Jackie and get back to her before she dies from heat stroke. She was making funeral arrangements when I left her."

"She's really something," said Gus as we moved up in line. "We appreciated her handing out copies of her novel last night. I don't usually read commercial fiction, and I never read romance, but I skimmed the first page and was sucked in by page two. I read half the book before I fell asleep. It's a real page-turner."

"I read a few pages, too," said Reno. "She's a dynamite storyteller. I was right there in the Big Apple, sipping that half-caf decaf caramel macchiato extra hot and suffering through those grueling Broadway rehearsals. But what's with our heroine? Sharing an apartment for two years and not knowing her room-mate bats for the other team? Get real."

I stared at Reno. Emma Anderson had a gay room-mate? Huh, what a coincidence.

"Remember," said Gus, "Emma's from the Midwest, so she's probably more naive than dense. Her naivete is part of her charm. Where are you in the story?"

"Her roommate just ran off with another actor, so Emma's scrambling to find a replacement."

"I think she's gonna ask the drop-dead-gorgeous detective to move in with her," said Vern, "even though he doesn't know he's a detective. Hell, he might not even know he's drop-dead gorgeous."

"Impaired vision?" I asked.

"Amnesia."

What?

"I couldn't buy the grandfather's accident," Reno admitted. "Too over the top. Real people don't die like that."

"Exactly how did he die?" I asked in a wary voice.

"The roof of his ice shanty caved in," said Gus. "Killed him instantly."

Oh. My. God. The ... the ... plagiarist! I was going to strangle her! Of all the sneaky, low-down, conniv-ing— She'd handed out a suitcase full of books! Did she think I wouldn't overhear details? Did she think I was entirely stupid? Her book wasn't about Emma Anderson; it was about me!

"I hope Jackie's working on a sequel," said Gus.

"I'd read the next installment," said Reno.

"Me, too," said Vern. "But I have a few words of advice for her: more exploding vehicles and more midget wrestlers."

I smiled as an evil thought took root. "You like her book so much, you know what would be fun? Why don't you tell her about all the scenes you like in person? I can hardly *wait* to see the look on her face."

All three men agreed to my suggestion, so after we bought our drinks, I led them through the maze of food stalls to our vacant tables, only to discover they were no longer vacant. "My whole group is back," I said in surprise. "That was quick. They usually take forever deciding what to order."

"That's not your group," said Gus. "It's ours."

"Yours?" I looked more closely. Aha. That explained the quick decisions. No one at the table was from Iowa; they were from Florida, and Jackie was making the rounds, schmoozing cordially with them all.

"Someone must have bought your friend a drink," Vern observed. "She's still alive."

Yup, but when the gang returned to find their seats gone, she was going to wish she was dead.

CHAPTER 4

I caught Jackie's eye and fired her a look that could have singed her eyelashes. To her credit, she excused herself immediately and hurried over to me. Being female had really increased her ability to interpret dirty looks.

"Emily, I'm so glad you're back. Would you gentlemen excuse us for a moment?" She seized my arm and dragged me aside. "What am I going to *do?* They arrived *en masse* and just made themselves at home!"

"Did you happen to mention the seats were saved?"

"How could I? They're my reading public. If I didn't let them sit down, they might have gotten even by giving me a nasty review on Amazon. People can be so petty. Besides, Joleen Barnum was so nice. She gave me her own drink and made Jimbob go back and get her another. How could I tell them to go plunk themselves down somewhere else?"

"The gang is not going to be happy about this, Jack."

"I know." She gnawed the nail on her pinky as she glanced back toward the tables. "Why am I driven by this exhausting need to please everyone? I never felt like that when I was a guy."

"I think it has something to do with the female hippocamus."

"Well, it's really annoying." She rolled her shoulders as if readjusting her bra straps. "I'm not sure I would have made the change if I'd known this was going to happen. Life was so much easier when I could be selfish and unaccommodating."

"Speaking of which—" I poked my finger into her sternum. "Emma Anderson? Gay roommate? Detective friend with amnesia? Grandfather dies when an ice shanty collapses on him? Sound like anyone you know?"

"It sounds like you."

"Don't lie to me, Jack! You can't bluff—" I paused. "You admit it?"

"Novelists are supposed to write what they know, Emily, and who do I know better than you? No one."

"You splashed my life all over the pages of your book?"

"Honestly, Emily, who's going to know? I gave you a new name, and I fudged most of the important details."

"Like what?"

"Like . . . Emma is addicted to half-caf decaf caramel macchiatos. You, on the other hand, never cared for them."

"You call that an important detail?"

"I'll have you know that caramel macchiatos play a crucial role at the end of the book."

"DICK, GET OVER HERE!" Helen Teig's voice flew off the decibel chart. "SOMEONE'S IN OUR SEATS!"

"Uh-oh, you better get over there, Emily." Jackie shielded herself behind me and nudged me forward. "Looks like trouble."

"And whose fault is that? So help me, Jack—"

The Dicks, their wives, and the rest of the group huddled near the occupied tables with their arms full of takeout and their eyes throwing daggers, paring knives, and a few spitballs—the Iowa version of *Gunfight at the O.K. Corral*. "Those are our seats," huffed Dick Teig.

Portia Van Cleef elevated her chin at an imperious angle. "Obviously, if we're sitting in them, they're our seats."

"We were here first," Dick Stolee protested.

"And then you left," said Portia. "Sorry."

"Emily was supposed to save those seats for us!" sniped Lucille Rassmuson.

Portia took a calm sip of her drink. "She didn't do a very good job of it, did she?"

"She doesn't do a very good job of anything," grumbled Bernice.

"There's been a terrible mixup," I explained as I

inserted myself between the two groups, "but I know we can fix the problem with minimum inconvenience to everyone." The number one rule of being a successful tour escort was to sound as if you knew what you were doing, even if you didn't have a clue.

Portia smiled without humor. "Really, Emily, our only problem is how to make your group disappear so the rest of us can enjoy our meals."

"Okay, blondie, I've had all I'm going to take of you." Bernice stepped out from the group like a self-deputized Wyatt Earp. "Give up the seat."

"That's not going to happen," said Portia.

"You better do what she says," warned Dick Teig. "She's armed with Diet Coke."

"And she just shook the can," added Helen.

I stabbed my finger at Bernice. "You will *not* open that can anywhere around here. Understood? We're going to find a way to accommodate—"

"You tiresome little troll," Portia flung at Bernice. "Are you vying for the title of most irritating person on the planet? News flash. You've won, so go crawl back under your rock. We'll be able to digest our food much better if we don't have to look at you."

Bernice's face glazed over with justifiable shock. Who would have thought that Portia could sound more like Bernice than Bernice herself?

"Come on, ladies," I appealed, "we don't have to resort to name-calling."

Portia laughed. "Calling her a troll was a compliment."

Gasps from the Iowans. Silence from the Floridians.

Bernice stood statue-still, looking small and unexpectedly wounded. "You'll be sorry you said that," she vowed in a steely voice.

Portia let out a tedious sigh. "I seriously doubt that."

"There's a table opening up by the water!" George Farkas yelled. "Run for it!"

They took off like stampeding wildebeest, proving that when it came to priorities, nursing a grudge would always lose out to nursing their appetites.

Click clack click clack click. Jackie's stilettoes sent up a Gatling gun clatter as she joined us. "Thank goodness that's over. Isn't it nice how another table opened up? Some problems are so easy to solve."

"Yeah, especially if you pass them off to other people." I narrowed my eyes. "Weren't you about to die from heat stroke?"

"I'm so much better now that I'm rehydrated." She touched Portia's forearm. "When I fly down for my book signing, I'll have to bring Joleen something special to repay her for her kindness."

"About your book signing," Portia demurred. "There's been a slight change of plans."

"You want me to come in August instead of July? I can do that. My schedule—"

"Actually, I don't want you to come at all."

Jackie looked confused. "Not come? Why not?"

"Because I finished reading that rubbish you gave me last night. You don't honestly expect people to buy anything so stupid, do you?"

In the blink of an eye, I watched one supremely

confident transsexual shrink from six-foot-four to four-foot-six. "You didn't like it?"

"Where should I begin? With the insult to my intelligence or the cardboard characters? It was poorly written, cartoonish, and perverted. Not only is your mind in the gutter, your overuse of exclamation points and Batman sound effects is positively juvenile. I refuse to have my name connected with either you *or* your book."

"But I've already contacted my editor. She's probably placing the book order even as we speak."

"That's not my problem."

"It is *so* your problem. We had an understanding!"

"It was *my* understanding that your novel was readable. It isn't." Portia glanced up and down the table. "Did anyone else make the mistake of opening up her book last night?"

"Vern, Gus, and Reno did," I piped up. "They loved it." I encouraged the men with a nod. "Tell everyone what you told me."

Gus massaged his beard, looking as if he wished he were somewhere else. "I give her an A for effort, but Portia's right. It's nothing more than sensationalized tripe."

"A bad soap opera," Reno agreed.

"Complete nonsense," Vern snorted, "and like Portia said, way too many exclamation points. I like periods myself. They're solid. Manly."

I stared at them, aghast. "You *adored* Jackie's book! You told me yourselves."

"You obviously misinterpreted what they said," Portia accused.

"Really? How would you interpret 'I hope Jackie's working on a sequel,' and 'I'd read the next installment'?"

"I hope you're not always this naive, Emily. They probably want to have sex with her."

"I wouldn't mind starting the book," said Lauretta Klick, "but finishing could be a big problem. There's just not enough time left for me to get through the whole thing. I'd be really bummed out if I had to spend Eternity not knowing how the story ends."

"There she goes again," June Peabody whined. "Spreading gloom and doom with her end-of-the-world scenario, trying to convince everyone it's curtains. Listen to me, Lauretta, if you and Curtis ruin another holiday for us, I'll start a petition to make sure that you're never allowed to sign up for another one."

"Knock yourself out," Curtis shot back. "Maybe you didn't get the message: there's never gonna be another one."

"Hush up," Portia chided the Klicks. "I've told you what would happen if people started popping antidepressants because of you. I'm giving you fair warning: you're teetering on the brink."

"You don't scare us," Lauretta said defiantly. "Not anymore."

"She scares me," cried Jackie. "I've never known anyone to enjoy trashing someone else's work so much—other than New York theater critics. Mean-spirited witch. Didn't your mother teach you that if you can't say something nice, don't say it at all?" She was six-feet-four again, and cranky. "I want my book back."

"Sorry. I performed a good deed before I left the hotel this morning. I threw it in the wastebasket to spare the next poor schmuck from having to read it."

"You threw my book in the trash?"

Portia shrugged. "It's exactly where it belongs."

Jackie puffed up with so much hot air that she looked like an inflatable sex toy. "Even with my author's discount, that book set me back fifteen bucks! Do I look like I'm made of money? You are *so* going to regret doing that."

"Don't you dare threaten me."

"It's not a threat." Jackie's eyes narrowed to vengeful slits. "It's a promise."

"MAN OVERBOARD!" an elderly voice yelled from dockside. "HELP! SOMEBODY HELP!"

I shot a look toward the water. "One of yours?" Jackie asked me.

"Not mine," I said with a surfeit of confidence, unable to see through the crowd. "I conducted a seminar on ocean safety before we left home. My guys aren't going anywhere near open water unless there's a guard rail."

"HURRY! HE CAN'T SWIM!"

"Oh, God, it's one of mine." I dodged around market goers and hurdled pools of melted ice cream as I pounded across the cobblestones. "Hold on! I'm coming!"

Clackclackcclackclackclack. "I'll get this one!" Jackie sped past me on her long legs, hair flying and arms pumping. "I owe you. Out of the way!" she yelled in a gruff baritone. "I'm comin' through!"

Onlookers leaped out of her path as she barreled toward the end of the quay. Kicking off her stilettoes, she made a spectacular running leap into midair and plunged into the harbor with a resounding—

"Wait! My sweater!"

Splat!

"That was actually quite refreshing," Jackie said as we hoofed it back to the hotel an hour later.

"I'm glad you thought so," I said tightly.

"I recognize that tone, Emily, so you might as well come right out and say it. You're still mad."

"It was my favorite sweater in all the world, Jack! Now look at it." The sleeves hung below her hands like sock puppets. The bottom drooped to her thighs. "It's a plus size minidress."

"Would you rather I'd let George drown?"

"No! But I could have saved him. And here's the important part: *I'm* not wearing cashmere!"

"Well, *excuuu*se me. Who packs cashmere to go on vacation anyway?"

"We're going to be traveling above the Arctic Circle. I even threw in a scarf and mittens because . . . *it's supposed to get cold!*"

She stopped in her tracks. "Really?"

"Didn't you look at the map?"

"Nah. I'm not good with maps anymore." She bobbed her head sheepishly. "You know, the girl thing."

I sighed with resignation. "All these other issues

aside, Jack, I really appreciate what you did for George. Thanks."

"No problem. He should think about getting that artificial leg of his replaced with a lighter material, though. It dragged him down so fast, I had to dive twice to find him."

"It's not the leg; it's the steel-toed boots. What he really needs to replace is his footwear."

I looked up and down the boulevard and across the street to the shaded lawns of Esplanade park, where an outdoor aerobics class was being conducted for stunning blonds with tanned legs and no body fat. "Do you see a shoe store around here?"

"Nope, but I wouldn't mind browsing in the one behind you."

The store was called Aarikka, and the shopfront displayed a unique assortment of Finnish-made necklaces that were strung with wooden beads stained in eye-popping colors.

"Ooo," Jackie cooed. "See the fuschia-and-plum one? That has my name on it. Or maybe the seafoam and teal."

"Tell me something, Jack, how did you know I was still ticked off about my sweater? If we were still married and I'd said I wasn't upset, you'd have believed me."

"That's because I've learned the secret code. 'No' means 'yes.' 'Yes' means 'no.' 'No, I'm not upset,' means, 'Of course I'm upset, you moron.' It all makes so much sense now. No wonder I acted so dense when I was a guy. I didn't know there was a code."

"You wanna go inside?"

She studied her soggy reflection in the plate glass. "They'll never let me in the door dripping seawater. Tell you what, you stay here and shop for a new sweater on my dime, and I'll change clothes and meet up with you later." She reached inside her purse and handed me a fistful of currency. "If that's not enough, I'll make up the difference back at the room."

"You don't have to do this, Jack. I know you meant well."

"I ruined your sweater, so I need to pay for it."

"You're making me feel guilty."

She flashed a smile with her blindingly white teeth. "I'm gettin' good at this female stuff, aren't I?"

"What time do you want to meet up?"

"Let's just wing it. I'll call your cell." She trotted off, pausing after a few steps to turn back to me. "Did Vern, Gus, and Reno really love my book?"

"I kid you not—three huge thumbs-up."

"So they lied to Portia."

"Through their teeth."

After chewing on that for a moment, she headed off again, the look on her face hinting that she intended to find out why.

"For a city that was founded as a trading post in the sixteenth century, Helsinki has blossomed into one of the most cosmopolitan capitals in the world," Annika told us as we trooped back to our hotel later that night. "So now that you have seen most of the attractions, what did you like best?"

"I liked the buildings that looked like gigantic pastel butter mints," said Lucille Rassmuson, obviously feeling the effects of her diet. "They looked good enough to eat."

"I liked the street performers," said Grace Stolee. "I thought that couple who were painted gold were actually statues until Emily threw a coin into their bucket and they broke out in a minuet."

"It's nice that street people have a way to take your money other than mugging you," Helen Teig conceded. "Maybe that'll catch on back home."

"I liked the electric trams," said Osmond. "But I can't figure out if they're green and yellow because they're made by John Deere, or because the Finns are Green Bay Packer fans."

"I liked that Bernice decided not to come with us," said Dick Teig.

Bernice was so sullen after her run-in with Portia that she'd decided to skip Annika's walking tour.

"It's too bad she's missing this," I commented as I strolled beside Nana and George. "It's not every day you get a chance to visit Helsinki. What can she possibly be doing in her hotel room that's more fun than soaking up local color?"

"Sulkin'," said Nana.

"Or complaining to the front desk," added George. "She's figured out that's a good way to get an upgrade."

"Could take her a while to get over her hurt feelin's," Nana predicted. "That Portia cut her right to the quick. All's I hope is that the bad blood between 'em don't end up causin' you problems, dear."

I shuddered at the thought of keeping the two women apart and their tongues in check for the rest of the trip. "How's your nose?" I asked George to divert my mind.

"Don't feel a thing." He fingered the purple bruises beneath his eye sockets and tapped the hard plastic nose guard the medics had given him to strap around his face. "Can't believe it's broken."

Nana gave his hand a squeeze. "Jackie done a crackerjack job pullin' him outta the harbor."

It would have been even more crackerjack if she hadn't broken his nose in the process. "In the interest of self-preservation, George, the next time one of Nana's Polaroids blows away, would you just let it go?"

He shook his head in disgust. "I woulda been okay if I hadn't run out of real estate. Another five feet— that's all I needed."

"Where *is* Jackie?" asked Nana. "Wasn't she supposed to call?"

"That's what she said." But I'd shopped all afternoon, dropped my packages off at the hotel, eaten dinner, and taken the walking tour without hearing a peep out of her. I checked my cell. "She hasn't left a message."

"Could be she hooked up with some a them Florida folks," Nana suggested. "They seemed real anxious to suck up to her. None a them is here neither, so maybe she's off readin' to 'em somewhere."

I'd thought it odd that the Floridians hadn't participated in the walking tour, but I'd attributed it to dinner schedules. Since none of the seniors had to worry about night blindness in Helsinki, they could actually hit a restaurant later than four o'clock.

We huffed and puffed our way up the slight incline to our hotel and pushed through the sparkling glass doors to the lobby. "Check the itinerary board before you head to your rooms," Annika advised. "It lists all your departure and arrival times for tomorrow."

As everyone crowded around the whiteboard, I asked the desk clerk for directions to the sauna, which she pronounced "sow-na," then made a proposal to the group.

"Anyone want to tag along while I check out the sauna? We can't visit Finland and not indulge in their national pastime."

"You're not getting me inside any steam room," Helen scoffed. "I just had my hair done."

"I don't think there's any steam," I corrected. "It's a dry heat."

The ladies exchanged meaningful looks with each other. "Do we have to strip?" Lucille finally asked. "Because there's no way us girls are going to sit in a room together without any clothes on."

"According to what I've read, the sauna is traditionally taken in the nude, but—"

"Is it coed or segregated?" asked George.

"In a family sauna, it's usually coed," I said, "but hotels might have different rules for—"

"If Emily gets naked, you can count me in!" whooped Dick Teig.

"Me, too," said Dick Stolee.

"I hope they have towels," said Osmond.

"I hope they have blindfolds," said Nana.

"You suppose they allow cameras?" asked Dick Teig. "Damn, I need film."

I rolled my eyes. "Okay, here's the plan: we'll find the sauna, read the house rules, then decide if the experience is for us. How does that sound?"

Everyone liked the plan, so we exited the lobby down a long corridor lined with fancy boutiques and rode the elevator to sub-level one—a well-lit underground concourse with passageways shooting off in every direction. "To the right," I said after reading all the signs.

"Yeah," said Margi Swanson, "but to the left is that huge shopping complex we passed on the way back to the hotel. We can reach it underground. Is anyone feeling the need to buy a bathing suit?"

"I am," said Helen.

"So am I," said Lucille. "Maybe we can find a Lane Bryant outlet."

"I can buy my film," said Dick.

"I'm gonna look for dark glasses," said Nana, "just in case they don't got blindfolds."

"Guys!" I called as they all began to scatter. "What about the sauna?"

"Dick and me will meet you back here in ten minutes," said Dick Stolee, pressing the push-pin of his stopwatch. "Don't strip down without us."

"Read the signs if you get lost," I yelled after them. "Establish landmarks!"

Normally, Iowans don't get lost, but I didn't know if their internal directional systems would work underground.

My phone started chirping halfway to the sauna. "Jack?" I said when I connected.

"Hi, Em, can you guess who this is?"

Jesus, Mary, and Joseph. "Mom?"

"That's right! I've never spoken to anyone overseas before, so I wasn't sure you'd recognize my voice."

"What's wrong? Is it Dad? Oh, my God, do you need me? Should I come home?"

"This is an excellent connection, Emily. You sound as if you're right next door. I bet you're paying big bucks for mobile service like this."

"Mom! What about Dad?"

"Your father and I are fine, dear. He's right here, waving hello."

"Steve and the boys. Mary Ann. Are they okay?"

"We saw them this morning. They're fine, too." She hesitated. "Under the circumstances."

Eh! Here it was. The phone call you always dread when you're traveling. "What circumstances?"

"Well, you know how Main Street cuts right through the center of town and passes by the church, the funeral parlor, and Lars Bakke's grain elevator?"

"I'm familiar with Main Street, Mom."

"We had a twister touch down last night that kind of rearranged things."

"Oh, my God. Was anyone hurt?"

"It was a miracle, Emily, but there was only one injury. Your friend Sharon missed a step on her basement stairs and ended up breaking both legs. But her mother tells me she'll be up and about in a few months, after they remove the pins and she goes through rehab."

I blinked numbly. "My maid of honor can't walk?"

"The wonderful thing is, not one house was destroyed. That pesky twister hopped over the residential district completely, so you can tell the Teigs, and the Stolees, and everyone else that there's no need to rush home, because their property is just fine. It's the rest of the town that's been declared a disaster area."

"Disaster area?"

"You'll notice such a change, dear. But like your father was telling Lars this morning, some of those buildings were so old, they needed to be torn down anyway."

I winced. "Did a lot of the buildings collapse?"

"All of them, dear. Windsor City Bank. Holy Redeemer Church. Skaartvedt's Roto-Rooter and Used Books. The funeral parlor. The bridal shop where you ordered your dress. Main Street is still there, but it's pretty much buried under rubble."

My vision dimmed. My head went fuzzy. "What about Ashgrove?"

"If the tornado had lifted up a hundred feet sooner, it would have been fine."

"It's gone?" I asked weakly.

"Flattened."

"Oh, God, Mom. How can I get married? I have no church, no dress, no reception hall, no maid of honor!"

"Don't you worry, sweetheart, I have it all figured out. Are you sitting down?"

"No, but . . . hold on." I rounded the corner toward the sauna. "They probably have chairs in—"

I tripped over something and went flying into the opposite wall with a bone-jarring *thunk*.

"Are you sitting down yet?" my mother chattered away. "I'm going to arrange everything while you're in Scandinavia. New church, new dress, new reception hall. I'm so excited, Emily. It's going to be even better than before."

I turned around, my back pressed to the wall for support. Portia Van Cleef lay faceup on the floor, body inert, eyes fixed, tongue lolling from her head. She was wearing the fuschia-and-plum necklace that Jackie had admired in the Aarikka store today, with one tragic difference.

Someone had used it to strangle her.

I let out a cry that could wake the dead.

"You should hear her, Bob," my mother gushed to my father. "She's thrilled with the idea."

CHAPTER 5

"At nineteen-hundred hours you had dinner reservations at Raffaelo, where Ms. Van Cleef ordered the chicken breast with Swiss vegetable cakes."

"We would have eaten earlier," April Peabody informed the policeman in charge of establishing a time line for Portia's activities, "but Portia insisted on stopping at a little jewelry store to buy a necklace she'd seen earlier. Who knows why she was so taken with it? Not her signature style at all. It was made of wood, for God sakes."

I'd given my statement to the chief investigating officer an hour earlier, but I was so rattled that I'd decided to attend the informal inquiry being held in the hotel's conference room rather than return to my room. Annika had knocked on doors, rousting everyone, so all the guests were present and accounted for, except for Jackie, who was mysteriously AWOL.

"You left the restaurant around twenty-one-hundred hours," Officer Rajanen continued. "Did your entire group walk back to the hotel together?"

"We sure did," said Joleen Barnum. "Me and Jim-bob were a little afraid of getting lost, so we never let anyone out of our sight. Wasn't easy with Reno leading the way, though. He walks so fast, no one can keep up."

"He does it to show off," claimed June Peabody. "He doesn't want anyone to forget he's a world-class athlete. I'm surprised he's not wearing his medals."

"I thought about packing them," Reno quipped, "but they would have put my luggage over the weight limit."

"Enough with the wisecracks," August Manning chided. "How about showing a little respect for the dead?"

"Did you try callin' Jackie on her cell?" Nana whispered to me.

"I don't know her number," I whispered back. I was getting a very bad feeling about the reason for her absence.

"Where did Ms. Van Cleef go after returning to the hotel?" probed Officer Rajanen.

"We all stopped in the lobby to read tomorrow's itinerary," Lauretta Klick volunteered.

"And then we rode the elevator back to our rooms," said Vern Grundy. "End of story."

Officer Rajanen jotted something on his notepad.

"Do you recall who stepped off the elevator with Ms. Van Cleef?"

"We all got off at the same time," said Curtis Klick. "They put all of us Florida people on one floor and the Iowans on another."

"Portia's room was closest to the elevator," added April Peabody. "The rest of us were farther down the hall. She always made sure she got the plum rooms. Location, location, location."

"Did she enter her room alone?" asked Rajanen.

"August challenged her to a game of gin rummy," said Curtis, "but she declined. Seemed pretty obvious he was trying to get her alone."

"Who knows for what sinful purpose?" added Lauretta.

"Don't try pinning anything on me," August called out. "Portia's in the gin rummy club with me. I throw out that challenge all the time because no one has ever beaten her and I'm aiming to be the first, even if it's not officially documented."

The officer made another notation. "Did any of you see or speak to her after she went inside her room?"

"That's the last I saw of her," Reno spoke up.

"Me too," said Vern, heads nodding in agreement around him.

"So no one saw Ms. Van Cleef again until Ms. Andrew found her outside the sauna. Is that correct?"

More head bobbing. George patted my shoulder. Nana squeezed my hand.

Officer Rajanen closed his notepad, his expression

pained, his tone apologetic. "Please accept my condolences for what has happened to your companion. I regret the black mark it places on our city, because other than for a few unlawful pickpockets, Helsinki is extremely safe."

"That's the line they gave us about Switzerland," scoffed Helen Teig, "*before* Emily found three dead bodies."

"She found four in Italy," Lucille bragged.

"She only found two in Australia," said Osmond. "That really brought down her average."

I slunk down in my chair, hoping to become invisible.

"Unfortunately, there are individuals who make the streets less safe in any country," Officer Ranjanen continued. "We've noticed an escalation of youth crime in our city center in recent years. Nonviolent crime, but crime nonetheless. When our youth feel disenfranchised, they seem capable of anything."

"Where's your city center?" asked Dick Stolee.

Rajanen spread out his hands. "You are sitting in it."

The room grew palpably quiet.

"Would have been nice if someone had told us that," barked Vern. "Portia might have been more careful. She might still be alive."

"What an ugly way to go," Jimbob empathized. "Garroted to death."

"Garroted?" said Bernice. "I thought you said she was strangled."

April Peabody stabbed an accusatory finger at Bernice. "You ought to know. What with the way you were talking to her earlier today, I wouldn't be surprised if you were there!"

Nods from the Floridians. Shock from the Iowans.

Rajanen paused in front of Bernice's chair. "Would you care to tell me about your exchange with Ms. Van Cleef?"

"Give me a break!" Bernice whined. "Those people stole our chairs at the waterfront market. I said I wanted them back, and Ms. Van Cleef said to forget it, so I told her she'd be sorry."

"How did you intend to make her sorry?"

"How should I know? People say stuff like that all the time. 'Switch the channel and I'll break your arm.' 'Eat that last Twinkie and I'll kill you.' Don't you ever say things like that?"

"No."

"Maybe they don't have Twinkies in Finland," offered Margi.

"You are Bernice Zwerg," Rajanen said, reopening his notepad and making a notation as he read her name tag. "Would you tell me where were you this evening between twenty-one hundred hours and the present?"

"You've got me all wrong," Bernice protested in a minor panic. "What could I do to make someone sorry? I'm old. I'm forgetful. I've got an arthritic back and bunions."

"I'll tell you how forgetful she is," Nana said helpfully. "She can't even remember that she had them bunions out last year."

Officer Rajanen grew ominously quiet. "Forgive me for asking again, Ms. Zwerg. Where were you—"

"I was in my room! That woman upset me so much, I went into seclusion."

"Can you provide a witness who will testify that you were in your room at the time Ms. Van Cleef was murdered?"

Bernice gave him a hard look. "If someone had been in the room with me, I wouldn't have been in seclusion, would I?"

Rajanen returned the look. "No, but at least you would have someone to verify your alibi." He stowed his notepad in his shirt pocket. "Would you mind coming with me, Ms. Zwerg?"

He was taking Bernice in for questioning? This wasn't good. My escort's manual didn't have a section covering incarceration etiquette! I stood up in protest. "You can't take her to jail, Officer. Bernice isn't capable of committing murder. Ask anyone." I prodded my group to back me up.

"Killing's not Bernice's style," agreed Dick Teig. "She'd rather grate on your nerves 'til you feel like killing yourself."

"Or cheat you," said Grace.

"Or insult you," added Margi.

"Or talk about you behind your back," said Lucille.

"Or lie about something she's dumping on eBay," said Dick Stolee.

"Wouldn't that go under cheating?" asked Margi.

"You hear that?" Bernice pleaded with Rajanen. "These people are my friends. They know me. You've gotta believe them."

Rajanen motioned her to stand up. Dick Teig hit

the Record button on his camcorder. "Here's Bernice, getting her ass hauled off to jail."

I looked on futilely, unable to think of anything that would save her butt.

"I'm telling you, I didn't do it!" Bernice cried as Rajanen escorted her away. "It wasn't me. It was the author!"

Blame someone else! That might work. But how did she know about Jackie's run-in with Portia? She hadn't even been there!

"She's got a point," said Lauretta Klick. "We all heard Jackie Thum threaten Portia."

"I had to cover my ears," said Curtis. "If she uses language like that in her book, I'm not reading it."

Officer Rajanen paused. "This is true?"

"I saw the whole thing," said June.

"So did I," said April. "Jackie was so mad at Portia that she swore to get even."

"She didn't swear," corrected Joleen. "She 'promised.'"

"I thought she said 'vowed,'" said Vern. "Seems to me an author might come up with a punchier verb than 'promised.'"

"The verb was irrelevant," said June. "The critical point, Officer, is that not only did Jackie Thum bear a grudge against Portia, she's physically capable of carrying out a vendetta because she's eight feet tall."

Rajanen looked out over the group, obviously trying to spot our resident giant. "Is Ms. Thum here?"

"Excuse me, Officer," Annika spoke up, "but I mentioned to you before that I was unable to locate Ms. Thum."

"Aha!" chortled June. "That should tell you something."

"She's guilty as sin," Lauretta accused.

"Probably skipped town," said Reno.

"Or went on a killing rampage and murdered more people," Bernice offered happily.

"Or had a late dinner!" I shouted to be heard above the escalating rumble of voices. "What is wrong with you people? Whatever happened to the concept of a person being innocent until proven guilty? Did you toss it out the window when you crossed the Atlantic?"

Awkward silence. Downcast eyes. Self-conscious foot shuffling.

"Emily?" Margi looked puzzled. "My airplane window wouldn't open. Do you think it was defective?"

Officer Rajanen dug out his notepad again. "Please, could I have a description of Ms. Thum other than her height?"

"She wears them real stylish high heels," said Nana. "But she's gotta order through the catalog on account a her feet are so big."

"Great legs," said Gus.

"Huge bazongas," said Vern.

"Skintight clothes," said Reno.

Those lechers. They *did* want to sleep with her!

Tilly rapped her walking stick on the floor. "I'll give you her description, Officer. She's mesocephalic and leptoprosopic, with no alveolar prognathism. Her nose is leptorrhine with a high nasal root. She has a non-Mongoloid eye with no epicanthic fold, and her hair is shoulder-length and brown, wavy as opposed to woolly or peppercorn. Is that exact enough?"

Vern scratched his head. "Did she mention the huge bazongas? I couldn't tell."

The door swung open and Jackie *clickclacked* breathlessly into the conference room, looking as if she'd just run a marathon. "The front desk clerk told me you were having a meeting in here." She sank into a chair and fanned her face. "So, what have I missed?"

"I can't figure how the locals sleep when it's so light out." Nana pulled the drape back on my bedroom window. She'd phoned a couple of hours ago, asking for an over-the-counter sleep aid, but when she'd arrived at my door with Tilly and George, I'd realized the visit had had more to do with keeping me company than coping with sleeplessness. "Looks more like six p.m. than one a.m. You s'pose that's why we're all awake?"

"I'm too creeped out to sleep." I sat cross-legged on my bed, hugging my pillow. "Every time I close my eyes, I see Portia sprawled on the floor, staring at the ceiling."

"Try this," said George, who was stretched out on Jackie's bed. "Keep your eyes open."

This is what I loved about men. They were so basic.

"Have you thought about your plan of action should the police find evidence that implicates Jackie or Bernice in Portia's murder?" asked Tilly. She sat on the settee with her feet elevated to relieve the swelling in her ankles. "Would you stay in Helsinki with them or fly to Lapland with us tomorrow?"

Annika had announced that her tour company was contractually bound to fulfill their obligation to their guests, so despite the misfortune with Portia, the tour would continue and refunds would *not* be given to those who terminated their trip prematurely.

"My escort's manual isn't exactly clear about where my duty lies. It kind of skips over all the scenarios where tour guests get jailed for murder."

"Call Mr. Erickson at the bank," Nana suggested. "He'll—" Her voice faded suddenly. "What am I thinkin'? The bank's not there no more."

"If the bank's not there, does that mean our travel club's not there either?" asked George.

I caught my breath as reality smacked me in the face. He was right. Without the bank to sponsor it, there *was* no seniors' travel club, which meant— "Oh, my God. I have no job."

"I imagine all of Windsor City's Main Street merchants are facing that same dilemma today," said Tilly.

"You've got somethin' more valuable than a job, dear," Nana soothed. "You got your young man."

"Not yet, I don't. How are we going to get married? I have no church, no restaurant, no gown. My maid of honor has both legs in a cast and won't be able to walk for months."

Nana waved her hand dismissively. "There's no problem bigger'n the two of us, Emily, 'specially when we put our heads together."

"Mom has put herself in charge of making alternate wedding plans while I'm away," I added.

Nana's face froze in horror. "Now we got problems."

The hallway door banged open and Jackie bustled into the room weighed down by so many shopping bags that she looked like a clothes tree that needed uncluttering.

"Welcome back!" Nana scuffed across the floor to give her a hug. "What a haul." She read the lettering on the bags. "Marimekko. Stockmann. Here we thought you was in the Big House, when all the time you was shoppin'. Where's the police station? In a mall?"

"Hardly. I left my bags at the front desk before I joined the little witch hunt in the conference room. The *nerve* of those people!" She dumped her stash onto the bed at George's feet. "Can you believe they dragged me off like a common criminal? I can see why they took Bernice in; she looks like Public Enemy Number One. But me? The only thing I'm guilty of is eating off all my lip gloss and forgetting to reapply."

"I'm so happy they let you go!" I hopped off my bed and gave her a welcoming hug. "Did they release Bernice, too?"

"Yup. We rode back in the same cab with Annika. Thank *God* they let Annika go to the police station with us. I don't know what we would have done without her."

"What made them decide to let you go?" asked George.

"They obviously had no evidence to implicate either of us. Besides, we both had airtight alibis."

I regarded her oddly. "Bernice didn't have an alibi. That's part of the reason why she came under suspicion."

"She musta made somthin' up," said Nana. "That Bernice can think on her feet real good. That's part a her mystique."

"She didn't have to make anything up," said Jackie. "She told them she'd been talking on the phone while she was in her room, and when the police investigated, it all checked out."

"Who could she possibly have been talking to locally?" asked Tilly. "Bernice doesn't know anyone in Finland, and she'd never pay for long distance."

"The front desk. She was on the phone with them for two solid hours complaining her little heart out. The desk clerk actually documented it, because he thought the hotel could use her call to instruct new employees about how to be diplomatic with cranky Americans. Since Bernice couldn't have been on her room phone and strangled Portia at the same time, they had to cut her loose."

"They've already established the time of death?" I asked. "That was fast."

Jackie looked unimpressed. "It was a no-brainer. There was a narrow window between the time the last person signed out of the sauna and the time when you found the body, so that had to have been when the killer struck. And the great irony is that if this had happened next week, the police would have caught it all on videotape because the city is installing surveillance cameras throughout the entire underground concourse. But the system isn't operational yet. Can you believe the bad luck? I can't think of an instance of poorer timing."

"Custer leading his troops into battle at the Little Big Horn," said Tilly.

"The *Titanic* steaming through that ice field in the North Atlantic," said George.

"Melanie Wilkes havin' that baby a hers on the very night the Yankees was attackin' Atlanta," said Nana.

We stared at her in silence.

"What?" she complained. "Don't Southern fiction count?"

"Out of curiosity, Jack, how did you come by all this detailed information?"

"Annika has a drinking buddy on the force, so she pumped him for details. I appreciated your offering to come to the station with us, Emily, but Annika was right to discourage you. We needed someone who could shmooze in the mother tongue."

"Did you come up with an airtight alibi, too?" asked Nana. "We was wonderin' where you was all afternoon and evenin'."

Jackie removed a fistful of loose papers from her purse. "Ladies and gentlemen, I give you the perfect alibi: shopping receipts stamped with the date and time of purchase. Isn't technology wonderful?" She fanned them out like a magician performing card tricks. "The police got out a map and pinpointed my movements from early afternoon until I left the cyber café and hit the ATM. According to their calculations, I was nowhere near the hotel when Portia was murdered, so I couldn't have done it—which has taught me a crucial lesson."

"Use the buddy system when you're in a foreign country?" asked George.

She flashed a broad smile. "It pays to be a shopa-holic."

I shifted my gaze to the computer perched on the corner desk. "Why did you stop at a cyber café when your laptop is already set up?"

"My screen kept freezing on me this afternoon, and I *had* to check Amazon for my book ranking. Obsessing about your Amazon number has become *the* most popular addiction to have among published authors. It sits right at the top of the list, just above chain smoking, binge drinking, and cross-dressing."

"Were you happy with your rank?" asked Tilly.

Jackie raised her arms in a victorious V. "One million three hundred and ten. I've moved up six whole points since yesterday!"

Gee, if the world didn't end, she might be able to claw her way to number one in—I did some quick mental math—four hundred seventy-six years. Hot damn!

"But would you believe I don't have a single Amazon review yet? The book has been out for two weeks! What are people reading? Comic books?"

"Diet books," said Nana. "Readin' about how to shed them extra pounds is way cheaper than liposuction."

Tilly boosted herself off the settee. "If Bernice is back, perhaps we should drop by to see how she's faring. Police interrogation can be traumatic, even for crusty cynics who lack social graces."

"Now, now," Jackie cautioned. "I think everyone might be wrong about Bernice. We had time for lots of girl talk on the way to and from the police station, and I saw a whole different side of her. She was chatty, agreeable, and surprisingly funny."

"Bernice?" said Nana.

"Bernice Zwerg?" said George.

Jackie buffed her nails on her tank top. "We actually bonded this evening. I think she's become much more pleasant since her bunion surgery. Who could possibly be in a bad mood wearing open-toed wedges with ankle straps?"

"Bernice Zwerg," repeated George.

"Come on, George," Jackie scolded. "Have a little sympathy. She suffered a terrible indignity when those Floridians ratted her out to the police. Can you believe that Hamlets bunch? Malicious little back stabbers.

"You'd have thought that throwing Bernice under the bus would have satisfied their bloodlust, but nooo, they had to throw *me* under there with her." Jackie narrowed her eyes into the kind of squint that could result in serious crow's-feet. "Which one of those miserable, two-faced hypocrites gave my name to the police? I tried to get it out of Bernice, but she refused to tattle because she said she didn't want to ruin my opinion of the person."

Wow, Nana was right. Bernice really *could* think on her feet. "Uhh . . . to be honest, Jack, there were so many people talking over each other, I'm not sure who first mentioned your name. Is that how you remember it?" I asked Nana, giving her the eye.

"I never heard nothin', except for Dick Teig belchin' a few times. George didn't hear nothin' either, did you, George?"

He tugged on his earlobe. "Waxy buildup. Didn't hear a thing."

Tilly regarded us as if we'd all lost our minds.

Uh-oh. Tilly wasn't going to play along.

"Unfortunately, I was so distracted trying to elevate my feet that I failed to hear who threw Jackie to the wolves. Sorry."

Jackie sighed with disappointment. "It doesn't matter. I'm just worried about publicity. Can you imagine what Hightower would do if they learned that one of their soon-to-be-famous authors was implicated in an international murder?"

"They'd probably sign you up for guest appearances on *Today*, *Dr. Phil*, and *Oprah*," I wisecracked.

Jackie stared at me, transfixed. "Emily, you're a genius!" She dug out her cell phone and punched in a number. "I can see it all now. Book sales will skyrocket. I'll hit number one on Amazon. I'll go into an immediate second printing. Hollywood will decide to make a movie of my life. Maybe I'll be asked to play myself. If it becomes a documentary, they might even film all of you!"

"I'll need to get my hair done," said Nana.

"My God, Jack, would you calm down? I was just teasing."

"But you're absolutely right, Emily! I need publicity, and you know what they say: bad publicity is better than no publicity at all." She looked suddenly crestfallen. "Damn. They shunted me to Mona's voice mail. What time is it in New York anyway?"

I rolled my eyes. "I apologize for being the voice of reason in this discussion, but wouldn't it be better for your professional image if you made an appearance on TV because you helped *solve* an international murder rather than because you were a suspect in one?"

Her eyebrows inched upward in thought. "Good point. Do you suppose if I solved the murder, they'd book me on *60 Minutes* instead? Think of it. Sunday night. Prime time. I bet their viewing audience is in a demographic that buys lots of books."

"I wanna see you get interviewed by the nice young fella on that mornin' news show," said Nana, "but I'm not sure it'll happen, on account a they mostly use him when they wanna make government leaders and Hollywood superstars look stupid."

"Okay, I'll do it!" Jackie executed a little patty-cake clap. "Finding Portia's murderer could be my best career move yet."

"Does she get to find the killer all by herself, or do we get to help?" asked Nana.

"If we get to wear disguises, can I have something that comes with a full head of hair?" asked George.

"How about one of those rainbow-colored wigs that NFL football fans wear?" asked Tilly. "You could pose as a man with no taste."

Jackie raised her hand. "Technical question. Do you have any suspects besides me and Bernice? Because if you tell George to tail me, I'm gonna recognize him if he's wearing a rainbow wig."

I could have sworn she'd said her IQ had risen when she'd become a woman. "Okay, here's the thing: the police's theory that Portia was killed by disenfranchised youth doesn't cut it for me."

"Me, neither," said Nana. "We seen a lot a dead bodies on our trips, and most of 'em got that way because someone they knew wanted 'em outta the way."

"Exactly," I agreed. "Some of the motives seemed pretty lame, but the killers didn't think so. The important point is, the assailants always knew their victims."

"Which supports the contention that Portia might have been killed by a member of the Hamlets' contingent," said Tilly.

"I dunno." George stroked his bald spot, which was essentially the entire space between his ears. "Those Florida folks seemed to buzz around her like bees around the queen. Looked to me like everyone was in love with her."

"Or pretendin' to be in love with her," said Nana. "You s'pose it was all for show?"

Tilly nodded. "I did notice the major sucking up going on throughout our city tour this morning. Perhaps it's a flaw in my personality, but I'm always suspicious of world-class brown nosers. And they *all* seemed to be like that—vying desperately for Portia's approval. Does anyone besides me wonder why?"

Jackie let out a melodramatic gasp. "The Klicks! They weren't sucking up when Portia scolded them at the outdoor market today. Lauretta gave her a really evil look and said something like, 'You don't scare us. Not anymore.' Do you think that's significant?"

"I wouldn't pay that no mind," said Nana. "Could be that with the world endin' in a few days, Curtis and Lauretta figure they don't got nothin' to lose by gettin' lippy."

"Or it could mean something else entirely," I said with sudden inspiration. "What if Portia wasn't the benevolent ruler that she appeared to be? What if the Hamlets people fawned over her not because they liked her but because they feared her?"

Tilly thwacked her cane on the bed. "By God, I knew there was something unnatural about the way everyone treated that woman. Dictators rule by fear. It makes perfect sense, Emily. Bravo."

"I don't get it," Nana objected. "What do folks got to fear from an old broad like Portia Van Cleef?"

"I'm not sure, Nana, but that's what we need to find out. Are you with me?"

Nods all around.

"Okay, here's the plan—"

Jackie raised her hand again. "If we do disguises, can I be blond?"

CHAPTER 6

When we flew over the Arctic Circle the next morning, I looked out the window expecting to catch a glimpse of glaciers, igloos, and the polar bears who do the Coca-Cola commercial. What I saw instead were dense forests and gleaming lakes that stretched as far as the eye could see. Hmm. Either Lapland had just experienced a catastrophic thermal event, or I'd apparently confused it with the North Pole.

"Isn't there supposed to be snow?" I asked Annika as we stepped off the plane into the ninety-degree heat at Ivalo.

"It melted."

Oh, my God. Scientists had warned us, but we wouldn't listen. "Global warming?" I choked out.

"Spring thaw."

I kept stride with her as we crossed the tarmac to

a one-story wooden structure the size of a Photomat booth. If the terminal was any indication, Lapland obviously lacked the appeal of more populous destinations like Prairie View, Kansas, or Chesuncook, Maine. "Have you heard any more about Portia?"

At breakfast she'd announced that once Portia's autopsy was complete and her body released, her casket would be flown back to Florida. "The head office is taking full responsibility for making the arrangements," she'd assured us. "We will see that she's returned to the bosom of her family with all the speed and dignity that is due a Midnight Sun Adventures guest." I figured the "speed and dignity" guarantee was supposed to compensate for the company's refusing to grant refunds to close friends who might want to accompany her body back to the States.

"I told you everything I know earlier, Emily, but I'll be talking to the head office again later today, so I promise to keep you informed. This holiday should have been the trip of Portia Van Cleef's lifetime. I can't believe what has happened."

I wondered how one said, "*I* can" in Finnish.

"How is your group coping?" she asked.

"They didn't know Portia, so it's not as traumatic for them as it is for her friends."

"Her traveling companions have my deepest respect. I was prepared for some of them to fall apart, but that hasn't happened at all. You Americans are a stalwart bunch. No tears. No emotional tantrums. No drama. The Finns are often accused of being dour and emotionless, but you wear the label much better than we do."

I guessed that was a compliment—kind of.

As we boarded our big yellow air-conditioned touring bus, I watched my spy team spread out and maneuver themselves into position.

"Isn't it supposed to be cold above the Arctic Circle?" asked August Manning as I sat down beside him. His face was red and sweaty, and matched the tartan on his flannel shirt. "The travel agent said to expect highs in the fifties. I wonder if she bothered to look at the weather forecast?" He gave his whiskers a vigorous scratch. "If it gets any hotter, the beard's going to be history."

"I brought boiled wool," I commiserated.

"Yeah, but it's not attached to your face."

"Ladies and gentlemen, I apologize for the heat," our local guide announced over the loudspeaker. His name was Helge, his English was impeccable, he lived across the border in Kirkenes, Norway, and he was wearing a pair of shorts and sandals that looked as if they'd been mothballed in his attic since the ice age. "Typically, it never gets this hot in Finnish Lapland, and I have the skin to prove it." He struck a pose that showcased his paste-white legs and feet. "But the happy result is that because of the heat, we have no mosquitoes this year."

"Portia would have been thrilled to hear that," August told me in a low voice. "She hated insects. Made me wonder why she ever moved to Florida. We have some butt-ugly bugs in the Sunshine State."

"Where was she from originally?"

"I know she lived in Massachusetts for awhile. She went the debutante route and ended up marrying a Boston blue blood with political connections. Hell of a nice guy."

"Did one of you call him to break the news, or did you leave it to the tour company?"

"Neither. Clayton's long gone. A polo accident years ago."

"Does she have any family?"

"Not in Florida. No kids, no pets, no lovers that I know of. Portia didn't like unnecessary attachments cluttering her life, but she never met a board of directors that she didn't want to serve on."

"If you were here in winter," Helge continued as we pulled onto the road, "you might enjoy a dog-sled safari through the wilderness, but summer is more suited for trekking. The four- to six-day treks are the most popular, and there are huts and campsites in the national park that can be used for sleeping, though people tend to sleep less when the sun never sets. You must carry all your food with you, but the river water is safe for drinking and the campsites are free. The huts may be rented for a minimal fee."

"Why would anyone want to spend four days trekking through the wilderness?" Dick Teig threw out.

"For health and exercise," said Helge. "It's a national pastime."

"Baseball is a national pastime," argued Dick. "Hiking to nowhere with a backpack full of beef jerky and peanut butter crackers is just plain warped."

Spoken like a man with a fifty-two-inch waist whose main cardiovascular activity consisted of punching buttons on the remote control.

"Let's hope this doesn't give Reno any bright ideas," Gus confided. "He's such an exercise junkie, it wouldn't surprise me if he tried to do the four-day trek in twenty-four hours. God only knows where he'd end up, and in what shape. He keeps forgetting he's sixty-seven instead of twenty-seven."

"He probably doesn't get a chance to do much wilderness trekking in Florida."

Gus laughed. "He could trek, all right, but he'd have to do it in a swamp or a strip mall."

I glanced down the aisle to see Jackie sitting with Reno, which had to be awkward considering the nasty crack he'd made about her novel. "What kind of exercise is his specialty? He looks like a tennis player, or maybe a swimmer."

"He's a runner. Sprinter. He does a lot of track and field for senior sports events, and travels all over the world. You wouldn't believe the ribbons and medals he's collected. He built an addition onto his house just so he could display them. If you're looking for modesty, you can skip over his address."

"Is he married?"

"Married twice; divorced twice. That seems to be the norm these days."

"For you, too?"

"I never took the leap. Too married to my work to commit to someone who might take me away from it."

"What kind of work did you do?"

"The same kind of work I still do. I'm a journalist, but I've switched from feature articles for the *Washington Post* to being editor-in-chief of *Everything Hamlets*. It's a much easier gig. I set the deadlines, decide what's newsworthy, and get to play boss with six staffers who always dreamed of writing the Great American Novel. They're not Hemingways or Steinbecks, but you couldn't find a better bunch to compile daily calenders for social and sporting events. I write the obituaries, feature articles, and op-ed pieces. I seem to have developed a few opinions in the last sixty-eight years that are itching to find their way into print."

"Like . . . opinions about debut novels?"

Looking sufficiently uncomfortable, he removed his glasses and polished them on his shirt. "I can't say I didn't deserve that. You're going to embarrass me into offering Jackie an apology."

"I don't get it. How do you go from praising a book to claiming it's nothing more than sensationalized tripe, all in a space of ten minutes?"

"I was placating Portia, telling her what she wanted to hear. We all treated her that way—dancing around her like monkeys around an organ grinder. Didn't you notice the way we always deferred to her? You had to be blind not to."

"Was there a particular reason you did that?"

"Damn straight. She kept threatening to move to a new gated community in Palm Beach, so we spoiled her rotten to convince her to stay. Portia wasn't just well-heeled and well-connected. She was the best board president the Hamlets ever had."

Nuts. Not exactly in keeping with my theory. "She was that indispensable?"

"Portia Van Cleef *was* the Hamlets. She made that place run as smoothly and efficiently as the Reagan White House. Without her expertise, the Hamlets would have been just another generic gated community. She put us on the map, on TV, on the pro golf tournament circuit. If we were a little too solicitous of her, it was a small price to pay for what she gave us in return."

Yup, back to square one. I *hated* when that happened.

"We are heading south now to Saariselka," Helge announced, "a drive of twenty-five kilometers. The wilderness surrounding Saariselka extends all the way to the Russian border and is home to bears, golden eagles, wolverines, and free-grazing reindeer. If you come back in winter, you can enjoy downhill and cross-country skiing, sledge runs, ski-trekking, snow-mobiling, reindeer-sleighing, twenty-four-hour darkness, and the phenomenon known as the northern lights."

"Are we gonna get to see any northern lights while we're here?" asked Margi Swanson.

"They could be sweeping across the sky right now," said Helge, "but the daylight makes them invisible. The original Laplanders thought the spectacle was caused by a giant fox swishing his tail across the Arctic sky, but science has provided us with a much less romantic explanation. Still, the Finns refer to the northern lights as *revontulet,* which literally means 'foxfires.'

You should see them at least once in your lifetime, because once you do, you'll never forget them."

"That was like Portia," Gus said wistfully. "She was so stunning that once you saw her, you never forgot her."

I patted his forearm in sympathy. "I'm sorry you're forced to continue this tour when you'd probably rather fly home to attend Portia's funeral."

"Why would you think that?"

"She obviously meant a lot to you. When a friend like Portia dies, it's only natural to—"

"Portia wasn't my friend."

I stared at him, nonplussed. "Excuse me?"

"I always deferred to her, but Portia wasn't anyone's friend. Portia Van Cleef was the most hated woman in the Hamlets."

"Did he tell you why everyone hated her so much?" Nana asked me after lunch.

"He had a laundry list of adjectives. He accused her of being mean-spirited, critical, self-important, humorless, conceited, profligate, bigot—"

"Prof—what? I never heard that word before."

"Profligate. It means wildly extravagant."

"I gotta write that down. I like to surprise folks with them kick-ass words sometimes."

While Nana jotted the word down, I turned a slow three-sixty to regard the terrain beyond the parking lot. Our restaurant sat atop a barren hill in the middle of nowhere. A giant erector set of a cell tower ensured good phone service, and straight winds rattled a trio of billboards displaying wilderness maps and trails. I'd never seen frozen tundra, but this is what I imagined it would look like if it thawed—desolate patches of bare earth intermingled with scrubby growth, deep ruts, and a boneyard of scattered rock. Ski-lift cables crisscrossed the area like telephone wires, and in the distance, the tundra spilled into dense woodland that looked even more ancient and forbidding than the forests of Tolkien's Middle Earth.

"Take a look at this, Emily. Did I spell it right?"

I stared at the indecipherable scrawl on Nana's notepad. Eh! Nana had the most legible handwriting in the world, but this looked as if it had been scribbled by a two-year-old. *Oh, my God!* She'd suffered a stroke.

I looked her square in the face. "Are you feeling okay?" Her lip wasn't drooping. She wasn't slurring her words. Her eyes were alert. Those were good signs.

"I been better," she said in a low voice.

I grabbed her arm to support her. "Do you feel woozy or confused?"

"I'm always confused, but I can't say I been woozy, except maybe when George read me one a them racy passages in Jackie's book in the airport this morning. He dog-eared the page if you wanna read it yourself."

I smiled despite my anxiety. "So why aren't you feeling up to snuff?"

"It's them cloudberries we ate for dessert, dear. My dentures are full of so many dang seeds, I feel like a watermelon."

"News flash, news flash," Jackie announced as she joined us. She batted a mosquito away from her face, then slapped it dead when it landed on her forearm. "What's this? I thought Helge said there were no mosquitoes in Lapland this year. Look at the size of this thing. Did it crossbreed with a pigeon?"

Nana stared at the flattened carcass. "Could be that one's from Russia. Maybe he was on vacation." She showed her notepad to Jackie. "Did I spell this right?"

"Profligate. Euw, ten-cent word, Mrs. S."

I checked out the notepad over Nana's shoulder. Squiggles. Lines. "You can read that?" I questioned Jackie.

"I spent a summer working in a medical office, Emily. I can read anything. And do I have news!" She drew us into a huddle, excitement oozing from every pore. "The government should hire me as a secret weapon, because I can literally squeeze blood from turnips. Reno O'Brien was putty in my hands."

I rolled my eyes. "That's because he wants to go to bed with you."

"Portia Van Cleef was the most hated woman on the planet," George blurted out as he and Tilly came up behind us. "I got it straight from the Klicks."

"That's not fair!" Jackie stomped her foot. "That was *my* news."

"It was my news, too," said Tilly. "The Peabody sisters told me Portia was so obnoxious and contrary that no one in Florida could stand her."

"How'd you get that outta them?" asked Nana. "I couldn't get nothin' outta Vern. He sucked me into playin' travel Scrabble with him on the bus and didn't have nothin' to say except, 'It's your turn.'"

A smile teased the corners of Tilly's mouth. "My ethnographic techniques are legend, Marion. Of course, it also helped that the ladies scarfed down their reindeer stew in two seconds, so that left plenty of time for chatting."

"Do you think they're ever bothered by heartburn?" asked George.

"I'd be worried about gas," said Nana. "Has anyone ever heard of U-L-N-A?" She lowered her voice conspiratorially. "Is it naughty?"

"It's a bone in your arm," said Tilly.

"No kiddin'? I had a notion Vern was makin' it up, but I didn't wanna challenge 'cause I thought it might embarrass him to give a definition in mixed company."

"Did Curtis and Lauretta happen to explain *why* they despised Portia so much?" I asked George.

He removed a slip of paper from his shirt pocket and angled his reading glasses over his plastic nose protector. "I knew you'd ask me that, so I made notes. They didn't say how much *they* disliked Portia, they just talked about how much everyone *else* disliked her. They thought that was more ethical than trashing her themselves."

"That's so noble," Jackie cooed. "Doesn't it make you all warm and fuzzy inside to know that *someone* on this tour is willing to take the moral high ground?"

Oh, God. "Anything else?"

"Yeah," said George. "The Klicks summed up their thoughts in one sentence, and I quote: 'We don't have anything bad to say about Portia Van Cleef personally, but everyone who knew her said she was a spiteful, uppity, dogmatic shrew.'"

"Aha," said Tilly. "A harridan."

Nana scribbled furiously.

"So where do we go from here?" asked Tilly. "Do you still want us to cozy up to people and pump them for information?"

"You bet," I said, as I watched guests amble back toward the bus. "If Portia was the most hated woman not only in the Hamlets and Florida but on the entire planet, too, why didn't anyone bother to tell that to the Helsinki police?"

"They were covering their own butts," sniped Jackie. "If someone leaked that bombshell to the police, they'd all be suspects."

"Lots of people are obnoxious and critical, but they don't get killed because of it," George countered. "Look at Bernice. She's a pain in everyone's neck, but no one's strangled her yet."

"George makes a good point," said Tilly. "We can usually tolerate obnoxiousness in a person, but when it gets meaner and is directed at us specifically, we tend to react by either circling the wagons or going on the offensive. I suspect Portia may have antagonized someone until it reached the proverbial tipping point. The question is, what was she using as leverage and why did it suddenly reach critical mass?"

"You s'pose them folks what live in the Hamlets have to fill out disclosure statements before they can move in?" asked Nana.

"Of course they do," said Jackie. "You practically have to file a disclosure statement to buy a chili dog from a street vendor these days."

"So if Portia seen them statements, she'd know an awful lot about them folks."

"Things no one else might know," I said with sudden clarity. "Financial history. Medical history. Family background. Do you think she was blackmailing someone?"

"Could be she was leaking confidential information," said George, "but you can't divulge what's in those legal documents. It says so right there in the fine print."

Tilly nodded agreement. "If she betrayed someone's trust, she might have angered them beyond the pale."

I suspected she'd angered someone, all right. Angered them so much that they'd decided to kill her.

CHAPTER 7

"Do you see the computer hookup?" Jackie asked as she glanced behind the television on our dresser.

Our hotel flaunted an alpine air, with dark wood interiors, acres of glass, and flower boxes brightening every balcony. A deck fronted one end of the building in German beer-garden style, and directly across the road sat an odd complex that looked like a misconceived experiment to cross a fairy-tale castle with the dogs from *101 Dalmatians*.

I searched the wall beside our mini-sofa. "Are these rooms supposed to have computer access?"

"They better have! If I can't check my Amazon numbers, you're not going to want to be around me."

Always something exciting to look forward to.

Knock, knock, knock.

"These rooms don't got no computer hookups," Nana

fretted when I answered the door. "How am I s'posed to dig up the dirt on folks if I can't Google no one?"

"We might have to do it the old-fashioned way," I said as I ushered her inside. "Ingenuity instead of technology."

"I'm old, dear. The switch might be too much for me."

"Do you think there's a computer room in the hotel?" asked Jackie.

"We might could look," said Nana. "They got a cell tower, so Internet access shouldn't be far behind."

A familiar digital tone sent me rummaging through my shoulder bag for my cell phone. "Hello?"

"I have such good news for you, Em! Oh, this is your mother."

"Hi, Mom," I said, distracted as Nana shook her head and mouthed, "*I'm not here.*" "I could use some good news."

"I knew you could. That's why I'm calling. You're going to be so proud of me, Emily. I've found a new venue for your wedding reception!"

"So soon? Wow. How'd you do that?" I nodded to Jackie as she herded Nana out the door.

"I talked to Arnie . . . *krrrrrk* . . . and he . . . *krrrrrkkk* . . . isn't spoken for on the weekend of your—"

"Wait a sec, Mom. You're breaking up." I stepped onto the balcony and leaned against the decorative wood rail. "Okay, say again?"

"Arnie Arnoldussen told me the auction barn is available on your wedding day, so I went ahead and booked it."

I paused. "The Auction Barn? What's that? A new restaurant in Ames?"

"The Windsor City auction barn, Emily. The one west of town. It's plenty big for the number of guests you're inviting, and Arnie promised to fix the roof. It blew clear off in the tornado and landed in the middle of Elmer Egeland's cornfield. We can set up tables. Sweep the sawdust off the floor. It'll be perfect."

"Mom, don't they auction off hogs in that barn?"

"Yes, dear, but it's close to home, and the building has lots of receptacles, so we can use those plug-in room fresheners to eliminate odors. They come in several delightful fragrances. We can even use the animal pens to display gifts. The key will be strategic use of crepe paper."

Oh, God. "Have you talked to Sharon to see how she's doing?"

"First thing this morning. She wanted me to tell you that she thinks she should bow out of the wedding, but I told her you wouldn't hear of it. So here's my idea: we rent a wheelchair and decorate it with crepe paper and tulle so it looks like a piece of wedding cake, and she rolls down the aisle as if she's riding a Mardi Gras float. I'd like to add a few helium balloons, but Etienne's relatives might find that a little tacky. What do you think?"

I hung my head. *Why me, Lord? Why?*

"Oh, before I forget, Emily, there's a rumor circulating that Olle Erickson might decide not to rebuild the bank."

"But he has to rebuild! Windsor City Bank is a cornerstone of the community. Where will people go to do their banking?"

"One of those newer national banks will probably take its place. Olle's already past retirement age, so word is he might hang up the day job and become a snowbird." She let out a tired sigh. "I don't know what's going to be harder on your grandmother—the prospect of never taking another trip with you and her friends, or standing in the rubble of the funeral parlor."

"Nana's the most resilient person alive, Mom."

"I know, I know. But Heavenly Host is her home away from home. The shock of not being able to attend visitations when she gets back is going to come as a terrible blow. Between you and me, Em, I'm afraid she might never recover. When old folks are forced into changing their routine, it often proves to be the beginning of the end."

"Nana is *not* old! She's only seventy-nine. Have you read *Cosmo* lately? Seventy-nine is the new sixty."

"Of course, it is. Have you noticed any changes in her since you broke the news about the tornado?"

"No, she's perfectly fine." I spotted her and Jackie on the lawn below me, making small talk with guests who were snapping photos of the dalmatian puppy castle across the street. "Except . . . her handwriting has gotten a little sloppy. Have you noticed that before?"

"Oh, dear. Handwriting is the first thing to go."

"I thought it was memory."

"Is it? I don't remember. But it sounds as if she's on a downward spiral. Will you be able to handle her,

Emily? Should I fly out there to help you? If I leave your father a list he can take over the wedding plans, though I'm not sure how well he'll do if he has to pick out your flowers. His color blindness could be a real problem, especially—*krrrrrk krrrrrk.*"

"Mom?"

"*KRRRRRK!*"

I killed the connection, then watched forlornly as Jackie helped Nana up the stairs to the beer garden. Oh, God. What if this *was* Nana's last trip? What if the handwriting business was symptomatic of a larger problem? What if she didn't live long enough to see me married?

I can't go there.

Battling unwanted tears, I punched a number into my phone.

"Miceli."

"Hi, sweetie, it's me. Do you have time to cheer me up?"

"Always," he said in an unhurried tone that wrapped dreamily around me. "Where shall I begin? By telling you how many days are left until our wedding, or by listing the things I love most about you?"

I dried my eyes, feeling better already. "Etienne, how would you feel if the wedding turned out a little different than we'd originally planned?"

"Different how?"

"Different church, different restaurant, different town."

"As long as the bride stays the same, I won't complain."

"So you'd be okay with a bridal reception in a live-stock auction barn with crepe paper streamers and plug-in room fresheners?"

Silence. "What happened to the elegant restaurant with the string quartet and candlelight?"

"Here's the scoop. Have you ever seen the movie *Twister*?"

As I filled him in on Windsor City's recent disaster, I watched Nana and Jackie hobnobbing with several guests who were seated around patio tables, drinking and swatting mosquitoes. August Manning waved a deck of playing cards in front of Reno O'Brien, drumming up a game of gin rummy, no doubt, while the Peabody sisters and Vern Grundy sat side by side, staring at mugs of ale. When Joleen Barnum shouted, "Go," Vern and the two Peabodys chugged down their brew, then slammed their mugs onto the table. Joleen consulted her stopwatch, announcing in a thundering tone, "And our winner is—by one and eight-tenths seconds—Ap-rrrril Peabody!"

Applause. Table pounding. Foot stomping. A deep-throated chant that sounded like, "Ape-ape-ape." Gee, these Floridians really knew how to celebrate a victory. Jimbob Barnum turned a cartwheel on the deck, which propelled him onto the surrounding rail like a gymnast on a balance beam. He flipped backward into a handstand, lowered himself onto his chest, then, with the ease of a Cirque du Soleil acrobat, coiled himself into a Chinese ball with his bony tush coming to rest on his head. Quite a trick for a guy who wouldn't have to jump to dunk a basketball.

"Your mother's offer of help is very generous, Emily, but are you sure you wouldn't rather elope? I could arrange everything. We could be married on the summit of the Jungfrau, or on the shores of Lake Como."

The shores of Lake Como sounded a lot more romantic than Arnie Arnoldussen's auction barn, and yet . . . "If we elope, does that mean no family present?"

"It can mean anything you want it to mean."

An alpine lake or a hog barn? The fragrance of Italianate gardens or the masking power of room deodorizer? The choice seemed pretty clear cut. "It wouldn't feel like a celebration if Nana, and Tilly, and George, and the rest of my family weren't there. Is that all right with you?"

"I'd prefer it that way, *bella*. Imagine what lively entertainment our grandmothers will provide when they meet."

I regarded Nana as she snapped a picture of Jimbob twisting himself into another contortion. *If they meet.*

"Tell Jackie I'm enjoying her novel, Emily. Do you know how much of it is autobiographical?"

"Probably all of it."

"Really?" His voice dipped an octave to a soft, throaty whisper. "Her love scenes are quite . . . stimulating. I didn't realize you were so . . . insatiable."

When had I been around any man long enough to be insatiable? "Are you sure you're not confusing me with Nana?"

"GET OUT HERE, DICK!" Helen Teig stood on the balcony to my right, pointing at the road. "AND BRING YOUR CAMCORDER!"

"Does the shouting mean you have to go?" asked Etienne.

"Oh, my God. You won't believe this." I regarded the spectacle in front of the hotel, wishing my phone could take photos. "We're being visited by Santa's reindeer."

They moved as quietly as a fog bank, their hoofs eerily silent as they poked down the road and into the hotel parking lot in seeming slow motion. Their pelts were gray and mangy, their legs spindle thin, their antlers soaring above their heads like giant wishbones with attached hat racks. They seemed as tame as a herd of house cats, and they continued their unhurried pace across the lawn as the guests in the beer garden flocked down the stairs for a closer view.

"Don't get too close!" Helen shouted to the onlookers. "They could attack at any moment."

"There's a couple of dozen of them," I said to Etienne, "and they're huddling like Irish sheep on the lawn right below me."

Dick Teig stormed outside to join Helen. "I'm standing on my balcony in Finnish Lapland," he narrated into his camcorder. "Here's the front lawn of our hotel. Here's some of the guests on our tour. Here's the pack of wild reindeer who are gonna attack the stupid shits if they get too close with their cameras."

Jimbob Barnum leaped off the railing with the grace of a ballet dancer, then cartwheeled across the lawn, collapsing to the ground when he slammed into August Manning's back.

"What *is* it with you?" August barked. "You can't walk on your feet like everyone else? You almost knocked my glasses off my face."

"Don't you talk to him like that," Joleen shouted, running toward Jimbob and wrapping him protectively in her arms. "Who do you think you are? Portia?"

"Neutral corners," said Vern, flattening his hand against August's chest. "You two have better things to do than knock each other's teeth out."

"That's what you think," Jimbob shot back. "There's nothing I'd enjoy more than taking this guy down a peg or two."

"You've had it in for us ever since we showed up at the security gate," Joleen lashed out at August. "All of you have."

"Don't look at me," said Reno. "I never laid eyes on either one of you until we had that group meeting about the trip."

"It might have helped if you'd tried to fit in a little better," April Peabody advised Joleen.

"You needed to buy a golf cart," said June. "No one walks anymore. It's simply too gauche."

"Things are heating up down there," Dick Teig said as he shut down his camcorder. "I'm going down for close-ups. Looks like it could get bloody."

"Is someone bleeding? Emily? Are you there?" Etienne asked.

"Don't panic," I soothed him. "That's just Dick Teig thinking out loud."

"Those commercials on television are so phony," Joleen ranted. " 'Come to the Hamlets to find the gold in your golden years.' What the ad should say is, 'Come to the Hamlets if you want to be laughed at for being different.' Intolerant snobs."

"If you find the Hamlets experience so distasteful, why don't you move?" suggested June.

Joleen helped Jimbob to his feet. "'Cause we didn't buy into the Hamlets concept to cut and run at the first sign of trouble. I don't care who egged our house, or toilet papered our trees, or exploded our barbeque grill. We're gonna stay the course, no matter what."

"Stick to your guns," encouraged Jackie. "Moses stayed the course, and look how well it turned out for him."

"Curtis and me never heard about the exploding grill," Lauretta Klick objected. "Did it make the paper?"

All eyes turned to August, who suddenly looked like the guilty guy in a police lineup. "I had a piece all ready to run, but Portia asked me not to print it. She didn't want to stir up emotions for what was probably a one-time incident."

"Of course it was one time," sniped Joleen. "We only had the one grill."

"Manning was covering up," alleged Curtis. "Makes you wonder what else went on that Portia didn't want made public."

"There wasn't anything else," August defended, "so let's drop the making mountains out of molehills attack."

"I'm not saying Gus covered up," said Vern, "but so what if he did? Coverups are part of our national heritage. Then someone gets paid ten million dollars to write the tell-all book. Hell, it keeps the economy booming."

"Ten million?" Jackie grabbed his arm. "What did they tell?"

"It's immoral," Lauretta sermonized. "If you think lying to folks is okay, then you're all in for a big surprise come Judgment Day." She glanced at her wristwatch. "And you don't have long to wait. Isn't that right, Curtis?"

"That's gospel, Lauretta."

"Would someone put a cork in those two?" April yelled. "I didn't come on this trip to hear it's going to be my last. Why do they always have to spoil everything? Freaking nut jobs."

"Blasphemer," Curtis barked at her.

"Bible banger," April barked back.

"Heathen."

"Holy Roller."

"Hold it!" Nana flipped open her notepad. "I wanna get some a this down."

"Democrat!" jeered Curtis.

Gasps. Mouth dropping. April staggered backward, all color draining from her face. "What did you call me?"

"You heard me," Curtis drawled, sounding like John Wayne, only shorter.

"How dare you! I've been called names in my life, but *this*—this goes far beyond the limits of common decency. And you call yourself a Christian? No one has *ever* stooped so low as to call me a . . . a—"

"Democrat," said Nana, reading off her notepad.

"Ohhh! You little—" Windmilling her arm, April flung her handbag at him, looking abashed when it sailed over Curtis's head straight into Dick Teig's face.

Eh! I gasped as Dick stopped, tottered in place, and went down like an imploded casino on the Vegas strip.

"Dick!" cried Helen. "She's killed Dick. Do something, Emily!"

"Etienne? I've gotta run."

"Hardly unexpected, *bella*."

I bolted out the door. Chances were April hadn't killed him, but she'd probably broken his nose.

Old Dick had said things were going to get bloody.

He sure got that right.

"See there?" said Nana. "Them's Joleen's clothes hangin' up. I told you she was gonna be here. I heard her tell Jimbob when you was tendin' Dick's nosebleed."

We were in the dressing room of the hotel's sauna, hoping we might catch Joleen alone and in a talkative mood.

"Oky-doky," said Jackie when she finished reading the instructions posted on the wall. "Everybody get naked."

"Does it say anything there about old folks bein' able to keep their bloomers on?" asked Nana.

"Don't get too hung up on modesty," I advised as I peeled off my top. "We all have the same body parts."

"I know, dear, but gravity's been working on mine

a lot longer. I don't want you to get depressed when you see what's in store for you."

Jackie handed each of us a fluffy white towel. "Here you go, girls. Antidepressants."

The sauna was a little bigger than our hotel room and a whole lot hotter. A small furnace sat in a pit in the center of the room, smoke steaming off the rocks piled around it. Surrounding the pit on four sides was a raised walkway, a protective guard rail, and wooden benches with slatted backs. Joleen sat at the far end of the room, her head and body wrapped in towels as she stared listlessly into the pit.

"Could you use some company?" I asked as we trooped into the room.

"So long as your name isn't April or June, you're right welcome," Joleen said in a down-home twang. "I'm developing a real dislike for the months of the year."

"Feels like Arizona in here," said Nana as we parked ourselves on Joleen's bench.

I peered at her through the haze. "Have you ever been to Arizona?"

"Nope, but I got a good imagination."

"Arizona's pretty nice," Joleen mused. "Mostly because it doesn't have Florida's humidity. Jimbob and me toured Arizona once. If we'd been smart, we would have retired there instead of the Hamlets, but Jimbob wanted to end up someplace close to home so we wouldn't be too far from the grandkids."

"Where's home?" I asked as perspiration beaded my upper lip.

"Sarasota. We used to winter there in the off season, but we liked it so much, we decided to set up housekeeping permanently."

"Where was you the rest of the year?" asked Nana.

"Just about everywhere. The Southern states, New England, Mid-Atlantic states, the Midwest. Anyplace there was a fairground big enough to erect our tents and carnival rides."

"You're circus people!" Jackie exclaimed.

"And proud of it," said Joleen. "Though having a circus background apparently puts you on the outs with the gatekeepers of the upscale retirement communities. Seems we're not homogenized enough for the 'normal' folk." She sat up straighter on the bench, perking up a little. "Bet you can't guess what I did."

"Lion tamer," I threw out.

"Are you kidding? One false move and you're the blue plate special. No thank you."

"Trapeze artist," said Nana.

"Afraid of heights."

"I know, I know," cried Jackie, bouncing with excitement. "Tattooed lady!"

I regarded Joleen's bare, unblemished skin before glancing at Jackie. "I think being a tattooed lady probably requires tattoos."

"She might have had them removed, you know. Laser surgery can correct a lot of the dumb things you do when you're drunk."

"I'll give you a clue," said Joleen, lifting my hand to her face. "Rub your knuckles over my cheek here."

Scratch, scratch, scratch. It felt as rough as an emery board. "Is that stubble?"

"I got it!" said Nana. "You was the bearded lady."

Joleen held her head high and preened. "I was the best sideshow act to ever hit the circuit. My beard hung all the way to my waist. I could braid it, set it in banana curls, put it in pigtails. Leo the Lion-Faced Boy was green with envy. He had a terrible time with split ends and breakage. I told him to try a good conditioner, but most men don't want to fork out the bucks for expensive hair care products. Give 'em a bar of soap, and they're happy. His pelt got so scruffy, he was forced to retire a decade earlier than he wanted."

"How was you able to grow a beard?" asked Nana. "I got a little mustache. Should I be frettin' that it's gonna spread to the rest a my face?"

Joleen giggled like a teenager. "Not unless you got the same skin condition I got. Hypertrichosis. It's something you're born with and it lasts 'til you die. It doesn't hurt or nothing, but it means I got way too much body hair. On an average day I can look like a shag carpet."

Aha! That explained the sparkly face powder. She was trying to camouflage a four o'clock shadow. "But you have no hair on your arms and legs. How do you manage your condition? Electrolysis?"

"Full body wax."

"*Euuw.*" Jackie grimaced in imagined agony. "Your threshold of pain must be off the chart. My first bikini wax was more excruciating than childbirth."

I regarded her oddly. "You've never been through childbirth."

"Excuse me, Emily, but Mrs. S. isn't the only one with a good imagination."

"Take it from me," said Joleen, "gettin' all the hair ripped off your body is worse than childbirth. I gotta take painkillers when I go in there. And not just the over-the-counter stuff. I gotta take the same prescription meds that Vern Grundy takes for his knees. Awful things, with all their side effects, but at least they make the procedure tolerable.

"Not that anyone cares. When they opened the new spa, one of Gus Manning's cub reporters interviewed me about the pros and cons of professional waxing, but the article never made it into the paper. I figured Portia didn't want to highlight anything about her resident freak. Bad enough for her that Jimbob and me actually got voted into the community. I tried being nice to her and giving her lots of attention so she'd like me, but I don't think it worked."

"You have to be voted into the Hamlets?" I asked.

"Yesiree. You got to appear before the board so they can look you over and make sure you're Hamlets material. They tell you it's a friendly meet and greet to discuss your financial disclosure statement, but it's not. It's a beauty pageant."

"So if Portia was so opposed to any kind of diversity, how did you end up being voted in?" I persisted.

"Must have been the other board members who voted their conscience instead of the party line. Probably wanted to avoid bad publicity. A bunch of people who'd been rejected had complained to the local TV stations about discrimination, so media folks started coming around requesting interviews. Portia blew them off, but I think the other board members got nervous. Maintenance fees are high in the Hamlets, but not high enough to cover legal fees in a class action suit."

"Who's the other folks on the board?" asked Nana.

"The Peabody sisters, August Manning, Lauretta Klick, and Vern. The whole board's on this trip."

I exchanged a meaningful look with Jackie. Gee, what an interesting wrinkle. "What about Reno O'Brien? He seems pretty thick with Vern and Gus. Was he ever a board member?"

"Don't rightly know, but I expect he wasn't. He's too busy traveling the globe for those races of his. And I can see why. I watched him run in one of the Hamlets sports events and he broke some long-standing record. I hear tell his nickname is Roadrunner. Gus ran an article about him in the paper, probably one of the few Portia didn't object to. Between you, me, and the bedpost, if I was a Pulitzer Prize–winning journalist like August Manning, I wouldn't have let Portia Van Cleef bust my chops about anything I wrote. Must have driven him crazy, having her dictate to him like that. Don't know why he tolerated it."

Why indeed?

"Would someone grab that ladle and splash more water on those rocks?" asked Joleen. "The instructions say adding humidity to the air makes you sweat, and you gotta sweat to get rid of all the nasty impurities in your body."

"I'll do it," said Nana. "I probably got more impurities that need gettin' rid of on account a I'm old." She dipped the ladle into the nearby bucket, then, with one hand holding her towel together, stood at the rail and poured water into the pit.

Sssssssssssssst! Steam spewed upward, enveloping us in the kind of fog you see in B horror flicks.

"Doesn't this remind you of Victorian England?" Joleen whispered in an eerie voice. "Can't you see it? The gas streetlamps, the men in their stovepipe hats, Jack the Ripper lurking in an alleyway in Spitalfields, ready to eviscerate his next victim?"

"Eviscerate," Nana repeated, savoring every syllable. "That's a good word. Emily, dear, remind me to write that down when I get to my room. I might can use it if I'm ever invited to play board games again. Did they ever figure out who that Ripper fella really was?"

"They never did," said Joleen. "Just like that big case in Boston back in the fifties. The police thought they'd solved the mystery, but looking back now, they're not so sure they got the right guy. Gus wrote about it in the article he published about Reno. Seems Reno was a beat cop back then and was right in the middle of the case. He even got to testify in court because he claims he saw the killer running from the apartment of one of his victims."

"Reno's an ex-cop?" Jackie exclaimed. "You'd think he might have mentioned that to me on the bus. I can see him as a cop." Her voice turned dreamy. "Cops are so sexy. Cops and paramedics. I think it's the attitude."

"I think it's them wraparound sunglasses," said Nana.

"What case was Reno involved in?" I asked Joleen. "Anything I might have heard of?"

"It was well before your time, so I'm doubtful. There was no cable news back then to give up-to-the-minute coverage of every cat that gets stuck in a tree. Still, you might have seen the movie. Tony Curtis played the lead." She looked at me through the fog. "You ever heard of the Boston Strangler?"

CHAPTER 8

"The territory in northern Scandinavia that you Americans call Lapland is known as Samiland to its indigenous peoples," Helge told us on the bus ride to our evening event. "You call them Lapps, but they call themselves the Sami, and they have been herding reindeer for eight thousand years."

"There's a bunch of escapees hanging around our hotel," Bernice complained. "How'd they get loose? After eight thousand years, you'd think someone would be bright enough to figure out how to keep 'em penned up."

"Reindeer roam wild in the far north," said Helge, "and they graze wherever they want, including the grounds of your hotel. Every reindeer belongs to someone, though. If you look at their ears, you'll see they're notched to prove ownership."

We turned onto a dirt road that snaked through a woodland of hardwoods and new-growth pine, the bus shimmying as we rolled in and out of the deeper ruts. "This entire area is a working reindeer farm," Helge informed us, "and your meal this evening will be prepared and served by its owners. Historically, the Sami were nomads like your native American buffalo hunters, but they have traded in their dogsleds for snowmobiles, their tents for condos, and their quiet evenings around the cookfire for dinner extravaganzas. The Sami have survived for eight thousand years because they have adapted to change." Laughter crept into his voice. "It has also helped that they are—what is the term?—bitching entrepreneurs."

Would gambling casinos be far behind?

"What happened to your hair?" April Peabody asked me as we stepped off the bus.

I fluffed the crinkled strands of what used to be my sexy Italian haircut. "The sauna treatment. It refreshes the spirit, invigorates the skin, and turns naturally curly hair into a Brillo pad. It's really wonderful. You should try it."

She leaned close to me and lowered her voice. "You should cover your head. You're going to frighten the reindeer."

Our Sami host greeted us by a rustic lodge that resembled a wigwam made of Lincoln logs. His name was Emppu, and he was a small-boned man with black eyes that snapped with intelligence, and facial features that gave him the look of Genghis Khan. He wore a blue wool tunic embroidered with bright primary colors, dark leggings, moccasins with turned-up toes, and a hat like a court jester. In Finland he'd immediately be recognized as a Sami reindeer herder; back home he might be mistaken for the head elf at the "Have Your Picture Taken With Santa" kiosk at the mall. The poor guy had to be cooking in that getup.

He led us across a clearing to a fenced enclosure, where a solitary reindeer shied away from guests who clamored to pet him. I worked the crowd, snapping shots of people dressed in full mosquito regalia—white shirts, light slacks, and flat-topped green canvas hats with enough face netting to outfit a bridal party. Annika had recommended the hats as protection against insects in the deep woods, so we'd flocked to the hotel gift shop and bought out the stock, which, unfortunately, hadn't been large enough to allow everyone to make a purchase.

Psssssssssssssst.

I looked over my shoulder to find Bernice spraying a halo of repellant around her wire whisk hair. "Do you want your picture with Emppu?" I asked cheerfully. "I should be able to get a good shot of your face since you're not hiding behind mosquito netting."

She stabbed a crooked finger at me as she wheezed on the fumes. "Don't think I'm gonna forget this. You should have done your research. That's what an escort is *supposed* to do."

Bernice had pooh-poohed the mosquito netting idea, deeming it a tourist rip-off, but she'd changed her tune when she'd discovered that repellant was even more expensive than a hat. Of course, by then it was too late, because the hats had been limited to one a customer, and I'd bought the last one for Nana.

"You better pray I don't come down with malaria," she warned.

"No chance of that happening," I assured her. "These are Finnish mosquitoes, not the tropical variety. And they're not as bad as Annika said they'd be." I stuck out my hand as bait. "See? They're not bothering me at all."

"It's your hair. You've scared them all away." *Psssssst.* "Ornery critters."

Annika clapped her hands. "Please to follow me, everyone!" She led us back to the clearing, where we formed a wide semicircle around a sawhorse reindeer whose antlers were as wide as a spreading oak. "Emppu is going to demonstrate how the Sami lasso reindeer, so please watch closely so you can test your own skill later."

"Here it comes." Gus sidled next to me, his mosquito hat cocked at an odd angle. "The part of the tour where we get to show the world how stunningly uncoordinated we are."

"People might surprise you," I said as Emppu sailed a coil of neon orange rope toward the wooden reindeer from twenty feet away, snagging all fourteen points of its impressive antlers.

Whoops. Applause. Whistles.

"Dick Teig killed in the hula competition in Maui. It was a real ego booster because after his big weight gain, he couldn't find his hips, much less swivel them."

Emppu gathered his rope into a tidy coil and then scanned our faces expectantly, hefting the lasso as if to give it away to the first taker.

"Any volunteers?" asked Annika.

A hush descended on the group. People adjusted their mosquito netting in an obvious attempt to look preoccupied. A few shuffled backward out of the front row. The Dicks bowed their heads and slunk behind their wives.

"Where is the sense of reckless adventure that you Americans are so famous for?" Annika scolded.

Gus leaned toward me and said in an undertone, "It's being quashed by the fear of looking like a total ass in front of everyone."

A gasp went up from the crowd as the lasso whipped through the air, encircling George Farkas around his shoulders. "Holy Hannah!" George chuckled as Emppu tightened the noose, dragging him toward the center of the clearing. "How'd he do that?"

Eyes twinkling, Emppu coiled the rope again and handed it to George, who threw off his mosquito hat, swung the lasso back and forth to gauge its weight, then hurled it into the air.

"Yo, George!" yelled Jackie as the line dropped over the reindeer's antlers.

"Foul!" sniped April Peabody. "He was standing too close."

"Iowans rule!" shouted Dick Teig, fisting his hand above his head.

George shrugged modestly. "Beginner's luck. I'd probably never be able to do it again."

"Did you see that?" Nana asked, elbowing Vern Grundy. "He's with me."

"I'm going next," demanded June Peabody as she marched into the clearing.

"I'm after her," cried April.

I got spun around as the Floridians stormed past me in a mad scramble to line up behind the Peabodys. "Eh!" I hunched my shoulders to give them room. "I guess they rediscovered their sense of reckless adventure."

"It's not the adventure," said Gus, "it's the competition. Everyone wants to be top dog. They're galled that George looked so outstanding. They smell blood."

"Are you going to join them?"

"Hell, no. They can eat each other alive, for all I care. I gave up the competitive thing a long time ago."

"Except for gin rummy."

He smiled through his layers of mosquito netting. "Yeah. It ticks me off that I never beat the champ before she died, so I guess that makes me more competitive than I'm willing to admit."

Hoots went up from the crowd as June's toss flopped to the ground at the reindeer's feet.

"You must have been pretty competitive when you wrote for the *Post*," I remarked. "I imagine everyone would like a Pulitzer. Did you run into a lot of professional jealousy?"

"How did you know about my Pulitzer?"

"Joleen told me. She was very complimentary of the article you wrote about Reno."

"That's hard to believe, but I can't take much credit

for the piece. O'Brien is a real chatterbox, especially when he's talking about himself. Besides, who's going to stop reading when you mention the Boston Strangler? O'Brien knew details about the case that never saw the light of day. It was pretty creepy, actually. If I didn't know him so well—"

A cheer exploded as April roped Osmond Chelsvig's foot.

"If you didn't know him so well?" I prodded.

He looked suddenly distracted as Reno advanced to the front of the line. "Let's just say he knows more about strangulation than ninety-nine and nine-tenths percent of the population. Definitely his area of expertise."

I stared at him in disbelief. "And you didn't mention that to the Helsinki police?"

"Was that my responsibility? Everyone knows about O'Brien's big case. It was in the article. I thought it was a non-issue."

Sure it was. Kinda like Tweetie Bird's feathers flying out of Sylvester's mouth was a non-issue.

"If you want to nail me for withholding evidence, you'll have to nail everyone else for the same thing, which could really bog down the sightseeing activities. Lighten up, Emily." He draped his arm around my shoulders and gave me a squeeze. "Reno O'Brien is the last person on earth who'd ever kill Portia."

"How can you be so sure?"

"*Because* he's the resident expert on strangulation. If he doesn't keep his nose clean, you know damned well he'll be the one they haul off to jail."

I liked his logic. Reno didn't do it because it was way too obvious that he *might* have done it. Why hadn't I thought of that?

Sniggers and jeers traveled through the Florida crowd as Reno snagged two points on the reindeer's antlers. "Let me try again," he pressed Emppu. "I can do better."

Emppu waved him off good-naturedly and nodded for Vern to step up.

A hint of sarcasm crept into Gus's voice. "If O'Brien had hit a ringer the first time up, he would have demanded I write a feature article about it when we got back home. When he makes good, he expects adulation from the immediate world."

I couldn't have engineered a better segue. "Do you have complete control over what you print in your newspaper?"

"I've always had creative control, but Portia liked to keep her thumb in the pie. She scheduled semiweekly meetings so she could look over some of my more high-profile op-ed and feature stories and give me a yea or nay."

"I can't imagine she'd nix much of what you wrote. I mean, you're the one with the Pulitzer."

"The award didn't matter to Portia. She was the Hamlets' heart and soul, which meant she wasn't above downplaying controversy and suggesting that I—" He cut himself off, his voice growing cautious. "You know something, Emily? I've had this conversation once today already, so I'm going to end it here. Discussions about editorial decisions make for boring conversation." He nodded toward Emppu and Vern. "Old Vern looks pretty steady right now, but who knows how long that'll last? I'll tell you one thing: if he sticks it, O'Brien will go ballistic."

I regarded Jimbob as he waited his turn behind Vern. "Is it true that Portia could barely tolerate the Barnums?"

"That's a question you should have asked Portia— before she died."

"She couldn't have been very happy with whoever voted them in. Pretty gutsy move to oppose the queen bee. Was she surprised?"

He laughed out loud. "She was apoplectic, but majority rules, so there wasn't much she could do except pout and act pissy."

Vern launched the lasso into the air and pumped his arm as it swooped over all fourteen antler points. "Bull's-eye!" he yelled, hobbling off balance as he was applauded by the Iowans and booed by his friends.

Gus grinned sardonically. "The person who coined the phrase 'Familiarity breeds contempt' must have lived in the Hamlets. It's so inspiring to spend your retirement years with people who cheer your failures and boo your successes."

"Did Portia ever find out which board members opposed her?"

Gus frowned, looking a little disturbed by my persistence. "We voted by secret ballot."

"But a majority would mean that four people opposed Portia. That's nearly the entire board. What would you call that? A coup or a rebellion?"

He narrowed his gaze. "Would you mind telling me where you're going with this? You ask more questions than the Helsinki police. Forgive my presumptuousness, but it sounds as if you're digging for evidence that would prove one of us committed murder."

"It does?" Damn, I hated it when I sounded so obvious.

"Is it time for dinner yet?" April Peabody whined. "I've had it with the mosquitoes."

"We're going inside," said June, swatting the air with abandon.

"It is very hot inside the lodge," Annika warned, "so until the food is ready, you must stay out in the fresh air."

Psssssssssssssssssst.

"It's not that fresh!" Lauretta objected, choking on Bernice's aerosol spray.

"Do not enter the lodge!" Annika repeated, chasing after the Floridians who were streaming toward the building.

"All of you just stay where you are!" Joleen bellowed. "Jimbob hasn't had his turn yet!"

"That woman never gives up," Gus grumbled. "If we wanted to see Elastic Man perform, we'd go to the circus."

"Is that what he was called? Elastic Man?"

"That's what Portia called him, when she was feeling generous. Would you excuse me? He loves making a spectacle of himself, so I'd prefer not to encourage him." He made a hissing sound as Jimbob eased into a handstand, bent his knees, and removed the rope from Emppu's hand with his feet. "Good God, the man isn't a showman; he's an aberration."

As he walked away, I realized I'd discovered the other board member who'd voted with Portia in opposition to the Barnums.

"Go, Jimbob!" Joleen cheered. "Show these folks how to do it the circus way."

I joined Nana and Jackie, who were watching the entertainment beneath their veils of mosquito netting. "See what he's doin', dear? He's gonna toss the lasso with his feet. Your grampa woulda loved this. When he was a boy, he had a notion to run off and join the circus. He wanted to be the fella what got shot outta the cannon."

"Little boys can be so dumb," Jackie tittered. "Can you imagine what that would have done to his hearing?"

I regarded her indulgently. Had she been like this when we were married? Wouldn't I have noticed? Or had I simply been in denial?

"I seen you talkin' to Gus," Nana whispered. "He tell you anythin' useful?"

"He thinks Jimbob is an aberration."

Nana's eyes brightened as she reached for her notepad and pen. "Does that got one r or two?"

"That is *so* unkind," Jackie huffed. "How can a Pulitzer Prize winner be so intolerant?"

Nana shrugged. "Maybe he's a right-wing Republican."

With a flurry of fancy footwork, Jimbob flung the lasso off his toes and bounced back onto his feet, breaking into a rebel yell as the noose dropped over the reindeer's rack.

Pandemonium erupted. Cheers. Whoops. I let out my signature whistle and clapped until my palms turned red.

"What'd I tell you?" Joleen hugged Jimbob so hard that I thought I heard his spine crack. "He's twice as good as those wannabes. Jimbob Barnum, the greatest contortionist ever to work the main ring of P. T. Barnum and Bailey Brothers Circus!"

"You s'pose he's related to the original P. T. Barnum?" Nana mused. "I seen a show sayin' that fella was pretty slick. Kinda like snake oil slick."

I inched closer to Nana and Jackie. "I also found out that not one, not two, but four people voted against Portia on the Barnum issue. Four board members wanted Joleen and Jimbob to move into the Hamlets."

"Ooo," Jackie gushed. "What does that mean?"

"Regime change," said Nana.

"I'm pretty sure Gus voted with her," I continued, "which means April, June, Vern, and Lauretta voted against her."

"And suffered her wrath," said Jackie. "Can you imagine being on that woman's bad side? I'd rather have a million needles plunged into my body."

"George had that done once," Nana reminisced. "He said the pain was excruciatin', on account a Medicare don't pay for acupuncture."

"Do you think Portia found a way to punish the four dissenting board members?" I asked.

"Either that, or they mighta knowed somethin' was

comin', so they made one a them preemptive strikes to get her before she got them."

"How do you punish an elderly resident of a retirement community?" asked Jackie. "Deactivate their golf cart?"

"Oh, my God, do you think the other four board members were in cahoots with each other to knock her off?"

Jackie let out a frustrated sigh as she wrestled with her hat. "Do you see a trap door in this thing? How are we supposed to eat dinner through all this mosquito netting?"

"I was plannin' to take my hat off," said Nana, deadpan. She tilted her head back to look far up to Jackie's face. "You're very tall, aren't you, dear?"

"Last one to the lodge has to sit with Bernice!" yelled Dick Teig, initiating a footrace of pounding feet and flying elbows. As people charged past us, I saw Gus and Reno at the far side of the lodge, hats tucked under their arms, engaged in the kind of heated discussion that often takes place between baseball managers and home plate umpires. Arms waved, words flew, and when they suddenly looked my way, I got the distinct impression that the topic under discussion was me.

I had a really bad feeling that this wasn't good.

The "authentic Sami lodge" was a modern spit-polished banquet facility with seating for two hundred guests. The log roof was shaped like a funnel, and in the center of the room was an authentic Sami open-flame grill that raised the indoor temperature to a degree that could melt the fillings in your teeth. Throughout our meal, people kept escaping to the outside for a breath of air, then crawled back to swelter in the smoke-filled haze, leaving many bowls of mushroom soup and plates of reindeer meat, mashed potatoes, and vegetable medleys half-eaten.

"If we was sittin' here in the all-together, I'd think we was in that hotel sauna," said Nana, mopping her throat with a tissue.

"I'd think I was in heaven," said George, the clear plastic of his nose guard fogging up.

"George Farkas, you are such a rascal." Jackie rubbed a playful hand over George's little bald head. "Men of your generation don't admit stuff like that. They get way too embarrassed."

"I've been reading your book, so nothing embarrasses me anymore."

"Eating in the nude is common practice among African bushmen," Tilly informed us. "They're so comfortable with their bodies, they don't quite realize they're naked."

"Must save 'em a bundle on their dry cleanin' bills," said Nana.

Jackie pushed her bowl of cloudberries aside and stood up. "George just reminded me of something. I have to call Mona. Every time I've phoned her today I've gotten shunted to voice mail, so I'm getting really pissed."

"How many times have you tried?" I asked.

She stared into space as she calculated. "Twelve."

"Are you kidding me?"

"If we hadn't sat in the sauna so long, I could have called more."

"Jack, no wonder she's not answering your calls. You're bothering her too much. Can you give it a rest? I bet she'd appreciate an occasional call much more than a barrage. She might even break down and talk to you."

She glowered at me. "Excuse me, Emily, but I'm perched on the edge of literary stardom, and you're telling me that Mona thinks I'm a bother? I don't think so." She grabbed her mosquito hat. "If anyone needs me, I'll be outside."

"I'm real partial to that girl," said Nana as Jackie stalked toward the exit, "but she don't got a clue."

"With bazooms like that, she doesn't need one," said George.

"I hope all of you have enjoyed your meal," Annika told everyone as she joined Emppu and his family near the cookfire. "If you would like more to drink, there are beverages for sale by the door. The heat is a little overwhelming inside, so I encourage you to overindulge with liquids. If I may offer my opinion, the Finnish beer is especially good."

"Alcohol is the last thing people need in this heat," whispered Tilly.

"I'll try the beer if I don't have to pay for it," Bernice called out.

Annika smiled stiffly. "I also recommend the water, which is free. Please settle back now as Emppu's wife and daughter perform a musical selection for you. This will be an authentic Sami song that urges all peoples to treat Nature with respect or suffer consequences, which usually involve boils, pestilence, and some form of horrific death. Enjoy!"

The two women stood side by side in their long skirts and decorative blouses, chanting in lively tones as they beat out a rhythm on handheld drums that looked as if they'd been crafted from reindeer skins. I was touched by the music's soulfulness but grateful I couldn't understand the chant. I wasn't sure what a boil was, but I was certain I didn't need to hear about it on a full stomach.

Jackie crept back to the table as the drumbeats ended and the room erupted in applause. "Did you get through?" asked George.

She tucked in her bottom lip as if to prevent it from quivering. "I don't want to talk about it."

"This next song relates the heroic feats that Emppu's ancestors performed during the reindeer migration hundreds of years ago," announced Annika.

The drumbeats resumed at a quicker pace. The women's voices throbbed with emotion, their expressions growing animated. I swayed with the rhythm, as did Nana and Tilly, but other guests yawned, looked bored, changed seats for a better view, or got up to buy drinks or visit the facilities.

None of this boded well for a late evening.

The entertainment continued with songs that celebrated Emppu's first visit to a snowmobile dealer, his discovery of polar fleece and gum rubber boots, and his purchase of an Oral-B electric toothbrush, which is when I realized what Sami chanting really was.

It was a blog!

A digital tone from my shoulder bag sent me scrambling for my cell phone, prompting *tsk*s and dirty looks from the guests at nearby tables. "I'm sorry," I apologized. "I forgot to turn it off." I slunk down on the bench, burying my head under the table. "Hello?"

"Emily? This is your mother."

I lowered my voice to a whisper. "I can't talk right now."

"Would you take it outside?" the guy behind me grumbled.

"Hold on, Mom." I slithered out from beneath the table and skirted the perimeter of the room to the exit, stepping out into the audible buzz of swarming mosquitoes. *Uff-da.* "Can I call you back?" I asked as I flapped my hand in front of my face.

"This can't wait, Em. I have wonderful news. You know the church on—KRRRRRK—Well, I spoke—KRRRRRRRRK—KRRRRRRRK—good news?"

"Mom? I'm catching every fifth word. Are you there?"

"KRRRRRRRK."

Nuts. If she'd found another church, that really would be wonderful news. "Don't hang up," I urged as I hiked across the clearing in search of better reception. "This place is full of dead spots."

I circled to the back of the lodge. "Are you still there?"

"*Krrrrk*—ily?"

"This isn't working, Mom. I'm going to hang up and—"

At the edge of the woods, I saw a man in light

trousers and a white shirt lying facedown on the ground, his mosquito hat covering his head, his body unmoving.

A chill raced up my spine. *Oh, my God.*

Heart pounding, I ran across the uneven ground and fell to my knees beside him, rolling him onto his back. But when I saw Emppu's lasso wrapped around his throat, I knew it was too late for CPR.

"Can you hear me now?" Mom's voice chimed happily from my phone. "Did you run into a dead spot?"

I turned my head away, gasping for air.

Oh, God. I'd run into a dead Pulitzer Prize winner.

CHAPTER 9

"I have reviewed the initial statement you gave to Officer Kynsijarvi, Ms. Andrew. Thank you for your cooperation. Would you mind going over a few minor details with me? It's very late, so I'll try to be brief."

I was in one of the hotel's private offices, sitting opposite Officer Jukka-Pekka Vitikkohuhta, who commanded the position of authority behind the desk. He was around my age, with intense eyes and a whipcord body that looked as if he might spend his off hours shooshing down ski slopes in spandex and designer goggles. His English was well enunciated and precise, but his voice was hoarse from the interviews he'd been conducting since he'd arrived from Ivalo. He and two fellow officers were shuffling guests from conference rooms to a main lecture hall, and once they were done with me, I figured they'd make a decision about what to do with us.

"Did you see the deceased leave the lodge at any time during your meal?" he asked me.

"I didn't see him at all while we were eating."

"Did you notice anyone else leave the room?"

"Everyone. People were up and down all evening. Buying drinks, getting fresh air, changing seats, using the facilities. You would have needed a score card to keep track of everybody."

He made a notation on his notepad. "Did any of your table companions leave the premises?"

"Jack. I mean, Jackie. Ms. Thum. When the entertainment began, she went outside to call her editor. She wasn't gone very long, because I suspect her editor shunted her to voice mail again."

Officer Vitikkohuhta smiled at the mention of Jackie's name. "My officers and I had never met a published author before tonight. She was kind enough to autograph my notepad"—he flipped to a back page and held up her sprawling signature—"and she signed Officer Hamalainen's forearm. Officer Kynsijarvi had her autograph his athletic sock. He hopes to auction it over the Internet."

"He might want to hold onto it for a while," I suggested. "She hasn't hit the bestseller list yet."

"Officer Kynsijarvi will make it work. He was once offered two hundred American dollars for a stale marshmallow that looked like Raphael's *Madonna and Child*."

"Seriously?" I had stale marshmallows back home.

Was I turning my back on a fortune by ignoring the resale value of snacks I'd kept beyond their freshness date?

"Sadly, he was never able to complete the sale."

"Did the buyer suddenly come to his senses?"

"No. His wife used it in a cup of hot cocoa and it melted." He referred back to his notes. "You were outside talking on your cell phone when you discovered the deceased. Is that correct?"

I nodded. "I was getting mostly static, so I was trying to find a spot that had better reception."

"Perhaps you could tell me, do you know of anyone in your tour group who had reason to want Mr. Manning dead?"

"He seemed to be fairly well liked, but I know some of the guests didn't see eye to eye about a variety of things."

"I'm told there was a confrontation in Helsinki between your group and the Floridians about seating in the outdoor market. Could someone in your group have taken exception to having his chair stolen from beneath him and gotten even with Mr. Manning?"

"No! That was just a minor blip on the radar. I'm sure my group forgot all about that. Besides, Gus wasn't in on the chair stealing. He was standing up."

Officer Vitikkohuhta scanned his notes, his expression tightening. "There was ill will between August Manning and Mr. and Mrs. Barnum. The deceased apparently found the couple distasteful, and they resented him for it. You were aware of that?"

He already knew? Relief flooded through me—I wouldn't have to be a stool pigeon. "Joleen mentioned a slight personality conflict earlier today."

"Mr. Manning and Reno O'Brien were seen arguing outside the Sami lodge. Did you witness that?"

"I saw them, but I don't know what they were so ticked off about. I thought they were good friends."

He flipped to a dog-eared page and read his notes aloud. "Mr. Manning apparently made a derogatory comment about a Boston team never being able to win a World Series, and Mr. O'Brien took exception to it. Something about a curse."

"Curse of the Bambino," I informed him. "It's a baseball thing. Dinosaurs will make a comeback before the Red Sox ever win the pennant."

"Mr. O'Brien is an expert in strangulation techniques, but an ex-policeman would never kill someone using a method he knew so much about," he theorized. "It would be far too obvious. In fact, someone might be trying to frame Mr. O'Brien by making it look as if only he could have committed the murders. I believe this is what you call a red herring."

Or a con job.

"Your group dislikes Lauretta and Curtis Klick because of their disturbing predictions, and they're unhappy with April and June Peabody because watching the sisters eat apparently gives everyone heartburn."

My, my, my. People had certainly been chatty with this guy.

"But the revelation I find most interesting is that

several of your Floridians serve on the board of directors of their retirement community, and now two of them are dead. Do you know what this means, Ms. Andrew?"

"Someone is targeting board members?"

"It means there is a killer in your midst and until we are able to identify him, you should assume that all guests are in danger."

"Even if we're not on the board?"

"Membership on the board might be coincidental."

"Even if we don't live in Florida?"

"Until we discover a motive, you are all at risk."

So even if the Klicks were wrong and the world didn't end, we still might not make it to the end of the trip. Nice. On the upside, at least I wouldn't have to hold my wedding reception in a livestock auction barn. "Are you planning to assign a special detail to protect us while you look for the murderer?"

His mouth widened into a grin. "We are not that kind of police force. Perhaps you are thinking of the Swiss Guard?" He placed a sheet of plain white paper and a pen on the blotter and indicated that I should slide my chair up to the desk. "Would you mind providing me with a sample of your handwriting, Ms. Andrew?" He placed another paper on the blotter.

I eyed the typewritten text. "This is what you want me to write? 'Twenty-five bottles of beer on the wall. Meet me in St. Louis. Take me out to the ball game. East side, west side, all around the town. Sixty minutes, a news magazine.' " I frowned. "You do realize this last sentence has never been set to music?"

"If you would please copy all five sentences, then you will be free to leave."

Had they found a note on Gus's body? Something written by the killer? Was that the reason I was being asked to copy pre-1950 song lyrics?

"How long does it take for handwriting samples to be analyzed?" I asked when I handed the paper back to him.

"Longer than it takes to provide the sample. Just one more formality, Ms. Andrew. Would you please hold out your hands, palms up? Thank you. And now turn them over? Very good. Please understand that I'm required to do this with everyone."

"I don't suppose you could tell me if you ran across anyone with fresh scratch marks."

"You're quite right. I can't tell you." He nodded politely. "Officer Hamalainen should be just outside the office. He'll escort you to the lecture hall."

"Can you at least tell me how you managed to pump so much information out of people in such a short amount of time? The policeman in Helsinki wasn't nearly as successful."

He looked embarrassed. "I would like to take credit for superior interrogation techniques, but the truth is that most guests were not very forthcoming. I didn't hit the mother lode until a woman with a voice like a rusty pipe walked through the door and underwent a system dump. I would almost guess she was retired CIA or FBI, or perhaps had watched too many James Bond movies."

I sighed. "Was her name Bernice Zwerg?"

He consulted the same dog-eared page on his note-pad before regarding me in astonishment. "How did you know?"

" 'Take me to St. Louis in twenty-five minutes,' " said Osmond, reading from the inside cover of a candy wrapper.

"You can't get to St. Louis that fast," objected Dick Stolee. "The Atlantic Ocean gets in the way."

"Maybe it's written in code," suggested Lucille Rassmuson.

"Is there a St. Louis in Lapland?" asked Alice. "Does anyone have a map?"

The lecture hall was set up amphitheater style, with bright overhead lighting, comfortable theater seats, and collapsible desktops for note taking. Annika and Helge were conspicuously absent, but the Floridians were spread out across the lower tier of seats, the majority of them slumped over their desktops, snoring. My Iowans hung out in the nosebleed section, scribbling on trash. I curled up in the seat next to Osmond, wondering if he'd invented a new version of charades. "Is this a private party or can anyone join?"

"Did that policeman ask you for a writing sample?" Dick Teig asked me as he pressed an ice pack to the nose that still bore the imprint of April Peabody's purse.

I nodded. "Five sentences, four of them song lyrics."

"And they didn't make no sense," said Nana, "so we're guessin' the strangler wrote Gus a note usin' some a them words, and we're tryin' to figure out what it mighta said. Could give us a clue about who done it."

"I had the same thought!" Which suddenly terrified me. *Uff-da*, I was thinking like a septuagenarian. That couldn't be good.

"Who wrote that one?" Dick Teig asked Osmond.

Osmond scrutinized the candy wrapper. "Can't tell. I don't recognize the writing."

I glanced anxiously at Nana. Was it hers? Had her handwriting deteriorated even more? Maybe I needed to get her to a doctor.

Osmond read the next one off a wrinkled tissue. " 'Take twenty-five bottles of beer to me in sixty minutes.' "

"That one is stupid," sniped Bernice. "It doesn't have a destination."

"It does so," Dick Teig chortled. "My mouth!"

He and Dick Stolee dissolved into laughter as Tilly raised her walking stick and thwacked it against her desktop, sending a loud *crack* through the room.

"Quiet in back!" a startled Floridian yelled. "You got something against sleep?"

Tilly nodded to Osmond. "If you would be so good as to read the next entry," she instructed, her gaze frosty as she eyed the Dicks. "If this were South America, you'd be pirhana bait."

Dick Teig's ice pack flopped onto the floor, which sent both Dicks into another fit of laughter.

Poor guys. They were so tired they were even more punchy than normal. But it was after midnight. Who could blame them?

Osmond waited for silence before reading from a small pink envelope. " 'Meet me on the east side in twenty minutes.' "

Eyebrows lifted. Heads nodded. "I like that one," Margi commented. "It sounds like something a real murderer would write." Her eyes widened as she surveyed the group. "Gee, do you think one of us killed him?"

Suspicious stares darted all around before Bernice crowed with laughter. "Duh? If one of us had killed him, the note wouldn't have said east."

"Why not?" asked Lucille.

"I know!" George said with sudden excitement. "Because the body was found on the west side of the lodge. No homegrown Iowan would make a mistake like that."

"So whoever wrote the note doesn't know east from west?" asked Helen.

Dick Teig slapped his thigh. "That eliminates all of us. Guess none of us killed the guy."

"That's a relief," said Margi.

I was sure there was logic in this exchange; I just wasn't sure where.

"This is the best one yet," Osmond declared as he squinted at the envelope, "but I don't know who wrote it, 'cause I don't recognize this handwriting, either."

"It's mine!" Jackie cried, shooting her hand into the air. "Fooled you, fooled you. None of you could possibly have committed the murder, because I wrote that one!"

I blinked numbly. A few more remarks like that could put her on a track to run for president.

Osmond held up the final entry and read in a steady voice, " 'This exercise is even dumber than the last one.' "

Margi frowned. "Are you sure that's one of ours? It doesn't have any of the right words."

All eyes riveted on Bernice.

"You people are an embarrassment to every card-carrying member of AARP," she taunted. "You couldn't tag the killer if he bit you on your collective butts. If you wanna play Dick Tracy, you gotta be like me and keep your eyes and ears open all the time."

I narrowed my gaze at her. "Even with your eyes and ears open, I don't see how you could possibly know the things you told Officer Viiii— Vit— the officer. You haven't been shmoozing with the people from the Hamlets."

"That's on account a she doesn't like them," said Nana.

"She doesn't like anyone," said Helen, yawning.

"You don't have a laptop," I continued. "You don't have a cell phone with Internet capabilities. How did you get all the information?"

"She eavesdrops," said Dick Teig.

"How?" I asked. "She has hearing aids in both ears!"

"She claims they're hearing aids," said Dick Stolee, "but have you ever looked at them up close?" He stabbed an accusatory finger at her. "I think they're bugs."

Margi gasped. "Do you remember the *Night Gallery* TV episode years ago where someone put a bug in Laurence Harvey's ear and it ate clear through to the other side of his head and then it laid eggs?" She grabbed Bernice's forearm. "I hope you weren't stupid enough to put that kind of bug in your ear."

Bernice rolled her eyes far up into her head. "Why do I bother coming on these trips?" She wiggled out of her seat and stood up. "I'm outta here."

"You can't leave," Osmond warned. "We're supposed to stay here until we're told it's okay to go."

Iowans pride themselves on following the rules. We obey traffic laws, see our dentist every six months, and always turn our cell phones off in movie theaters. When someone in authority gives us an order, we treat it like a Commandment.

"You think I can't leave?" Bernice cackled as she squeezed around feet and knees to the center aisle. "Watch me."

Bernice obviously had a different take on the Ten Commandments.

"Hey, Blondie," she called to Officer Hamalainen, who was standing guard by the door. "This is an emergency. Where's the potty?"

The young officer's expression went from sober to confused. "I'm sorry, madam, but the kitchen is closed."

The Dicks collapsed onto their desks in belly-jiggling laughter.

"Don't they have potties in Lapland?" asked Margi.

"Try 'little girl's room,'" suggested Alice.

Tilly snorted. "Have you ever asked yourself at what age a woman becomes old enough to use the 'big girl's room'?"

The ladies exchanged bewildered looks, apparently unprepared to debate such a deep question at this hour of the morning. "Trick question," said Jackie. "There *is* no such thing as a big girl's room."

"WHERE'S THE TOILET?" Bernice yelled down to Hamalainen.

Before he could react, the door opened to admit Annika, Helge, Officers Vitikkohuhta and Kynsijarvi, and a non-uniformed man I hadn't seen before. Officer Vitikkohuhta walked to the podium and turned on the microphone. "If you would please take your seat," he said, nodding to Bernice. "You should be able to leave in a few minutes. Could I have everyone's attention, please?"

He waited for the Florida people to snort and stretch and elbow each other awake before he continued. "We are fortunate in Ivalo to have our own handwriting expert." He gestured to the man standing beside Officer Kynsijarvi. "Mika-Matti Arctopolitanus."

If the Finns were given a choice between world peace or shorter names, I wondered which one they'd choose?

"He has studied the samples you were kind enough to provide and has drawn some preliminary conclusions. Unfortunately, this means more inconvenience for a few of you, so please accept my apologies ahead of time."

Uh-oh. Sounded as if the remaining board members were about to get the third degree.

"Would the guests from Iowa please identify themselves?"

We stuck our hands in the air, a little smug to be released first.

"Would all of you except Ms. Andrew kindly follow Officer Kynsijarvi to the bus outside the hotel? I need to take you to Ivalo for further questioning."

What?

Bernice jumped out of her seat. "Further questioning? Why are you picking on us? We didn't kill that guy. We didn't even know him!"

"Forgive me, Mrs. Zwerg, but you knew a great deal about the deceased, and everyone else."

"That's because she eavesdrops," shouted Dick Teig.

"You ever heard of barking up the wrong tree?" Bernice demanded. "Those people sitting down front are the guilty ones. Why don't you drag them in for further questioning?"

"Because their handwriting samples do not warrant it."

"Should I pack pajamas?" asked Margi. "I can't sleep in street clothes. And if you don't have hypoallergenic pillows, I'll have to bring my own."

"Someone grab insect repellant," said Grace.

"And toilet paper," said George. "Government issue can be awful scratchy."

"I have to take my medications in the morning," Lucille piped up, "so you're going to have to let me run up to my room for my pill caddy."

"Me too," everyone chimed at once.

"Are you gonna handcuff us?" asked Nana. "I wouldn't mind being cuffed."

"Is it okay if we bring our camcorders?" asked Dick Teig. "You got someplace in your jail cell where I can recharge my battery?"

"I'm not going to jail!" Bernice yowled. "I want a lawyer. I wanna talk to the American ambassador. I don't care what time it is. Wake him up. I demand justice!"

"There, there, honey." Jackie popped out of her seat to wrap her arms around Bernice. "It won't be that bad. They'll take your beverage order, ask you some questions, then cut you loose. You know the drill. Just like we did in Helsinki. It might actually be fun! Think of it as a sleepover with boys along."

Nana raised her hand. "If this is a sleepover, can I be handcuffed to George?"

"I'm not going to jail!" Bernice cried.

Jackie crushed Bernice's head against her breasts with such force, I wasn't sure if the idea was to soothe her or kill her. "Be brave, Bernice. You can do this. And if they allow you to make one phone call, would you mind terribly calling my editor and asking her why *the hell* she's not answering my phone calls? I'll give you the number."

Officer Vitikkohuhta motioned to Jackie. "I nearly forgot, Ms. Thum. You need to come with us, also."

Jackie gasped. "Me? What do you want with me? I'm not from Iowa."

"I'm sorry, but your penmanship sent up many, many flags."

"Of course it did!" she cried, shoving Bernice aside. "I told you I haven't written script since high school. I print! Do you know how hard it was for me to remember how to make a capital S?"

"Your sample was very suspicious."

"Capital S isn't so bad," Lucille interrupted. "If you want to talk hard, what about the capital Z?"

"I've been known to leave off the little hump on the side of the Z," Osmond confessed. "Makes my Zs look like tadpoles."

"I thought the hump was on the Q," said Margi.

"I didn't kill August Manning!" Jackie wailed. "Look at my nails." She flashed her fluorescent pinks at Vitikkohuhta. "I had a manicure four days ago. Given the outrageous price I paid, do you honestly think I'd risk breaking one of these babies by strangling someone? I bet you don't even offer emergency nail repair above the Arctic Circle."

As Officer Kynsijarvi headed up the aisle stairs to assist us from our seats, Jackie's voice grew more plaintive. "You can't lock me up. I'm almost famous! Don't you read the entertainment rags? This would never happen in Hollywood."

"There, there," Bernice mimicked. "Spending the night in jail might actually be fun. Think of it as a sleepover with a bunch of old farts who'll be up peeing all night." She stared down at Officer Vitikkohuhta and added in a loud voice, "But at least we don't have to worry about getting whacked at the jailhouse, because all the *real* suspects will still be here in the hotel!"

Bernice sometimes surprised me by making a lot of sense. The gang *would* be out of harm's way at the jail, which meant I wouldn't have to fret about their safety. But still . . .

While Officer Kynsijarvi helped people down the

stairs and directed traffic, I ran ahead to take Officer Vitikkohuhta aside. "I know my handwriting passed muster, but I'm the official chaperone of the Iowa contingent, so I think you should take me to jail with them."

"Annika has asked Helge to accompany your group to Ivalo, so thank you for the offer, Ms. Andrew, but it won't be necessary."

"But you don't understand. My grandmother is Marion Sippel—the lady who'd like to be hand-cuffed—and she needs medical attention. I think she may be exhibiting signs of stroke, so I really need to be there with her."

"I'll arrange for someone to see her before she's questioned. Will that be acceptable?"

Officer Vitikkohuhta obviously didn't have a grandparent who was his best friend. "I'd really like to go with her," I repeated.

"Our facilities are very small. Please, Annika tells me this is the protocol that must be followed. Helge is a Midnight Sun Adventures employee, so he will chaperone the group, and you must stay here. Annika can use your support. She is devastated by this incident."

"Would one of you people in charge tell us what in tarnation the rest of us are supposed to do while you're gone?" Vern Grundy asked in a stentorian voice.

"You're free to return to your rooms," said Vitikko-huhta, "but please do not wander far. I may have more questions for you in the morning."

Grumbling. Snorting. Foot scuffing.

"I don't think I can sleep," announced Vern. "Anyone up for a game of Scrabble?"

"I'll play," said June Peabody. "I could use a distraction."

"If she's playing, I'll play, too," said April.

"What the hell," Reno muttered. "Count me in. I probably can't get back to sleep anyway. How about we meet in the lobby in ten minutes."

"Does anyone have any snacks?" asked June. "This emotional anxiety has made me hungry."

"Me, too," said April. "Reindeer meat doesn't stick to your ribs very long."

It probably would if they didn't swallow it whole.

Fifteen minutes later, I waved good-bye to my group as they headed off for Ivalo in the subdued sunlight that was 1:30 a.m. As the bus headed down the road, I was thankful that Nana would have an opportunity to be checked out by a doctor, but I worried about the prognosis. What would I do if she was really sick? Would she be able to fly home? Would she have to be hospitalized here?

The constriction in my throat eased as I reminded myself what I had told Mom. Seventy-nine wasn't as old as it used to be. Seventy-nine-year-olds were jumping out of airplanes and bungee jumping off bridges. Seventy-nine was the new sixty. And sixty-year-olds were a hearty demographic, especially if they ate their vegetables and had obscene amounts of money. So chances were that Nana would be all right, and the rest of the gang would be out of harm's way at the police department.

I looked back at the hotel, battling a sudden sense of dread.

Yup. The only Iowan in any danger tonight was . . . me.

CHAPTER 10

I didn't know what time it was anywhere else in the world, but in Saariselka, it was 3:05 a.m., and I was still awake.

I sat propped against my headboard, staring bleary-eyed at the list I'd written but failing to be inspired by my notes. I'd separated my suspects into two columns: Board members, which included April, June, Vern, and Lauretta, and Others, which included Curtis, Joleen, Jimbob, and Reno. My instincts told me that the killer's name was right in front of my face, but the challenge was, how could I whittle eight names down to one with any certainty?

I put an asterisk next to O'Brien, wondering if Officer Vitikkohuhta was right about the killer trying to frame Reno. Sure sounded good, but I wasn't entirely convinced. Reno was quick and he was strong.

He could have strangled Gus in no time flat and returned to the lodge before anyone missed him. But why would he have killed a friend? Or had the friendship just been a ruse? Had they had differences they'd never telegraphed, differences that could have led to murder? Reno and Gus had supposedly been arguing about the Red Sox outside the lodge, but who'd given that information to Officer Vitikkohuhta? Reno or Bernice? If it had been Reno, had he been telling the truth, or had he tried to cover his butt by making up the story?

I studied the names as I listened for suspicious sounds outside my room. Were the Peabody sisters capable of murder? Was either one of them strong enough to strangle a man who had greater upper-body strength? I doubted they could have succeeded alone, but could they have joined forces and done it together? They'd probably scarfed their meal down so fast that they would have had plenty of time to slip Gus a note and lure him outside.

I scribbled a note to myself: Find out who Gus was sitting with at dinner.

Chances were he hadn't been sitting with the Barnums, but I wondered if his deliberate avoidance of them had been so blatant that it had pushed them over the edge. Could this final humiliation have turned Joleen and Jimbob into murderers? Like Nana was fond of saying, you might not remember what someone said, but you'll always remember how it made you feel.

I doodled a question mark by Vern's name. Military

men were trained to kill the enemy, but had Gus been the enemy? Could Vern even attempt to overpower anyone with his bad knees? And what about Lauretta and Curtis? How could they have strangled Gus? They were too short! The only way they could have placed that noose around his neck was if they'd been piggyback, and I doubted they had either the strength or balance to execute a move like that. Jimbob, on the other hand, could have tightened the noose with both hands tied behind his back, using only his feet.

I placed two asterisks beside Jimbob's name.

Hearing voices in the hall, I ran to the door and squinted through the peephole. Aha! The Scrabble players were returning from the lobby. Sure had taken them a long time. It made me wonder if they'd been playing Scrabble the whole time, or doing something else—like reminiscing about Gus or plotting something nefarious. Could Vern, April, June, and Reno be in cahoots? Were they devising a strategy to get Reno elected to the board of directors? Could that be why existing board members were dropping like flies? But what benefit would it be to anyone if Reno joined the board? And were the benefits enough to warrant two murders?

I returned to my bed knowing exactly what the hangup was.

I just didn't know enough.

Hoping to remedy that, I grabbed my cell phone, calculated what time it was in both Lucerne and Windsor City, and punched in a number. "Hi, Mom," I said when I connected.

"Emily! I've been waiting on pins and needles for you to call back. Are you ready for the good news?"

"Before you give it to me, would you do me a huge favor?"

"Another favor?" She oozed enthusiasm through the phone. "Oh, my goodness, this is so exciting. I *love* being helpful."

"Grab a pen and paper, then. I need you to do an Internet search for me." Under Nana's tutelage, Mom had developed some kick-butt computer skills over the last year, progressing from sending simple emails to hacking into the files of any agency, organization, or institution in about three minutes flat. Nana was so proud of her success with Mom that she'd approached the Senior Center about offering weekly computer workshops, but the only slot open was after lunch, which was the worst possible time of day for the senior set. Nana had said, "Them old folks won't be listenin' to me. They'll be too busy takin' cat naps and fallin' outta their chairs. There won't be no end to the broken hips."

"Okay, Mom, I'm interested in any information you can find about the following people." I gave her the names of the four current board members. When it was morning in Lucerne, I'd ask Etienne to do the same for the four non-board members. With both of them searching the Internet, they were bound to turn up something that would raise a red flag or two. At least, I hoped they would.

"April and June Peabody," Mom repeated. "What happened to May?"

"Excuse me?"

"If you're naming your children, why would you jump from April to June? There has to be a May there someplace."

"Maybe the Peabodys didn't like the name May."

"I bet there's a May. There could be a story there, Emily. Maybe you can use it in your next travel club newsletter." A pause. "Oh, that's right. There might not be a next newsletter. You could still write it, though. I bet the *Register* would love to publish it." Another pause. "After they rebuild the newspaper office and replace all their equipment."

I let out a discouraged sigh. "Have you run your idea about the wheelchair with the crepe paper and helium balloons past Sharon?"

"She loved the idea, Emily, but her rehab is going to take much longer than she first anticipated, so unfortunately she has to drop out of the wedding. She feels just terrible, but I told her not to beat herself up about it. You'd understand."

Totally.

"So you need a new maid of honor and if you could send me her measurements within the next couple of days, I'll start working on the dress orders. Have you seen the new L.L. Bean catalog, Em? They have some very stylish dresses that could be modified for an evening wedding. You don't have a problem with flannel, do you?"

I padded into the bathroom in search of antacid tablets. "You're ordering my bridesmaids' dresses out of a catalog that specializes in camp and fishing gear?"

"They offer free shipping for orders over twenty-five dollars. That's a real cost saver."

I broke open the bottle and shoved a fistful of tablets into my mouth.

"But here's the news you've been waiting for, Em. I've found a church for the wedding!"

"*Wwwllly?*"

"What?"

I chewed faster. "Really? An honest-to-goodness Catholic church that has an opening in September for a Saturday evening ceremony?"

"Mmm—it's not exactly a church."

I read the label on the bottle. Seventy tablets. Not nearly enough to last until tomorrow. I braced myself. "What is it exactly?"

"It's a lovely synagogue, Emily. It's only thirty miles away, and the rabbi is so nice. He said all faiths have to come together in times of need, so he's offering us use of his building on any Sunday in September. He'd like to make Saturdays available to us, but that's his holy day, so we have to work around him."

I scratched a sudden itch on my throat. "So the plan is for me to get married in the Jewish synagogue with the reception to be held in the hog auction barn."

"Would you like the Knights of Columbus to attend the wedding in their ceremonial dress, Emily? Your Uncle Bill could arrange it. Swords and capes are so dashing, and the plumes in their hats would add lots of color."

"Are the Knights of Columbus the guys who ride the tricycles in the Fourth of July parade?"

"Those are Shriners, dear. And they don't ride tricycles anymore. They've graduated to Hummers."

Scratch, scratch, scratch. I looked in the bathroom mirror to find a string of angry red welts crawling up my throat. *Uh-oh.* "I've gotta go, Mom. Something's come up."

"What about the synagogue, Em? Should I tell Rabbi Karp it's a go?"

I rummaged through my toiletry bag for my antihistamines. "I'll get back to you on that, okay? Talk to you later." I read the drug interaction statement on the label, then popped two capsules and washed them down with water. I stared forlornly into the mirror, hoping the antihistamines would quiet my hives before they migrated to my face.

God, could anything else go wrong?

"What's wrong with your face?"

I'd hit the breakfast buffet early and found a secluded booth in order to avoid that question, but it apparently wasn't secluded enough. "Allergies," I told April Peabody.

"Are you contagious?" asked June, standing a safe distance behind her sister.

I patted the Calamine-lotion-covered welts on my jaw and cheeks. "Hives aren't contagious. They just look like they are."

"What are you allergic to?" asked April.

"Apparently, my mother."

June looked relieved. "As long as you're not contagious, do you mind if we join you? I don't know where these other tourists are from"—she sent a withering glance through the dining room—"but they've taken over all the other tables."

I gestured to the seat opposite me. "Be my guest. So who won the Scrabble game last night?"

"We quit halfway through," said April, as she slid into the booth ahead of June. "Reno spelled 'baked,' and when June added an 're' to form 'rebaked,' Reno said it wasn't a word and refused to count it."

"It would have given me a triple word score and put me in the lead," said June. "That's why he didn't want it to count. He always has to win. He's such a poor sport."

"Did anyone have an official Scrabble dictionary?" I asked.

"We never needed one when Gus was alive," April lamented. "Words were his specialty, so he was a walking dictionary. He knew instantly if something was derived from the Latin or the Greek."

"And he was familiar with all the unusual words, like *qoph* and *zyzzyva*," added June, "not to mention your two-letter tricksters like *op, aa,* and *ka.* Plus, he knew *all* the words that could be prefixed with un- and re-. Gus would have known that rebaked is a word."

"June is right," said April. "Take your typical Idaho potato. You bake it once, do something fancy with the insides, and stick it back into the oven to *re*bake it. People call that a 'twice-baked' potato, which is another way of saying you're baking it again. Rebaked. It's a word."

"I can eat a rebaked potato in twenty-seven point three seconds," June bragged, tilting her chin at a cocky angle.

April grew stiff-lipped. "That wasn't a fair contest. They threw fresh scallions into the potato mixture, and you know I can't eat scallions. My stomach is extremely sensitive to foods in the onion family."

She could swallow a Virginia ham in thirty-eight seconds, but she couldn't do onions? Go figure.

"Did you eat scallions at dinner last night?" asked June. "I just about died, sleeping in the same room with you. Give me carbon monoxide any day—at least that gas is odorless."

"Thank you for sharing that," April said stiffly. "Why don't you announce it to the entire dining room?"

"It wouldn't do any good. These new people don't look like they speak English." She lowered her voice. "I think they're foreigners."

"Maybe the vegetable medley didn't sit well with you," I offered, seeing my opening. "Fruits and vegetables can do a real number on you. Who did you end up sitting with last night anyway? I don't recall seeing either one of you in the dining room."

"We started out sitting with Gus and Vern," said April, "and then—"

"We sat with the Klicks," June corrected.

April rolled her eyes. "That was at breakfast yesterday."

"It was not. We both finished eating in thirty-two point six seconds, then moved to the Klicks' table because they were farther away from the cookfire.

Remember? We were sweating like common laborers. Daddy would have disowned us."

"*I* stayed put. *You* went and sat with the Klicks. Reno joined me and Vern when Gus went to the men's room. What's wrong with you? Did you forget to take your medication?"

"Reno was never at your table, because you were sitting opposite me with the Klicks!" insisted June.

"That was at breakfast, I tell you!"

I looked from one to the other, determined to pin them down. "So it's safe to say the two of you were sitting with Gus for at least thirty-two seconds last night?"

"Yes," said April.

"No," said June.

This is what I loved about investigative work. Crack witnesses.

"Vern!" yelled June, motioning him to our booth. "Come join us." Then to April, "He'll tell us who's right." She pulled a stopwatch out of her purse and set it on the table.

"What are you timing?" snapped April. "We don't even have our food yet."

"I'm going to see how long it takes you to eat your words."

"Mornin', ladies." Vern arrived with a bowl of Mueslix in one hand and a cup of coffee in the other. "Appreciate the invite. Space is tight this morning. Did you notice the two tour busses outside? Germans. Hard to believe that sixty years ago we were lobbing grenades at each other." He threw a cautious look over his shoulder. "If things should get dicey in here, go for the four-minute eggs. They're the only ammo in the place, but they make almost as big a mess as grenades. Aim for the head. And try not to throw like girls."

"Who did you eat dinner with last night?" April blurted out.

"Jimbob and Joleen."

"You did not!" April squealed. "You ate with me and June. Remember? I helped you with the cap on your prescription bottle."

Vern looked confused. "I thought that was at breakfast the day before."

"Naa-naa-na-naa-na," sang June.

Vern set his breakfast down and eased himself onto the seat beside me. "Hell, I don't remember who I saw five minutes ago. How do you expect me to remember who I sat with last night?"

Could their memories actually be this faulty, or were they putting on a very clever act?

"I heard tell if you look in some of those natural food stores, you can find herbal supplements that are guaranteed to improve your mental capacity," Vern declared. "Something called Memorex is supposed to be the gold standard. I'm thinking I should buy some."

"Memorex isn't an herbal supplement," scoffed April. "It's a brand of videotape."

"You're such a know-it-all," scolded June. "Maybe someone discovered that eating cellophane is good for your memory."

Not to mention all the health benefits to your colon and small intestines.

"What's that white stuff on your face?" Vern asked me. "Aren't you a little old for acne?"

"Calamine lotion. Minor skin condition. It'll pass."

As Vern and I reached for our coffee cups, our elbows cracked together like hockey pucks, numbing my arm all the way to my fingertips.

"Sorry," Vern apologized, wincing as he massaged his elbow. "Righty?"

I nodded as I massaged my own. "Lefty?"

"That has to smart," June commiserated. "Vern has the sharpest elbows in the Hamlets, and most of us have the bruises to prove it. He can be very dangerous to sit beside in a confined space. You want to trade places with me, Vern? Emily might not get to finish her breakfast otherwise."

A lightbulb went on over my head. "Did you bruise any of your companions at dinner last night, Vern?" Surely no one would forget getting hammered by his elbow.

"I don't recall hearing any bones crack," said Vern, "but Jimbob's not made like the rest of us. I think he's got pipe cleaners for bones."

"You weren't sitting beside Jimbob," persisted April. "You were sitting beside Gus, and Gus knew to stay to your right."

"Poor August." June removed a tissue from her purse and dabbed the corners of her eyes. "Everyone called him Gus, but I always called him August." She crushed the tissue to her chest and lifted her chin. "August is such a noble name."

"Sure it is," said Vern as he shoved a spoonful of

Mueslix into his mouth. "Right up there with November and December."

That's right, August was a month, too! *April. June. August.* There were so many guests named for months of the year on this tour that they could probably publish their own calendar—which reminded me of the question my mom had asked earlier. "Is there a May Peabody?" I asked the sisters.

They exchanged wary looks before April asked me, "Why do you want to know?"

"You're April. She's June. Seems as if you should have a May there someplace."

"That's none of your business," April said in a tight voice.

"Who told you about May?" June demanded. "Was it August? He had a lot of nerve telling— Ow!" She glared at her sister. "Why did you kick me?"

"I'm trying to light a fire under you. Get moving before all the food disappears."

"But I want to find out how she knew about—"

"Move!" April slid into her, forcing her off the bench.

"You are so bossy!"

"If you don't waltz your buns over to the buffet table before the scrambled eggs are gone, we're going to get stuck eating toast, and you know what happened the last time."

June got a faraway look in her eye and a pained expression on her face. "I nearly choked to death. Euw. Remember how angry Daddy got with us?" She helped April out of the booth. "If the scrambled eggs are slimy, let's do the prunes. Prunes will go down great if they don't have pits. Ready? Go!"

They charged toward the buffet table while Vern and I stared after them.

"Those two gals are odd ducks," Vern mumbled around his Mueslix.

"Have you ever heard them talk about a sister named May?"

"The only thing they ever want to talk about is food. But when you're as high up in the competitive eating hierarchy as they are, you have to stay focused which is a good thing, because they can't play Scrabble worth beans. Rebaked. Can you believe they tried to pass that off as a word?"

I suspected Mom had been right. There *was* a May Peabody. But who was she, and why did April and June want to keep her under wraps?

"Ow." I grabbed my arm as Vern nailed me again with his elbow.

"Doggone, Emily. I'm really sorry."

"Uncle." I sighed. "How about we change places."

"I know I'll be sorry for asking, *bella,* but has someone died?"

"I give you a few names to research, and you jump to the conclusion that someone has died?" I was sitting on a rock on the front lawn of the hotel, observing the reindeer, who were curled up comfortably on first-floor patios, and regretting that the signal to Switzerland was so strong. Where were the dead spots when you needed them?

"It's your pattern," explained Etienne. "When a guest dies, you become Sherlock Holmes and immediately begin gathering background information on possible suspects."

"Nooo. I do that?" It smarted to know I was so predictable.

Etienne uttered a very long word in a language I couldn't identify. "*Bella, bella,* how many dead?"

"Two?"

A pause. "Are you telling me or asking me?"

"I'm trying to be accurate. It's two so far."

"By what method?"

"They were strangled."

Another pause. "I assume the police are involved?"

"Two police forces—Helsinki and Ivalo. In fact, there's a whole group of people being questioned by the authorities even as we speak."

"Do they have any leads?"

"They're pretty sure the killer is one of our tour members, but they haven't come up with any motives yet."

"Which is where my computer and I come in."

"I'd do it myself, but there aren't any cyber cafés here."

I could almost hear his forehead crease with worry. "Would it do me any good to implore you to allow the police to handle this, Emily?"

"But what if they miss something? I doubt there's much crime above the Arctic Circle, so they're probably not current with new forensic methods. They can probably use all the help they can get. I have a dozen people to watch out for, Etienne. We have to catch this guy before he strikes again."

"I almost lost you five months ago, *bella*. Have you forgotten?"

"No, but—"

"Are you so willing to put me through the same anguish again?"

Oh, my God. What was this? A suggestion? An edict? I froze with sudden dread. Was this a side of Etienne he'd deliberately kept hidden from me? Would he continue to respect my independence and choices after we were married, or would he try to put a leash around my throat? Were there problems awaiting me that I hadn't even imagined? "Are you trying to make me feel guilty?" I asked softly.

"You bet," he said, mimicking Nana. "Is it working?"

"No. You know I can't stand around and do nothing."

"I realize that, *bella*. It's what I love about you. But in all seriousness, I'm concerned for your safety. Should I fly to Lapland to join you?"

Oh, boy. "I'd *love* to have you join us, but I'm not sure about the logistics. By the time you arrive in Saariselka, we could be gone."

"Are you sure the tour won't be confined to the hotel until the killer is found?"

"Grounded in Saariselka? Can the police do that?"

"I should think someone in authority might at least suggest it. I know nothing about the Finnish criminal justice system, but I imagine that common sense looms large in their decision making. It seems foolhardy to send you on your way with a killer in your midst."

I watched the Klicks and Barnums exit the hotel dining room onto the beer garden patio, looking as chummy as new best friends. So the outcasts had found each other. I guess there was a certain poetic justice to that. Isn't that what we all wanted? Simply to be accepted by the people around us? "I miss you," I whispered, cradling the phone as if it were his hand.

"A few weeks more, *bella*. How do you say, we have to hang in there."

I smiled. "Have you been studying your dictionary of American slang?"

"You bet. And while we're discussing the two of us, have you run into any more impediments with the new wedding plans?"

"My mom has gone ecumenical. We're getting married in a synagogue. Is that okay with you?"

"My uncle Salvatore turned Jewish to marry his fourth wife. He'll feel right at home."

The morning quiet was suddenly broken by the roar of a diesel engine motoring up the road.

"I'll get busy on the names you gave me, *bella*. Don't turn off your phone; I'll call you when I've finished. I'll also look into flights. Let me know what the status of your tour is as soon as you find out. *Ti amo*."

"I love you, too."

Our big yellow tour bus turned into the hotel parking lot and rolled to a stop across ten vacant car spaces. When the door hissed open, Bernice was first down the stairs, followed by Margi with her hypoallergenic pillow, and Lucille and Helen with their super-ultra-deluxe pill caddies packed in their super-ultra-deluxe over-the-shoulder carrying cases.

"Are you off the hook?" I asked, meeting them halfway.

"I could have told you that before we left," sniped Bernice. "Idiots. Are we too late for breakfast?"

I checked my watch. "Ten minutes before they close the line. You can make it if you hurry. They didn't feed you at the police station?"

"TEN MINUTES BEFORE THE BREAKFAST LINE CLOSES!" Bernice yelled back to the group.

I counted heads as they stampeded past me, concerned when my count stopped at nine. I was missing Nana, and Jackie, and George. I let out my signature whistle. "Hey, guys, where's Nana?" But my query fell on deaf ears as all nine of them tried to squeeze through the dining room door at the same time.

I trotted down to the bus, my knees spongy as I fended off what I hoped was unwarranted fear. "I'm missing three people," I announced to Helge. "Do you know where they are?"

"There was an issue with one of the guests. The elderly lady was having a bit of a problem."

"What kind of problem? A health problem?" I *knew* there was something seriously wrong with her. Oh, God, why had I let her out of my sight?

"It was headed in that direction, so the officer had to call in a specialist."

Every bone in my body turned to gel. "Can you take

me to Ivalo? I need to be with her. She's my grandmother. I—"

"Officer Vitikkohuhta can tell you about the incident." Helge nodded to the police car pulling into the
parking lot. "I suspect that's him now."

I ran across the parking lot, breathless when I
reached the squad car. "Where's my grandmother?" I
gasped out at Officer Vitikkohuhta as he opened his
door. "Is she conscious? Has she asked for me? I *told*
you she wasn't well! Why didn't you listen to me?"

"I apologize, Ms. Andrew, I should have listened.
It was a night we hope never to repeat. One minute, your grandmother was acting perfectly normal,
and the next—" He shook his head. "This has taught
me to pay much greater attention to your American
octogenarians."

"She's not eighty yet. She's only seventy-nine. She's
practically a kid!" Tears stung my eyes. A knot lodged
in my throat. "Was it a stroke? It was a stroke, wasn't
it? Oh, God. What am I going to tell Mom?"

Officer Vitikkohuhta regarded me gravely. "You
might tell your mother that I am letting your grandmother off easy this time. But the next time she pulls
something like this, I will throw the book at her."

CHAPTER 11

"What?" My mouth dropped open at his vehemence. "How . . . how can you talk that way about a helpless old woman who may have suffered a stroke?"

"Your grandmother is many things, Ms. Andrew. Helpless is not one of them." He tipped his head politely. "If you'll excuse me, I have business inside the hotel."

"But where's Nana?"

A second squad car pulled into the parking lot. Officer Vitikkohuhta gestured toward it. "Ask and you shall receive."

The squad car eased to a stop in the middle of the parking lot, close enough for me to see Nana press her face against the backseat window and wave to me.

"Why didn't you come back with everyone else?" I asked when Officer Hamalainen opened the back door to let her out. "What happened? Are you all right?"

"What's wrong with your face? Uh-oh. You must a been talkin' to your mother again."

"Never mind my face. What happened?"

"It's on account a we had to stop at a little bookstore down the road from the police station so's Jackie could sign some book plates. Word spread like wildfire that a real live author was holed up in the jail all night, so the nice officer here was put in charge a crowd control. Turned out to be a real big crowd for these parts—one Russian hiker and two stray reindeer."

I glanced into the car to see Jackie and George struggling to untangle their legs in the cramped backseat compartment.

"Why did you and George go along?"

"Jackie asked us to, dear. We was her entourage. All the famous authors got 'em."

Officer Hamalainen patiently held the door while George and Jackie literally crawled out over each other. "Thanks ever so much," Jackie cooed, giving Hamalainen a peck on his cheek. She patted the forearm that she'd signed for him the night before. "Take good care of my signature. It'll be worth a fortune one day soon."

"It has been my honor to be part of such an historic literary event," Hamalainen announced proudly. After shaking hands all around, he slid back into his squad car and sped off, leaving me to ponder an obvious problem.

"I hope you signed your name in permanent ink," I said to Jackie.

"All I had was a pink sparkle gel pen, but he's going

to wrap his arm in plastic food wrap to make sure the ink doesn't wash off, fade away, or get obliterated by repellant."

"Isn't globalization somethin'?" marveled Nana. "Who'd a thought they'd have Glad Wrap in Lapland?"

I cupped my hands around her shoulders and peered into her eyes. "What's the story, Nana? Did you see a doctor at the jail?"

"He was waitin' for us when we got there. Took our temperature and blood pressure, listened to our hearts. Shined his little penlight in our eyes. I guess it's good to have a doctor around when you're arrestin' old folks."

"No one arrested us, Marion," George corrected. "They brought us in for questioning."

"Did the doctor seem concerned about anyone's health in particular?" I asked, trying not to alarm her.

"You bet," said Nana. "He said we was too fat, and if we all didn't lose twenty kilos, we wouldn't be around in twenty years."

I winced. "How did that go over?"

"Didn't faze Osmond none. Twenty years from now he'll be a hundred and nine."

"So the doctor gave you a clean bill of health?"

"Yup."

"But what about your handwriting?" I persisted. "I can't read it anymore, Nana. It's illegible. I'm sure it's nothing to worry about, but the change happened so quickly that I think we should get you to a neurologist for a second opinion. If there's a problem, we can get it taken care of before it gets any worse."

"My writin's back to normal again, dear, so you don't gotta bother."

I raised a skeptical eyebrow as I dug a notepad and pen out of the side pocket of my shoulder bag. "Would you show me, please? Any phrase will do."

She dashed off something and handed the notepad back to me. I read aloud the neatly formed letters of her precise script. " 'Do you believe me now?' " I stared at the paper, stupefied. "Your handwriting's back to normal. Oh, my Lord. It's a miracle!"

Nana looked at George. George looked at Nana. They both looked at me.

"What?" I asked. "Okay, so it's not the loaves and the fishes, but it's close."

"It wasn't no miracle, dear," she said in a sheepish voice. "It's 'cause a the handwritin' expert. He found us out."

I narrowed my eyes. "Found you out?"

"None of us could write a word the same way twice," George confessed, "so the fella knew something was fishy."

"And the reason you couldn't write a word the same way twice was because?—"

" 'Cause we don't want Osmond knowin' who's votin' for what, so we been disguisin' our writin'. "

Oh, God. "You gave the police a phony sample of your handwriting because you're trying to outsmart Osmond?"

Nana nodded. "We was just tryin' to be consistent. Besides, we needed the practice. Makin' your handwritin' sloppy is hard work."

I regarded her in disbelief. "Nana, do you know what this is?"

"If it's a felony, I reckon I'll be here longer than my denture cream's gonna last."

"It's wonderful!" I threw my arms around her, hugging her within an inch of her life. "It's absolutely wonderful! You're not having a stroke! You're healthy! I don't have to break any bad news to Mom." I planted kisses all over the top of her head and squeezed her some more, feeling as if the weight of the world had been lifted from my shoulders. "No wonder Officer Viti— whatever wanted to throw the book at you. You were obstructing his investigation, or providing false evidence, or—"

"*Mmmilly?*" she mumbled against my chest.

"Oops. Sorry." I stopped squeezing and straightened her *World's Number One Gramma* shirt. "What were you trying to say?"

"It wasn't our handwritin' what set off the nice officer."

"It was the handcuffs," said George.

I looked slowly from one to the other. "Go ahead. I'm listening."

"Well, they treated us real nice at the jailhouse and didn't lock us up or nothin'. We got to roam wherever we wanted so long as we stayed inside."

"They even let Jackie use their computer," said George.

Jackie bit into her bottom lip and turned her face away, looking pained. "I don't want to talk about it."

"So one time when I was on my way back from the

potty, I seen a pair a handcuffs lyin' on a filin' cabinet, so I picked 'em up and tried 'em on for size. They fit just like a charm bracelet, Emily. I was wonderin' if they was one size fits all, so I snapped the other one on Dick Teig while he was snoozin' and sure enough, it fit him, too. And that's sayin' somethin' 'cause Dick's wrists are thick as tail pipes. Who do you s'pose invented one size fits all?"

"I bet it was the Chinese," said George. "Probably right after they invented gun powder and origami."

"Isn't origami Japanese?" asked Jackie. "I can make a crane. Does anyone have a large sheet of paper? Oo, wait, I have one."

I knew exactly where this story was going. "There was no key, was there?" I asked Nana.

"It was right in my hand, dear. I wouldn't a dared try 'em on if the key hadn't been layin' there beside 'em." She flashed me a pointed look. "I'm not Bernice."

"So what was the problem?"

"Dick woke up," said George.

"I stuck the key in the lock, but it got jammed, so Dick give it a twist, and *crrrkk*—he broke it clear off. I never had a notion Dick Teig was so strong. Who woulda thought he had so much muscle under all that blubber? Anyway, he wasn't real happy with me, 'specially since the only reason he woke up was to go potty."

"Ooo—kay." I covered my ears. "Too much information. Don't need to hear any more."

She stood in front of my face and kept talking. "They had to call a locksmith in the wee hours of the mornin', and he couldn't do nothin'—"

Damn. I could read her lips.

"So they tried cuttin' through it with a hacksaw, and that was takin' too long, so they ended up havin' to bring in a specialist."

"A metallurgist?"

"A magician. He had them cuffs off in no time, which was a good thing seein's how Dick's back teeth was singin' anchors away. But the nice officer was a mite put out with me, so I been keepin' my distance."

"Ta-da!" said Jackie, holding up her paper crane.

Nana regarded it oddly. "It don't got no head."

"The paper wasn't big enough, so you have to imagine the head."

Nana nodded sagely before turning back to me. "We didn't get no breakfast at the jail, dear. Can we still get served in the dinin' room or do we gotta imagine that, too?"

"You have three minutes," I said, checking my watch again. "How fast can you move?"

Nana grabbed George's hand, and off they went at a trot—an extraordinary speed for two people who had only three good legs between them. "Are you going to join them?" I asked Jackie. "You probably haven't eaten either."

"I couldn't possibly eat." Bottom lip quivering, she inhaled melodramatically before breaking into a pathetic sob. "I'm so miserable, Emily. I want to die!"

"No, no. We already have enough corpses on this trip. Poor Jack. What's wrong?" I wrapped my arms around her and patted her back while she slouched down to sob into my neck. "Is it because of your crane? I'm sure the hotel can find you a larger piece of paper so you can give it a head."

"I got my first review on Amazon," she wailed, causing rubbernecking and stares from the guests on the patio. When six-foot transsexuals cry, people listen.

"That's great, Jack. See? The reviews are starting to pour in."

"It was only one star!"

"Oh, dear."

"My readers hate me!"

"I'm sure that's not the case," I soothed. "The review probably said some nice things, too. I know you; you're just obsessing about the bad stuff."

"It was *all* bad! Someone from North Carolina said she bought my book because she knew she was going to be temporarily vertical. She found it so unreadable that she threw it away! She said I had no talent, my book was a waste of paper, and she'd never buy another. And here's the thing, Emily. She sounded *thrilled* to have the opportunity to slam me."

"Why was she vertical?"

"What?"

"When people are laid up, aren't they usually horizontal? She was vertical. What is she? A bat?"

Jackie's sobs morphed into a little chuckle. "I didn't catch that."

"Come on, Jack, don't let some petty review get you down. You have more sense than to let someone who doesn't know the difference between vertical and horizontal ruin your mood. Remember: Those who can, do; those who can't, criticize."

Sniffling loudly, she straightened to her full height and dried her eyes. "I suppose. Thank you for pointing that out, Emily. You always make me feel so much better. If I didn't already have a husband, I'd marry you."

I flinched. "You might need to reapply your eyeliner, Jack. It's running down your cheeks."

"I guess I should feel sorry for the twit," she speculated as we crossed the parking lot to the hotel. "I checked out some of her other reviews, and you know what? She gives *everyone* one-star reviews. She hates everything! And she loves to send them out on Christmas Day. Can you believe it? What kind of lowlife tries to ruin someone's Christmas?"

Bernice popped into my head, but I figured even she had more class than that. "Did you ever get a call in to Mona?"

"They wouldn't let me use the department phone because the call was long distance. But—drumroll, please—I talked the officers into ordering six copies of my book online! Isn't that terrific? This is *really* going to boost my sales, Emily. And you know what else? I did some sleuthing and figured out what was written on the note the police don't want to admit they found on Gus's body." She paused for effect. " 'Meet me outside in twenty minutes.' "

Which made a lot more sense than Dick Teig's "*Take twenty-five bottles of beer to me in sixty minutes.*" I regarded her with new respect. "And you weren't even in disguise. How'd you do it?"

"There was a wrinkled note with those words on it

in a clear plastic bag on Officer Viti's desk. Probably waiting to be processed. No one said where the crime lab is, but I was getting vibes that it's far, far away and not used too frequently."

"Fingerprints," I said. "If there's a note, the police should have taken prints! Why didn't they do that?"

"They did do that." Jackie flashed her slightly stained fingers in front of my face. "When the handwriting analysis fell flat, they dragged out the fingerprint cards."

"But they didn't get everyone. What about the Hamlets people?"

"They weren't at the police station, Emily. Kinda hard to take prints from people who aren't there."

"But he can't let them off the hook that easily. One of them's a murderer!"

"Have you figured out whodunit yet?"

"No, but I've narrowed the field down to eight."

"Gee, you're almost there. Allow me." She yanked open the front door of the hotel. "Oh, and by the way? I'm not speaking to you."

"What?"

"With all the excitement, I nearly forgot. I'm mad at you!"

I rolled my eyes. "A few minutes ago you were willing to marry me again."

"That's the beauty of being female. You can change your mind every three minutes and people think you're perfectly normal."

Annika walked past us, clapping her hands for attention. "Please to gather in the lecture hall immediately. I have an important announcement. Hurry, please. This is most urgent."

"Do you think they've found the killer?" Jackie asked me.

I hoped it was that, and not that someone had discovered another dead body.

"Are we all here?" Annika asked from the podium.

"Don't answer," Bernice advised from a seat in front of me. "It's a trick question."

"Thank you for arriving so promptly," Annika continued. "I will now turn the microphone over to Officer Vitikkohuhta."

He took her place at the podium, his eyes steely as he studied our faces. "One of you killed Mr. Manning. I know this for a fact. Unfortunately, I have no evidence that implicates any of you specifically." His features bunched into a scowl. "If I hold you, I must charge you. Since I cannot do that, the law dictates that I must let you go. You are therefore free to continue your journey."

"What if we don't want to continue?" asked Joleen Barnum. "What if we want to get out so's we don't end up being sent home in a box?"

"I assume you are free to leave the tour at any time," Vitikkohuhta replied.

"Not without losing all our money," objected April Peabody. "It's a lose-lose situation. We'd get swindled out of our holiday *and* our hard-earned cash."

"What hard-earned cash?" Jimbob taunted. "I bet you never had to work a day in your life."

"She has so worked," defended June. "Have you ever heard of charity benefits?"

"It won't do anyone any good to go home," announced Curtis Klick. "The End is coming, maybe today, maybe tomorrow, so you might as well stay here and enjoy the sights while you can."

"Will someone yank that guy's batteries?" demanded Reno. "If I hear one more doomsday prediction out of him, I'll see to it personally that it becomes a self-fulfilling prophecy."

Lauretta popped out of her chair, trembling with righteous indignation. "If you were a God-fearing man, Reno O'Brien, you wouldn't be so quick to mock us. Repent before it's too late. Repent lest you be condemned to the everlasting fires of Hell for all eternity!"

"I plan on finishing this trip," Bernice called out, "but not with these nutcases. Send the Floridians home! One of them's a killer. Why should us Iowans have to spend our vacation worrying about getting strangled, when you can send the nut jobs home and take care of the problem real easy?"

That brought June Peabody to her feet. "She's only saying that because she's still ticked off about the seat-saving business in Helsinki. You should send the Iowans home. They hold grudges!"

"You should talk!" Dick Teig ejected himself from his seat like a fighter pilot whose plane had been hit. "Your sister tried to kill me yesterday. Look what she did to my face!"

Two black eyes. Swollen nose. Bruised cheeks.

The poor guy looked like a member of the eggplant family.

"She tried to kill me, too," Curtis piped up, "only I was smart enough to duck."

"Are you saying my Dick isn't smart?" demanded Helen. "Hey, Shorty, we're not the dummies who forked out eight thousand bucks to see the world end. If we'd known that was going to happen, we'd have stayed home and seen it for nothing!"

"Send them home," barked Bernice.

"Send *them* home," countered April. "If they weren't here, I bet the killing would stop."

Annika stepped to the podium. "Due to the unfortunate circumstances surrounding this tour, the head office has issued a temporary policy change. Since your patronage is so important to us, Midnight Sun Adventures is prepared to refund the entire cost of your package, plus provide discount vouchers redeemable on your next Midnight Sun adventure. So you may leave now without penalty."

Whistles. Hoots. Clapping.

"Oh, sure," crowed Bernice. "Give us a chance to hang ourselves, why don't you? The minute we volunteer to leave, you'll be all over us. Just because we're old doesn't mean we're brain dead. If we opt to leave, it's as good as admitting we're guilty. What killer isn't going to want to be a billion miles away from the scene of the crimes?"

Bernice was addicted to C-Span, so she was good at making rhetorical hash out of any issue.

"That is not the case," Annika said nervously, indicating that it actually *might* be the case. "Mrs. Barnum has indicated a desire to leave. Is there anyone else who would care to join her?"

Joleen raised her hand less enthusiastically. "If it's all the same to you, I'm thinking I might not want to leave after all."

"Very well," said Annika. "Anyone else?"

An uncomfortable silence filled the room as the Floridians sat on their hands, trying to look nonchalant.

"So you all want to continue?"

Nods. Murmurs. Head bobbing.

"Nice way to deal with undesirables," quipped Dick Teig, slapping Bernice's back. "Convince 'em to come with us."

"Do the Iowans also wish to continue?" asked Annika.

"We're Norwegian," Margi Swanson said proudly, "so there's no way you're going to keep us from seeing the motherland, especially if the world's about to end."

"It is agreed then?" asked Annika. "No one from Emily's group chooses to depart?"

"Me and Dick were talking at the police station this morning," Dick Stolee spoke up, "and we figure we're pretty safe. They're not killing us. They're only killing each other."

Oh, yeah, that was a big comfort.

"How are you handling Gus's body?" Vern Grundy spoke up. "What happens to him once we leave?"

Officer Vitikkohuhta took over the microphone. "His body will remain here until we notify his family and arrangements can be made to transport his remains back to the States."

"Who are you going to notify?" asked Reno. "Gus didn't have family."

"He had a sister," Vitikkohuhta informed us. "I have been unable to speak to her directly yet, but I have left a message."

"He never told anyone he had a sister," Reno puzzled. "I wonder why she never came to visit?"

Vitikkohuhta shrugged. "She was listed on his tour form as next of kin."

My brain kicked into overdrive. "Could you tell us her name?" I called out.

"I'm sorry, Ms. Andrew, but as you are all aware, the information on the tour form is confidential. When I speak with her, I'll ask permission to share her name with your group."

"Maybe he had a falling out with her," suggested Vern. "Would have been nice to meet her. You suppose she was the wordsmith that Gus was?"

I didn't know if she was a wordsmith, but for some illogical reason, I'd bet her name was May.

"Are we free to leave now, Officer?" asked Vern. "Annika might be too polite to say, but we have a schedule to maintain."

"About our schedule." Annika looked apologetic. "I have had to make a slight adjustment. Instead of leaving today as planned, we will remain in Saariselka and head out early tomorrow morning in time to board the Norwegian coastal steamer before its departure from Kirkenes at thirteen hundred hours."

"What about the lunch we were supposed to have today with the Eastern Sami family?" complained June. "The brochure said they were going to serve several courses of their traditional food."

"What about the iron ore mines?" asked Osmond. "I even brought a magnet along to see if it would stick to some of the scrap ore."

"Are you telling us we won't be stopping at the Grenseland Museum?" Vern grumbled. "That's the only reason I'm on this tour. It's supposed to have the finest collection of World War II artifacts anywhere in Scandinavia."

"There are resistance museums in many of the port towns," Annika assured him. "They are not the Grenseland, but I promise you will not be disappointed with their exhibits."

"Why do we have to sit in this hellhole for another day?" Bernice demanded.

"Because I still have unfinished police business to attend to," said Vitikkohuhta. "Would the group from Florida kindly file out to the parking lot and board the waiting bus?"

"Where are you taking us?" asked Joleen.

"Will we be back in time for lunch?" inquired April.

Vitikkohuhta allowed himself a tight smile. "We are going to Ivalo, where you will do me the honor of providing me with your fingerprints."

I leaned back in my seat and smiled. Hot damn! He got my brain waves.

"We already gave you writing samples," fussed Jimbob. "Why do you need our fingerprints?"

"Because even though you depart for Norway in the morning, you have not outwitted me. Our extradition laws with our neighbor to the west are very favorable, so do not be too quick to congratulate yourselves." He paused, his gaze touching every face in the room. "You can run, but you cannot hide."

CHAPTER 12

"During the war, the town was occupied by one hundred thousand invading Nazi troops, who were bombed almost daily by the Russian military." Helge spoke with emotion as we motored down a quiet residential street in Kirkenes late the next morning. "After the war, only forty buildings remained standing. The rest of the town was reduced to rubble."

Just like Windsor City.

"How far away is the Russian border?" Vern Grundy called out.

"Fifteen kilometers. Kirkenes is essentially a lawn ornament on Russia's front yard."

We'd departed Saariselka in the wee hours and driven straight through to Norway, not stopping for our usual midmorning snack, so I was starving.

"The two-level homes on your left were pre-built

in Sweden in 1945 and paid for with funds provided by your American Marshall Plan. They were
erected quickly for immediate occupancy and originally housed four families, but they have since been
completely remodeled and converted to two-family
homes."

The houses were as square as Rubik's cubes, severely
plain, and crowded together like Boston brownstones.
They were landscaped with only an occasional fence,
bush, or tree, and painted an array of high-gloss colors that were apparently the rage in Norway: caramel,
butterscotch, candy apple, and Grey Poupon. My
stomach growled as we passed one that was painted
like a giant Sta-Puf marshmallow.

Yup. High gloss paint was definitely more appetiz-
ing than brick.

"How come so many folks paint their houses red?"
asked Lucille Rassmuson. "We don't see much red
in Iowa. We're not comfortable drawing that much
attention to ourselves."

"Are they red?" Helge did a double take out the
window. "I hadn't noticed."

"That is *so* like a guy," Jackie whispered beside me.
"The only time they notice color is when it's attached
to a pair of breasts."

"You noticed color when you were a guy," I
reminded her.

She patted my thigh. "That should have been your
first clue that something was wrong."

Downtown Kirkenes could easily have passed for
Hometown USA. Wide boulevards. Attractive store-

fronts. Automatic teller machines. Sidewalk planters overflowing with colorful summer flowers.

"When we arrive at the coastal steamer terminal, please make sure that your luggage is offloaded from the bus before you board the ship," Helge cautioned. "You may then proceed to the reception desk on the gangway deck to receive your cabin assignments and key cards, and then to deck four, where your luncheon buffet will be served. Annika and I regret that today's itinerary had to be canceled, but we thought it more critical that you arrive in Kirkenes on time so you could begin the sea portion of your tour."

"Do you suppose the ship offers manicure services?" Jackie asked me as she gave her nails a critical look. "I'm tired of fluorescent pink. I think I need something more subdued, like *Purple People Eater* or *Green Tambourine*."

"I thought you weren't speaking to me."

"Damn. I keep forgetting. Sorry." She stared out the window, fidgeting for a half minute before turning back to me. "Emily, you know when a girl says she's not talking to you? How long does the not-talking part usually last?"

"It's killing you, isn't it?"

"I'm such a failure!" she sobbed. "I'm so far behind the learning curve, I'll never catch up to the rest of you. I don't understand any of the nuances, Emily. If a girl gets mad at you, she's supposed to act snotty and tell you she's not speaking to you. If a guy gets mad, he lets the air out of your tires, drinks all your Bud Light, and hides the remote control. It's over and done with!

Doesn't that make more sense? Why do women have to threaten the no-speaking thing?"

I shrugged. "It's part of our software package."

"Do you know why guys never threaten to use the silent treatment? Because they don't get a word in edgewise most of the time anyway, so no one would ever notice."

I was impressed with her insight. "My dad hasn't spoken for years. Well, other than, 'Mornin',' 'Evenin',' and 'How's it goin'?' My mom must be hearing voices in her head, because she sometimes scolds him for hogging the conversation. Dad is master of the opportune moment. A couple of well-placed words can sound like a whole lot more."

"I'll never get the hang of it," Jackie sniffed. "I've thought about therapy."

"Therapy might work."

"But who do I see? A man or a woman? If I don't choose right, the damage could be irreparable."

"Where's that famous confidence of yours, Jack? You have a degree in theater arts. You've appeared on Broadway. You're a natural! Trust me, with a little practice, you, too, can turn into a bitch of some renown."

"Really? You're not just saying that to make me feel good?"

"Let's try it again. You're not speaking to me: what do you do?"

She lifted her nose into the air, turned away coyly, and regarded downtown Kirkenes for nearly a minute before heaving a sigh. "Screw it." Fisting her hands on her hips, she turned back. "So exactly *when* were you planning to tell me about the change in your wedding plans?"

"I didn't tell you?"

"No, you didn't tell me. I felt so out in left field when Mrs. S. started talking about it at the jail. We're roomies. Best friends. How could you leave me out of the loop?"

"Oh, my God, no wonder you weren't speaking to me. I thought I told you. I know I meant to. It's all my fault. I was totally not thinking. I'm so sorry!"

"Well . . ." She softened her voice and lowered her gaze. "I suppose you *have* been a little distracted by weather disasters and dead bodies. And you haven't seen much of me because of my stint in jail. Oh, my God, Emily, it's not your fault at all. It's mine. I'm so sorry!" She flung herself at me, sobbing. "Can you ever forgive me?"

"That's perfect, Jack! See? You're getting it. Women always blame themselves for all the bad stuff that happens."

"Really?" She straightened up and executed a dainty clap. "I should document this. An honest-to-goodness female reaction." She paused thoughtfully. "Do you think I'm getting some of this through osmosis?"

We passed through a chain-link security fence that enclosed the port facilities and followed the designated road around the parking lot. "And I want you to know that I'm going to give your mother all the help she needs with the alternate wedding plans, Emily. What a nightmare she's been handed, with your gown under rubble and your invitations ending up in Kansas City."

"They probably blew north rather than south."

"With your invitations ending up in Milwaukee. Will you give me her phone number so we can kibitz? Can you imagine what incredible ideas the two of us will be able to come up with?"

God help me.

"She doesn't still hate me, does she?"

"She never hated you, Jack."

"She could never remember my name. What would you call that? Oh, never mind. Do you have any romantic beaches around Windsor City? Something with a gazebo and palm trees?"

"We have Monsoon Lagoon Water Park."

"Hmm. That could work. Does it have a slide?"

We slowed to a stop on the asphalt, and our driver cut the engine.

"And Emily, you don't even have to ask me to stand in for your poor, crippled maid of honor. I gladly volunteer to be your second choice. And I've already been thinking about a color scheme for my gown. Picture this for an autumn wedding: a floral pattern that combines pumpkin, mustard, and a dash of zucchini on a leaf lettuce background."

"Are you thinking bridesmaid gown or salad bar at Pizza Hut?"

"Ooo, how about a crinoline? We'll look like Southern belles at a garden party! How do you feel about that?"

I stood up as the door *whooshed* open. "How do you feel about flannel?"

The MS *Nordmarken* was cruise ship sleek for a working steamer that delivered cargo and passengers up and down the coast of Norway. However, there were no private balconies, no signs of water slides or miniature golf courses, no glass-enclosed fitness rooms overlooking the bow. There were plenty of lifeboats attached to the upper decks, which were painted the same neon orange as the rope I'd found tied around August Manning's neck.

I shivered as my cell phone went off.

"Emily, darling, where are you? Are you able to talk? I have your information."

"Etienne! I'm at the steamer port waiting for my luggage to be offloaded from the bus, and I think— Yup, there it is." I watched the driver remove my tapestry roll-away from the cargo bay and set it on the asphalt. "So what did you find out?" I retreated to a less crowded area of the parking lot, where a trio of hikers with backpacks and bedrolls were tossing around a Frisbee.

"Joleen and Jimbob Barnum. Jimbob is a descendant of P. T. Barnum and, due to a family trust, is a man of considerable means."

Wow. Nana had been right. "How considerable?"

"The article I read referred to him as 'independently wealthy.' He and his wife are retired circus performers. Or more correctly, Jimbob was a contortionist par excellence who performed in the main ring under the Big Top, and Joleen was part of the accompanying sideshow, appearing as both the Bearded Lady and the Fat Lady."

"You're kidding. Joleen used to be fat? She isn't anymore."

"Perhaps she is one of the millions of Americans who has discovered Weight Watchers. Your Barnums have established a foundation that makes it possible for differently abled children to attend circus performances, rodeos, and monster truck events, and for two weeks a year, Jimbob performs for all the children at St. Jude's Hospital."

"They're really community minded, aren't they?"

"I would characterize them more as budding philanthropists." I heard a paper rustle on his end. "Curtis Klick. According to the records I accessed, he's the former owner of a small business establishment called Visions."

"Is that like a LensCrafters?"

"It's like a strip club. 'All Nude Girls All the Time.'"

"WHAT?"

"In Las Vegas."

"No way. You must have the wrong Curtis Klick. My Curtis is a pint-sized zealot who'd probably rather cut off his right arm than drink, swear, smoke, or shmooze with nudies."

"He was forced to close down after a patron slipped on a boa feather and sued for damages. Mr. Klick was woefully underinsured, so the patron ended up in traction and Curtis ended up in bankruptcy."

"I can't believe it. Are you absolutely sure? I thought that guys who ran seamy establishments like that were— You know, like—"

"Parasites feeding off the underbelly of society?"

"Taller."

A pause. "Ah, I see. Hence the 'small' in the term 'small business owner.' You Americans can be very literal, Emily."

I startled as the hikers' Frisbee swooshed onto the asphalt and skipped across my feet. "I still can't believe that Curtis had an X-rated past," I said, picking up the Frisbee and sailing it back to the hikers.

"People change, *bella*. Perhaps he saw the light after he was forced into bankruptcy." More paper rustling. "Reno O'Brien. Did you know that Reno is another city in the state of Nevada?"

"Yup. Can you tell me something other than he's had two wives, built an addition onto his home to display his athletic awards, and was a rookie cop who worked the Boston Strangler case?"

"Do you know about the drugs?"

"Reno's a drug dealer?"

"A user, purportedly. He attended an international meet in Barcelona, and in an effort to show the world how senior athletes don't rely on performance-enhancing drugs, the sponsors conducted random drug tests. Unfortunately, Mr. O'Brien failed his. He blamed it on the prescription medication he was taking for a chronic sinus infection, but the organizing committee took it quite seriously and notified the Spanish authorities."

"Was he banned from the meet?"

"Mr. O'Brien wields a great deal of clout because of his impressive athletic history, so he was able to convince the organizing committee of his innocence."

"You're kidding me. They took him at his word and let him off the hook?"

"It's not the Olympics, *bella*. Senior athletes on the amateur circuit aren't governed by the same laws that regulate Olympic events."

"Yeah, but after he failed his test, how could the committee be sure his athletic history was the real thing?"

"Mr. O'Brien was likewise worried about how the charge would affect his reputation, so his lawyer flew to Barcelona with threats that if this story ever saw the light of day, he would initiate legal action that would keep the sponsors in court for more years than they had left to live."

"Wow, strong-arm stuff." I frowned. "So if this story was supposed to be kept so secret, how did you find out about it?"

"My third cousin on my father's side is married to—what is your American expression?—the Big Kahuna at the Barcelona police department. He owed me a favor."

"You have a lot of cousins."

"The Italian side of the family is very prolific, *bella*."

I kept my eye on the gangway as people streamed onto the ship. "Were you able to find out anything about May Peabody?"

"Is this woman on your tour, Emily?"

"No. I'm not even sure there is a May Peabody, but—"

"She does indeed exist."

"No kidding?" Damn, I was good! "Where is she?"

"In a woman's federal detention facility in West Virginia."

"She's in prison? Oh, my God. What did she do to land her in—ow!" The Frisbee slammed into my hand like a buzz saw. My fingers numbed. I lost my grip. My cell phone fell to the ground with a sickening *thunk*.

I stared in horror, my brain going haywire. Cracked case. Shattered display screen. I fought to remain positive. Maybe it wasn't as bad as it looked.

The hikers pounded across the parking lot in their clunky boots, spewing what might have been apologies in a language I couldn't understand. One of them snatched up my phone and handed it back, leaving shards of plastic and tiny metallic droppings all over the ground.

As I cupped my beloved phone in my palm, the hiker smiled confidently. "You have five-year protection plan against theft and damage, yes?"

"I think Etienne was about to tell me something really important. What if the information about May Peabody is the clue we need to break the case?" I was curled up on the convertible sofa bed in our cabin, obsessing over the ruined cell phone in my lap while Jackie scurried between her bed and the closet, unpacking her suitcase.

"So call him back already." She dug her mobile phone out of her pocketbook and slapped it into my hand. "Knock yourself out."

"Really? You're a prince, Jack."

She flipped her hair behind her head. "Better a prince than a queen."

I punched the power button, my excitement quickly dashed. "There's no signal."

"Maybe when we're closer to land."

"You think?" I groaned wearily. "Mom is supposed to call me with the results of her Internet search. What'll she think if she can't reach me?"

"That you're out of cell tower range?"

"Her brain doesn't work like that, Jack. She'll think the worst."

"What's worse than being out of cell tower range when you absolutely *have* to talk to someone?"

"How about being dead? That's what she'll think." I winced. "Poor Dad. She'll give him an ulcer over this."

Jackie shook out a short skirt in a Marimekko print and held it against her waist. "You're overlooking the upside of being dead, Emily. Dead people don't have to pay international roaming charges. That's a tremendous savings. Does this make me look fat?"

Knockknock, knockknock.

"Isn't this cabin somethin'?" asked Nana when Jackie opened the door. She trooped into the room ahead of Tilly and George. "It's like livin' in a cracker box without the crackers. But it's got all the essentials. Vanity. Closets. Potty. Blow dryer." She stopped to eye Jackie's new skirt. "Is that one a them Marimekko prints? I was ditherin' about buyn' me one in Helsinki, but I was afraid a short skirt like that would make my ankles look thick."

"We heard about your cell phone," George commiserated as he sat down across from me on Jackie's bed. "You want me to have a look-see? I might be able to patch it back together."

I handed him the plastic carcass. He gazed at it.

"Was a nice thought," he said before setting it on the narrow shelf that separated the beds.

"We got more problems than telecommunications," Nana cautioned as she sat down next to George. "Tilly's grip has went missin'."

"Define missing," I said.

"Define grip," said Jackie.

"The bus driver removed my suitcase from the luggage bay and set it on the pavement," Tilly said with conviction. "There's nothing wrong with my eyesight; I saw him. But it hasn't been delivered yet. Marion's was sitting outside our cabin when we returned from lunch, as was everyone else's, but mine has mysteriously disappeared."

"Have you checked the baggage room?" I asked.

"I checked the baggage room; I told Annika; I reported it to the crewman at reception. They assured me it would probably turn up shortly, but I'm not so sure that someone didn't take it deliberately."

"I bet it was one of the Floridians," accused Jackie. "They hate us. It's a trap. Someone is probably waiting for Tilly to go looking for her suitcase, and when she does—*wham!*" She smacked her fist into her palm. "*Adios, muchacha.*"

"But it don't stand to reason that someone would wanna kill Til'," puzzled Nana. "Not unless she's seen somethin' she don't know she's seen, or knows some-thin' she don't realize she knows."

"Duh?" said Jackie. "It's because she's the only one with a weapon."

"What weapon?" I asked.

Jackie rolled her eyes. "Her walking stick! You think the perp wants to risk getting clobbered with that thing? No way. He probably figures he'll take out Tilly, and once she's gone, the rest of us will be easy to pick off."

"Is it possible that her suitcase accidentally got delivered to the wrong cabin?" George inquired.

"Nothing that simple ever happens to this group," said Jackie. "Trust me on this. The handwriting is on the wall."

I threw my pillow across the room at her. "Cut it out, Jack! You're scaring people."

"I'm not afraid," Tilly assured us as she settled onto the sofa with me. "I'm quite capable of holding my own against any physical attack. In fact, the thought of confronting a killer isn't half as frightening as what awaits me on July thirtieth back in Windsor City."

"What happens then?" I asked softly.

"Root canal. I'd rather face death than the dentist's drill."

"I'd rather face death than talk in front of an audi-ence," admitted George.

Jackie sighed dramatically. "I'd rather face death than pee into a cup. It's so much harder with the new plumbing."

Nana regarded her with rapt interest. "You're very tall, aren't you, dear?"

"What cabin are you in?" I asked Tilly. "Maybe I can rattle some cages about your luggage."

"Three-sixty-three. The other side of the boat toward the stern. And my suitcase has a bilious green pom-pom attached to the handle."

Nana's face creased with worry. "You really think Til' could be in danger?"

"I'm sure Tilly is going to be just fine," I soothed, "but why don't you play it safe and stick together when you're outside your cabin? The buddy system is a great invention."

Nana linked fingers with George. "I wish that nice police officer from Saariselka would tell us if the crime lab got any hits off them prints on Gus's note. I hate not knowin' nothin'."

I jackknifed to attention. "Prepare to be blown away. Are you ready for the latest from Etienne?"

When I finished relating my recent conversation, I looked around the room for reaction. "Well?"

"My compliments to your Inspector Miceli," said Tilly. "This casts an entirely new light on the situation." Her voice grew steely. "There is a guest on this tour who would rather commit murder than have his secret revealed."

"You s'pose Gus mighta found out about Reno's alleged drug use when he was researchin' the article he done on him?" asked Nana. "Seems nothin' stays a secret forever. One a his old newspaper buddies mighta leaked somethin' to him. If Etienne found out, other folks mighta been able to find out, too."

George scratched his head. "What pushed Reno

over the edge? He and Gus were friends, unless they had a big falling out."

"I can't get past the friend part either," I said. "I saw Gus and Reno arguing outside the Sami lodge, but friends don't kill friends. At least not on a regular basis."

"I'll tell you why Reno whacked him," offered Jackie. "He discovered that Gus was doing a big exposé on performance-enhancing drugs in senior athletics and was planning to out Reno, so—*bam!* Reno offed him before he could squeal."

Nana looked confused. "Is Reno gay?"

"Hold on, Jack," I challenged. "Gus was retired. He wasn't writing Pulitzer Prize–winning exposés anymore."

Jackie rolled her eyes. "He was a writer, Emily. Writers don't write because we want to; we write because we *have* to. He probably felt as if he was fading into oblivion in the Hamlets, so he might have been tinkering with groundbreaking material that would open people's eyes and get him noticed. He was a huge celebrity once. Don't tell me he wouldn't sell out his own mother to be a celebrity again. The taste always stays in your mouth. Take me, for example. How could I ever go from being Jackie Thum, bestselling author, to Jackie Thum, Tom's wife again? I mean, it's unthinkable."

"I would warn you against putting all your eggs in one basket," said Tilly. "What about Curtis? Can you imagine the consequences he'd suffer if his religious community found out about his checkered past? Neither he nor Lauretta would ever be able to show their face again. The long term effect could be tragic."

"Might not be too long term seein's how the world's s'posed to end," offered Nana.

"You think Gus ran into that story on Curtis when he was researching his exposé?" asked George.

"I have a problem with Curtis being the killer," said Jackie. "He knows if he kills someone, he's going straight down, so there's no way he's going to whack anyone."

"Maybe he's not really religious," suggested George. "Maybe he puts on a front to disguise the Curtis who enjoys drinking, gambling, and fraternizing with exotic dancers. Works for some of those popular televangelists."

"Them women dance?" asked Nana. "I bet it's part a their diet program. Dancin' probably burns more calories than just standin' around naked."

"What about Jimbob and Joleen?" I piped up. "Should I delete them from our list of suspects?"

"Because they're rich?" asked Jackie.

"Because they're philanthropists," I shot back. "Philanthropists are driven by a need to help people, not kill them."

Jackie arched an eyebrow. "They're into helping children. They might not give a damn about what happens to adults."

"We could vote on it," suggested Nana, "but if Osmond ever finds out, it wasn't my idea."

Tilly thumped her walking stick on the floor for attention. "Aren't we forgetting something?"

"Ballots?" asked George.

Tilly regarded us patiently. "We have theories why Reno and Curtis might want Gus dead, but what about Portia? How does she fit into the picture? Was she killed for the same reasons Gus was killed?"

"Gus might have shared his bombshells with her," I postulated. "She was at the newspaper office all the time, so they were practically connected at the hip. But on the other hand, Gus didn't really like her, so I'm not sure that theory is valid."

"She mighta found out on her own, if she was given to snoopin'," said Nana. "Could be that Gus killed Portia for sticking her nose into his business, then one a them other fellas killed Gus for different reasons."

"Two killers?" I choked.

"Wouldn't that be somethin'?" said Nana. "It don't get much worse than that."

"What was Inspector Miceli able to dig up on Gus and Portia?" Tilly asked me. "Did they have personal secrets they were trying to hide?"

Prickly heat shot up my throat. "Gus and Portia?"

"You did ask your young man to investigate the two victims, didn't you?"

Uh-oh. I lowered my voice to an embarrassed whisper. "No?"

"Emily!" Jackie chided.

"Hey, I wasn't focused on the murder victims. I was focused on the suspects who might have *murdered* the victims."

"No harm done." Tilly waved off my omission.

"Perhaps you could call him back and ask for further assistance."

Nana leaned forward to inspect the directory that hung from the cabin's wall phone. "She's not gonna do it from this phone. It don't do outside calls."

"She can use mine when we reach our first port," offered Jackie. "Does anyone know when that'll be?"

George pulled a schedule from his shirt pocket. "We arrive in Vardo at sixteen hundred hours, and we'll be there for an hour."

"How can I do any meaningful shopping in an hour?" Jackie fussed.

I checked my watch. "Good. We have plenty of time to eat lunch now and check out the situation with Tilly's luggage. I'll keep you posted if anything new pops up."

"I wanna know more about that May Peabody person," said Nana. "You think she done someone in? I bet that's why she's in the Big House. Could be them three girls got bad genes. Maybe killin' runs in the family."

I held my head, thinking it was about to explode. "No more theories! I'll talk to Etienne and then maybe we'll be able to sort things out."

"I'd like something sorted out," Jackie sniped. "How did I end up giving a free book to Joleen and Jimbob? If they're so rich, they could have bought their own. Freeloaders."

CHAPTER 13

The common areas of the MS *Nordmarken* gleamed with polished brass fittings, lustrous wood detail, nautically themed wall murals and paintings, and windows whose exteriors wore streaky coats of salt spray. A long arcade of swivel chairs and glass-topped tables lined the entrance to the dining area, allowing passengers to enjoy quiet views of the Arctic Ocean while sipping lattes from the nearby café. The dining salon was nestled into the stern and set up with a central food island that rivaled Blimpie's once-a-year-only Easter buffet—hot food, cold food, mouthwatering desserts. Tables with white linens and flowery centerpieces flanked the central island, and because of the off hour they were mostly unoccupied, so Jackie and I had the whole place to ourselves.

I couldn't figure out what a lot of the cold food

was, and I wasn't turned on by the hot entrees, so I filled my plate with slices of aged blue cheese, crackers, smoked salmon, shrimp cocktail, and olives, and rounded out my selections with chocolate cake, a brownie, chocolate mousse, whipped cream, and a whole bowl of maraschino cherries. Protein. Dairy. Fish. Fruit. Looked like most of the essential food groups to me!

Halfway through our meal, an announcement blared throughout the ship, summoning all passengers to the panoramic lounge on deck seven for a mandatory couriers meeting. At least, that's what I thought it said. The message was repeated in a multitude of languages, none of which sounded like English, so it was anyone's guess.

We scarfed down the rest of our meal and climbed the forward staircase to the plush viewing salon on the top deck. After hooking up with the rest of the group, we were introduced to the *Nordmarken*'s captain and crew, and given instructions about what to do should our ship capsize in the frigid waters of the Arctic Ocean, complete with a demonstration of how to crawl into a one-size-fits-all survival suit. When the formal meeting ended, Annika announced that she'd set up a schedule board by the information desk on the dining deck, and that we should consult it several times daily to keep abreast of activities, meetings, and port walks.

"Just so you know," Jackie confided when Annika cut us loose, "if the ship goes down, I'm not jumping into blaze orange Doctor Dentons; just let me drown.

The literary *paparazzi* could be everywhere. Can you imagine how appalled Hightower would be if I appeared on the front page of *The National Enquirer* dressed like a giant carrot?"

"Literary *paparazzi*?" I questioned.

"I'm sure they're out there," she assured me as we followed the crowd down the stairs to the lower deck. "They just haven't found me yet."

Pausing on deck six to let the crowd thin out, I glanced down a long, wide passageway with cabins on either side, wondering if any of the Florida group had paid to upgrade to the larger rooms on a higher deck.

"*MESDAMES ET MESSIEURS . . .*" I practically leaped into Jackie's arms as a woman's voice exploded from the speaker system with another multilanguage message.

"Jeez!" Jackie clapped her hands over her ears. "Did Norway export all its volume control buttons?"

When the woman hit a language that sounded vaguely familiar, we learned we were nearing the port of Vardo and should prepare for disembarkation through the gangway on deck three.

"Are we going ashore?" Jackie tittered. "We can look for a cyber café and check my numbers on Amazon."

"I'd better start searching for the suitcase with the bilious green ribbon tied to the handle. Maybe there's another baggage room somewhere."

"I thought we were supposed to stick together."

She'd actually listened to me? "That would be great, Jack! To be honest, I could use your help."

She gave me a long-suffering look. "I meant stick together while we look for a cyber café."

"Oh."

"How about this? You look for Tilly's suitcase, I'll look for computer access, and when I get back I'll attach myself to you so permanently, they'll need the Jaws of Life to pry us apart!"

I forced a smile. "Sounds delightful."

She handed me her phone. "I hope you can get a signal. Stand outside when you try. All the metal in the ship could be causing interference. Don't miss me too much!"

"Remember that we're only going to be here for an hour," I called after her. "If you're not back on time, the ship won't wait for you!"

She flashed me a thumbs-up before disappearing down the stairs. She was really on her own in Vardo, because the rest of my group had announced at our meeting that none of them were going ashore. Nana had spoken for everyone. "We'd be cuttin' it too close. An hour only gives us enough time to walk down the gangplank, turn around, and walk back again. That's way too much pressure."

I tried to think positive thoughts about Jackie's onshore adventure, but I couldn't suppress a niggling fear that something dreadful was going to happen to her, the least of which was plummeting Amazon numbers.

Pushing my fears aside, I explored passenger deck six from stem to stern, finding no suitcases still sitting outside cabin doors, or any secret baggage rooms. I did find two Jacuzzis on the narrow aft deck, but I didn't think guests would be lining up to use them. They were stuck into dark corners and covered with tarps, so they weren't very inviting.

Working against the clock, I thoroughly examined the dining and gangway decks, rechecked the baggage room, then searched the two passageways on deck two, which felt a little like the bilge. It was darker down here. Danker. I found nothing resembling Tilly's suitcase in the fitness room or sauna, and when I opened a reinforced steel door at the end of the passageway, I was hit in the face with a blast of diesel fumes and deafened by the revving motors of vehicles, which streamed through the open cargo door. Car deck. Oops. Forcing the door shut, I climbed back up to level five and exited onto the promenade deck, with its Astroturf carpeting.

Vardo sat at the foot of low, green mountains—a sprawling town of two-story blue, red, mustard, and white houses that were exact replicas of the Marshall Plan houses we'd seen in Kirkenes. Tires hung from the quay like hubcaps on a gas station wall. Gulls screeched overhead, dive-bombing at boats laden with heavy nets and orange buoys. Warehouses with peeling paint jutted into the harbor, looking crooked and fatigued. As I stood at the rail, watching the managed chaos of passengers, forklifts, and cars vying for space on the asphalt quay, my nose twitched involuntarily.

Fish. The smell was overpowering—not because it smelled bad but because it was so alien. The only place you can smell fish in Iowa is at a Red Lobster.

Retreating to a quiet section of the deck, I dug

Jackie's phone out of my shoulder bag and powered it up, thrilled when I got a signal. I punched in Etienne's home number.

"This is Miceli," he said in his sexy French/German/Italian accent. "Please leave a short message. I'll return your call as quickly as possible."

I waited for the beep. "This is Emily. *Please* get back to me. I have to know why May Peabody is in jail. It's really important. I also need to beg another favor, which includes another Internet search, so if you could call me back at—"

Shoot! I didn't know Jack's cell phone number. I rotated the unit in search of a cheat sheet or label, but no such luck. Damn.

"Okay, here's the thing. I didn't expect to be talking to your machine, so I didn't think to get the number. So I'll have to call you back. Unless— Wait a sec. If you're not at home, you're out. Don't move! I'll try your cell." I punched in another number.

"This is Miceli," said his voice mail. "Leave a message and I'll get back to you."

"Nuts! Where are you? I'm using Jackie's phone, so would you call me back at the number that popped up on your screen . . . whatever it is? And let me know what you found out about airplane flights. We're in Vardo now, but I'm not sure we're going to be in any port long enough for you to catch up to us. I'll hope for the best. Love you."

I tried Mom next, relieved when she picked up. "What a coincidence, Em. I just tried calling you, but all I got was nothing."

"My phone died. Literally. It's in a thousand pieces. I hope you didn't jump to conclusions and think I was dead or anything."

"I thought you were probably out of cell phone range."

I frowned. "You didn't think the worst?"

"What's worse than being out of cell phone range when you really have to talk to someone?"

Oh, my God. Mom and Jack were on the same wavelength. The world really *was* going to end.

"I finished researching the names you gave me, Em. Are you ready for the results?"

"Fire away."

"Lauretta Klick's legal residence is a retirement community in Florida called the Hamlets. She's married to Curtis Klick—isn't that a cute name? I love the alliteration. And they bought one of the first homes constructed in Phase One. They've been there so long, I guess you could almost call them the project's founding fathers. Lauretta's maiden name was Hauck. I had a hard time finding that out, but I finally hit pay dirt."

"Special website?"

A pause. "I'd better not say. That way, if the Feds arrest you, you'll be able to pass the polygraph test. She and Curtis were married in Las Vegas about a century ago, and she worked for years as a dance instructor for Arthur Murray Studios. Just like Grace Stolee! Wouldn't that be something if they knew each other, Emily? When Arthur Murray was popular, I think they held big conventions for all the instructors."

Lauretta had met Curtis in Las Vegas. Had she married him knowing about his past? Was it her influence that had helped him find religion? Would she kill him if she discovered that he'd committed murder to ensure that his former life remained a secret? "Anything else on Lauretta?"

"She was a real maverick. When other women were working as telephone operators, dime store clerks, and waitresses, she was a professional, even before she got married."

"What did she do?"

"I think she made eyeglasses. The company where she worked was called Visions. Do you suppose that's the founding company that became Pearl Vision?"

Oh. My. God. Lauretta had been one of Curtis's exotic dancers? You've got to be *kidding* me!

"That's all I have on her. She's pretty different from your Peabody sisters, who are a couple of social butterflies. I found a lot of old newspaper articles that went on and on about the parties they attended and where they were wintering. And the society pages were filled with gossip about their string of broken engagements. It was almost as if the two of them were competing to see how many former fiancés they could rack up."

Gee, what a surprise.

"The family owned mortuaries across the country, but when the father died, the girls closed up shop in every state and moved to Florida. I can't figure out why they didn't sell out to someone who wanted to maintain the company under the family name. Peabody was apparently *the* brand name in burial services. Why would the girls turn up their noses at preserving their father's legacy?"

Why indeed? "Did you run across any mention of another sister?"

"Yes, I did! Mr. Peabody's obituary listed a daughter named May, but I never saw her name on any of the society pages. Isn't that odd? It was almost as if she didn't exist. How could two sisters attract so much publicity, and one attract none at all?"

"Maybe she was shy," I suggested. And serving time.

"Would you like me to see what else I can find out about her, Emily? I was only concentrating on April and June before."

"Could you? And would you check out Portia Van Cleef and August Manning while you're at it?" I gave her a brief rundown on each of them. "Do you have time?"

"Of course I have time." She repeated the names and wrote them down. "My whole day is open, except for driving to Ames to meet with the caterer, sampling food for the reception, writing up your wedding program, delivering it to the printer in Des Moines, picking out new invitations, and meeting with Rabbi Karp to discuss how we can pack a few more guests into the synagogue. A day doesn't get more quiet than this."

I waited a beat. "You have to drive all the way to Des Moines to find a printer? You can't find one closer to home? Like in Ames?"

"I'm going to spread the services around this time,

Em. Just a precaution. You never know when another tornado is going to hit."

I massaged a sudden sharp pain between my eyes. "What did you find out about Vern?"

"The military can be so aggravating, Emily. They put up so many fire walls to protect their records."

"So you couldn't find anything?"

"Shoot, fire walls don't faze me. What would you like to know?"

"I'm not really sure. I know he's a retired general with bad knees who enjoys playing Scrabble. Did you read any profiles that gave more insight into his personal life?"

"I know he has awards up the ying-yang."

"For his military service?"

"For the cha-cha. He apparently owned that dance when he was younger."

"You're kidding me. Vern was a dancer? It must have been a really long time ago, because he can hardly walk anymore."

"That's so sad. If he was in better shape, you could probably hold a dance competition. Isn't it funny how so many people in your tour group have ties to ballroom dance? Grundy, Lauretta Klick, Grace Stolee."

I wasn't sure it was funny, but I thought it might be significant in some unfathomable way.

"He's also a skilled equestrian, kayaker, cyclist, and ping pong player. Isn't it nice that the military makes sure its officers can be all that they can be?"

A long tone blared above me like an angry foghorn.

"Jesus, Mary, and Joseph," cried Mom.

"Sorry! Ship's whistle. Probably a warning blast to tell us we're about to leave." I looked over the rail to see passengers hotfooting it toward the gangplank and men in orange vests standing by to cast off the lines.

"You run along then, Em. I don't want you to miss the boat. I'll call you after I look into these new names."

"You can't call me. Remember? I'll have to call you. Thanks, Mom."

The activity in the dock area grew more frenetic. Quick hugs. Quick good-byes. A man in a tie-dyed T-shirt racing down the street toward us, waving his arms and shouting. A final blast of the ship's whistle. A rush up the gangplank. Lines being cast off. The whine of the gangplank as it creaked upward. The man in the T-shirt pelting across the pavement and windmilling his arms on the edge of the quay as we pulled away.

"*Halten sie an!*" he yelled, shaking his clenched fist at us. He stomped his foot and kicked a nearby pylon, then turned around to yell at the bystanders.

Tardiness? Yelling? I didn't know where the guy was from, but I knew it *wasn't* Iowa.

As we nosed into the harbor, I cast a nervous glance back at Vardo. The captain hadn't been kidding when he'd said if we weren't back in time, he'd leave without us.

I hoped Jackie had made it back in time.

When I climbed back down to the dining deck, I ran headlong into a throng of familiar guests, who were gathered in a noisy circle.

"Lay one finger on her and you're a dead man!" barked George.

"Get the hell out of the way," warned Reno. "Can't you see he's hurt?"

"Act not in anger," cried Lauretta. "Turn the other cheek."

"Make way!" yelled Margi. "I'm a nurse."

"Hey!" I shouted above the din. "What's going on?"

"She started it," accused April.

"Did not," said Bernice.

"Did so."

"Bite me."

"This is Vern Grundy," Dick Teig said into his camcorder. "He's flat on his back 'cause he just got the crap kicked out of him."

What?

I pushed my way to the center of the crowd to find Vern staring dazedly at the ceiling. "What happened?" I cried, dropping to my knees beside him.

A dozen sets of eyes riveted on Nana. I stared at her in disbelief. "*You* did this?"

She nodded sheepishly.

"Why?"

"'Cause he was lookin' at Tilly funny. I didn't wanna take no chances."

CHAPTER 14

"I have assurances from Mrs. Sippel that this will never happen again." Annika had gathered us into the Fembfiringen Bar for an embarkation meeting that began as a lecture about how we should conduct ourselves aboard ship. "Isn't that right, Mrs. Sippel?"

"You bet," said Nana.

Tucked between the conference room and the library, the bar was a cozy salon with overstuffed chairs and sofas arranged in intimate groupings around small pedestal tables. At least, that was the idea. By the time everyone had finished rearranging the furniture, we were a room divided, with Iowans on one side and Floridians on the other. Kinda the nautical version of the War Between the States.

"How did Marion do it?" asked Joleen Barnum, who had staked out a neutral chair between warring factions. "She really decked Vern, and she's a foot and a half shorter."

"She did *not* deck me," growled Vern. "I stubbed my toe on the carpet and my knees gave out."

Nana leaned toward me and whispered out of the corner of her mouth, "I decked him."

"Spinning roundhouse kick?" I whispered back.

"Flyin' drop kick."

"They teach drop kicks in beginners' Tae Kwon Do?"

"I'm not a beginner no more, dear. I graduated to intermediate. My instructor says I'm a geriatric wonder."

April Peabody waved her hand lazily at Annika. "Some of us have been talking, and we think you should throw Mrs. Sippel into the brig."

"Over my dead body!" threatened George.

"If Marion goes, I go," Tilly spoke up.

"Me too," said Margi. "I can monitor blood pressure for the folks who are claustrophobic."

"I'm not committing to anything until I find out if this place has *en suite* toilet facilities," said Bernice.

"If you don't throw that woman in the brig *this minute*," April warned Annika, "I'll write you up for showing partiality to felons."

"Marion didn't hurt me!" Vern maintained. "I tripped. She had nothing to do with it."

I guessed his military status forced him to say that. Better to fudge the facts than admit you'd been clocked by a seventy-nine-year-old dwarf.

Osmond stood up. "Show of hands, and I'd like to

be neighborly and include the Floridians in this. How many folks would like to be locked up with Marion?"

"Sit down," Annika snapped, with the kind of irritation that also implied *and shut up.* "None of you will be sent to the brig because there *is* no brig."

"What about an infirmary?" asked Dick Teig.

"There should be an infirmary," agreed Margi.

"The matter is closed," Annika decreed. "There are more important matters to discuss. Officer Vitikkohuhta has given me permission to tell you that he has received a preliminary report on the fingerprints found on Mr. Manning's note."

An uneasy hush fell over the room.

"The only clear impressions they could identify were of Mr. Manning's own fingerprints."

Margi gasped. "Does that mean he strangled himself?"

I hung my head. *Oh, God.*

"It means that for the moment, you are exonerated. If your fingerprints were on the note, they could not be found."

But . . . but . . . This was terrible! Someone in this room wrote that note. Someone in this room was a killer. How could they not find prints?

"Officer Vitikkohuhta also wishes me to tell you that they are pursuing other avenues of investigation, so you should not congratulate yourselves prematurely on eluding justice."

I glanced at the Floridians, who all looked pretty smug about the fingerprint results.

"I end with a few housekeeping notes," said Annika.

"I am in cabin three-ninety-two should you need me. Three-nine-two. I suggest you write it down. We have already suffered our first passenger loss—a man left behind in Vardo. So I caution you to double-check the posted departure times before disembarking, and to synchronize your watches with the ship's clock. You would also be wise to return to the ship earlier rather than later."

I exchanged a look with Jackie, who had found a cyber café and returned to the ship more depressed than she'd been yesterday—but at least she'd gotten back in time. I wondered if I'd ever learn not to be such a worrywart.

"Dinner will be served in fifteen minutes. We have assigned seating at the window tables on the port side, so please sit within the designated area. After dinner, coffee and tea will be served here in the bar. Do plan to partake of the refreshments. It's quite rude not to. And if any of you are prone to suffer from motion sickness, I would advise that you take a prophylactic to ensure your continued good health."

Nana's eyes rounded in shock. "Usin' a condom can prevent seasickness?" She raised her hand. "What size?"

"She's talking about Dramamine," April jeered. "Get a dictionary."

"Does anyone have further questions or comments?" Annika interrupted.

Curtis stood up. "Lauretta and me have been going over our notes real carefully, so we have new information that the group might enjoy hearing."

"Very good," said Annika, looking relieved not to be refereeing another fightfest or shouting match. "We encourage outside reading, especially guidebooks that point out areas of local interest. Go on."

"The world isn't going to end in a few days." He smiled broadly as he took Lauretta's hand. "It's going to end tomorrow."

"Lauretta was one a them hoochie-coochie girls?" Nana asked after dinner. "I'll be." She took a sip of her tea as she considered this latest revelation. "You s'pose that pays good?"

"I imagine the income is based largely on tips," said Tilly. "A woman with a Colgate smile and breasts the size of kettle drums could do quite well for herself."

Nana glanced across the room to give Lauretta the once-over. "She's kinda lackin' in the kettle drum department."

"Maybe she had breast reduction surgery," suggested George.

Jackie stared at Tilly in confusion. "Did you say tips or tits?"

We were once again in the Fembfiringen Bar, gathered in a cozy corner, dazzled by the scenery outside the port window. Rocky headlands. Solitary beacons perched on lonely islands. Waterfalls. Snowcapped peaks. Unexpected homesteads in the middle of nowhere. The five of us hadn't been able to sit together at dinner, so I'd related my earlier conversation with Mom as we oohed and aahed over the Norwegian coastline.

Nana drained her teacup and set it on a nearby table. "Don't sound to me like we know much more now than we did before, except Vern was a cha-cha king, Lauretta couldn't keep her clothes on, and April and June deleted May from their family calendar. You know what I think?" She cast a wary look at the guests seated throughout the salon. "I think they're tryin' to confuse us."

"We know a little more than that," Tilly spoke up. "If Curtis and Lauretta both had checkered pasts, they each had a stake in wanting to keep their secret buried."

"So they're probably working in cahoots," said George.

"What's to prevent 'em from walkin' off the boat tomorrow and never bein' seen again?" asked Nana.

"I hope the world does end." Jackie sagged deeper into her chair, pouting. "That should wipe Amazon off the Internet, right?"

"Emily, you s'pose Portia knew about the Klicks and was holdin' it over their heads?" asked Nana. "You said she sounded like she was threatenin' 'em back in Helsinki. Maybe they had an understandin'. Portia wouldn't tattle on 'em if they'd stop scarin' folks with their end a the world talk."

"Makes sense to me," said George. "They knocked off Portia to keep her quiet, then they popped Gus because they probably figured he was the fella who told her. I say they did it."

"It puts the nail in their coffin for me, too," said Tilly.

"You want Osmond to take a formal vote?" asked Nana.

"Would anyone care to hear about my reviews?" Jackie said in a small voice.

"It could be the Klicks," I agreed, "but how are we going to prove it before they disappear? And I'm still not convinced they're tall enough to strangle anyone."

"Son of a bitch," growled Vern as the room echoed with the sound of crashing china.

Laughter. Razzberries. "Steady Eddie strikes again," teased Reno.

"Step around the mess," ordered Vern, directing traffic away from his broken coffee cup and saucer. "Let me find someone to clean this up."

"Uh-oh," Nana lamented as he left the salon. "You s'pose him dropping that cup is my fault?"

I gave her a puzzled look. "Why would it be your fault?"

"On account a when I drop-kicked him. Maybe he hurt his hand. You think he'll sue? If it was Bernice, she'd sue."

Jackie sucked in her breath like a Darth Vader action figure. "Oh, my God, Emily, you're right. Women blame themselves for everything. This is so cool!" Settling back down, she continued in a more subdued tone, "I have new reviews on Amazon, if anyone is interested in hearing about them."

"Do *not* play the heavy in this," I begged Nana, rubbing my bruised hand. "Someone probably ran into him."

"Is that where the Frisbee run into you?" Nana

fussed, wincing at the color. "Looks like one a them inkblot tests what tells you if you're nuts."

"The Wombai in New Guinea played Frisbee," Tilly said reflectively. "With human skulls. Poor creatures had no concept of aerodynamics."

"I have three new reviews," Jackie burst out. "All one stars. I need sympathy!"

"Oh, no!" I leaned over to pat her knee. "I'm so sorry, Jack. Who knew that being a published author could be so traumatic? Is there anything I can do to make you feel better? I have chocolate in the cabin."

"You could write a nice review," she whimpered. "*Pleeeeease*, Emily. I'm going down in flames."

"Are them one stars the bad ones?" asked Nana.

Jackie dabbed her eyes, sniffing delicately. "For an author, there's only one thing worse than getting a one-star review."

"Having your book go out of print?" asked Tilly.

"Getting *four* one-star reviews," she sobbed.

"Isn't there nothin' you can do to make 'em disappear?" asked Nana.

Jackie shook her head. "Bad Amazon reviews don't go away. The only time they're deleted is if a reviewer reveals whodunit, or if the person being reviewed is married to the vice president."

"Why don't you write yourself a review?" George offered. "I bet other authors do that all the time."

Jackie looked horrified. "But that's so lowbrow. I'd much rather have you guys do it."

"Seems to me you need lots a folks writin' good reviews if you're gonna get your average up."

"Would you write one for me, Mrs. S.? I'd pay you . . . or . . . or I could have Tom give you a free cut and style the next time you're in Binghamton. You'd look really hot with another choppy cut."

Oh, God. The last time she'd gotten the choppy cut, she'd ended up looking like the losing poodle in a cockfight.

Nana's eyes crinkled in thought. "What you need is for that nice husband a yours to offer discounts to folks who'll post nice reviews for you on Amazon. Marketin' 101. Everyone loves discounts and free stuff. You think that'd work?"

Jackie's gaze froze on Nana's face. "It's brilliant. Absolutely brilliant!" She peered out the window at the iron-ribbed coast. "Do you see any cell towers out there?"

I dug her phone out of my shoulder bag and handed it back.

She punched the power button, cursing under her breath. "Maybe I can get a signal if I go outside."

George consulted the ship's schedule. "If that doesn't work, our next landfall is in four hours."

"I'll give it a try."

"Doesn't Amazon recommend that you actually read the book before writing a review?" I asked when she'd gone.

Nana eyed me curiously. "I never thought I'd be sayin' this, dear, but I think you got some a your mother in you."

"Would you like brochures over here?" Joleen asked, waving them enticingly. "They're the latest literature on the Hamlets." She lowered her voice as she handed them out. "The community could use an infusion of new blood. Might make it less stuffy, which would be a whole lot easier on me and Jimbob. You folks seem real nice. You ever thought about moving south?"

"I been thinkin' about buyin' an island off the coast a the Bahamas," said Nana, "but my accountant hasn't worked out the tax implications yet."

I stared at her, dumbfounded. "You're going to buy an island?"

"I gotta get rid a my money somehow, dear. I'm makin' it faster than I can spend it."

"Well, if the deal falls through, you come down and visit Jimbob and me. We'll give you the grand tour, take you to all the golf courses, and list a hundred good reasons why life in the Hamlets is so much better than life in the snow belt." She lowered her voice again. "It'll be even better if we can force the bad eggs out. But like Jimbob likes to say, 'Everything comes to those who wait.'"

I felt a twinge of alarm, wondering if Jimbob had gotten tired of waiting and decided to help things along. But that wasn't likely. He was a philanthropist, for crying out loud.

"The brochure covers all the important information, like housing costs, services, guidelines, clubs. There's maps of Phases One through Eight, and pictures of the new mortuary and hospital wing. Did you know we have our own zip code?"

Vern hobbled back into the salon, accompanied by a crewman pushing a cleaning trolley. Guilt spread across Nana's face as the cleanup began. "I seen you over there when Vern dropped his cup," she said to Joleen. "Was that on account a someone bumped into him?"

"Nope. He did that all on his own." She wiggled her fingers discreetly. "Problem with his hand."

Nana went ashen. "What'd I tell you? It's all my fault."

"Not unless you're telekinetic," Joleen said. "It's because of his pain medication. Does the same thing to me. When I pop one of those pills, I get the tremors so bad, the only way I can eat soup is through a straw."

Nana nodded thoughtfully. "You probably gotta avoid Chunky Chicken and Dumplin's."

"Yeah, I'm mostly stuck with consomme and tomato."

"Do you have an extra brochure we can give Jackie?" George spoke up. "She might get rich enough on her royalties to retire early."

"That wouldn't surprise me at all," said Joleen as she handed him another of the glossy leaflets. "That girl has so much going for her. Beauty, brains, talent. What did she do before she became a writer?"

"She was a Broadway actor," Nana said proudly, "starrin' in *Joseph and the Amazing Technicolor Dreamcoat*."

"I *love* that musical," Joleen enthused. "What part did she play?"

Nana regarded me nervously. "She had one a them speakin' parts, didn't she, Emily?"

"She pinch-hit," I said offhandedly. "She played the pharaoh, Asher, and even Joseph once, when the whole cast came down with the flu."

Joleen's jaw went slack. "How could anyone with a figure like Jackie Thum's be made up to look like a man?"

I shrugged. "It's show business. Everything is smoke and mirrors."

"Wait 'til I tell Jimbob. He'll never believe it. Too bad Jackie didn't know about the 'I've Got a Secret' competition we had at the Hamlets. I bet she would have won hands down."

Nana's eyes brightened. "Back when my Sam was alive, we was awful fond a watchin' that old 'I've Got a Secret' game show. You wouldn't believe some a the crackpots that come on that show, Emily. It was real must-see TV."

"That's what our contest was based on!" cooed Joleen. "It was Portia's idea. The person who revealed the most startling secret about himself could come on this trip free of charge, and let me tell you, the competition got pretty fierce."

"I thought most folks wanted to take their secrets to the grave with them," claimed George.

Joleen flashed him an "Aw, go on" gesture. "Not when there's a free trip involved. International travel with all expenses paid? People will do anything to get something for nothing."

"What'd I tell you?" said Nana.

"So who won?" asked Tilly.

"Geraldine Jordan, who started out life as Jerome

Jordan. Can you believe it? An honest-to-goodness transsexual living there among us, and we didn't even know it. That's some secret, isn't it? You could have blown us over with a feather."

I took mental inventory of our tour roster. "There's no Geraldine Jordan traveling with us."

"That's because she had to cancel at the last minute. Emergency surgery."

"Bunions?" I asked.

"Brazilian butt lift. Her plastic surgeon had a cancellation."

"So who got her ticket?" asked Nana.

"No one. No substitutions allowed. The runners-up complained, but Portia said there was nothing she could do about it. Didn't make them too happy that they'd blabbed their secrets and no one got rewarded."

My brain started turning over like a jump-started engine. "Do you recall who the runners-up were?"

"Oh, sure. The Klicks came in second with their entry. Curtis used to own a girlie place in Las Vegas and Lauretta was one of his strippers."

"You already knew that?" I squealed.

"That's no great shakes. I worked in a sideshow; we're all exhibitionists in one way or another. But I'll tell you what surprised me more than the Klicks—Reno saying he'd once been accused of using performance-enhancing drugs."

"You know that, too?"

"Honey, there's nothing I don't know anymore. Gus got ticked off that Reno didn't mention the doping incident for his big feature article, since scandals sell newspapers."

This wasn't fair. My whole case was going up in smoke!

"The Peabody sisters thought they had a lock on the free trip with their, 'Our sister is in federal prison for embezzling Daddy's fortune and driving us into poverty with only a million dollars to our name,' but it didn't have much curb appeal. If the sister had been a hotel heiress or a former *Survivor* contestant, interest might have been higher, but no one was wowed by a relative who cooked the books and deposited everything into Swiss bank accounts. Plots like that have been so overdone in the movies."

"Did you and Jimbob participate in the contest?" asked Tilly.

"Shoot, no. We don't need someone paying our way anywhere. Besides, Jimbob and me don't have any secrets." She glanced over her shoulder before continuing in a whisper. "Do you want to know Vern's secret?"

"He was a cha-cha king?" I offered.

"Nope. Before he went into the military, his hair was so bushy, people used to call him Stein, for Albert Einstein. He won an honorable mention because no one could picture him without his buzz cut."

George passed his hand over his bald pate. "I've been mistaken for Yul Brenner."

"Where's the other folks in your group?" Joleen asked, waving her brochures.

"They're enjoying their refreshment in the library

and being standoffish," said Tilly. "They figure that's much more polite than being two-faced."

"The library." Joleen's face brightened. "The perfect place to leave a few brochures. Which way do I go?"

"First door on the right," I said, pointing aft. "The one with the porthole."

"That's mighty thoughtful of her to invite us to Florida," said George when she'd trundled off. "Does she have a mustache?"

"*Shhh*," cautioned Nana. "It's 'cause she's got a skin condition what makes hair grow all over her body."

He looked suddenly hopeful. "Is it contagious?"

I slumped in my chair, discouraged. "So much for our grand theory. Why kill someone to prevent them from revealing a secret that everyone knows?"

"Could I change my vote on the Klicks?" asked George.

"We have no clear motive as to why anyone would kill either Portia or Gus," said Tilly, "so I believe that lands us back on square one again."

"But it was such a great theory," I complained. "I really liked it."

"One a your better ones, dear," Nana agreed.

"What do you propose we do now?" asked Tilly.

My head was so overloaded with useless information that I couldn't see a clear path leading anywhere. "I'm stumped. We might already have the clue that opens everything up, but if we do, I don't know what it is."

"That's unfortunate," said Tilly. "Keeping our eyes on the Klicks wouldn't have been so difficult, but monitoring the entire Hamlets group will be next to impossible."

"Good new, good news," Jackie announced as she rejoined us.

"Your husband liked my idea?" Nana asked, beaming.

"I couldn't get through to him—no signal. But I did run into Annika when I went down to the cabin to recharge my phone. She asked me to tell Tilly that they've found her luggage. Isn't that great?"

"Sure is," said Nana. "She don't got no toothpaste and all's I got is Polident, which don't work real good if your teeth don't come out."

"Did she say where it was?" questioned Tilly.

"They accidentally delivered it to cabin three-thirty-six instead of three-sixty-three, and the elderly German occupants took it inside for safekeeping. When no one came to claim it, they notified reception, so it's now sitting outside your cabin. Mystery solved. We're on a roll!" She dropped her voice to a conspiratorial whisper. "So when do we nail the Klicks?"

In an effort to keep the group together, we joined them in the library, where I found a welcome stash of playing cards, board games, and jigsaw puzzles. The Dicks and their wives partnered up for euchre; Alice and Osmond worked on a jigsaw of a scenic fjord; Nana, George, and Tilly played Monopoly; and the rest of us played the game of global domination—Risk.

By the end of the evening, Helen was giving Dick

the silent treatment for stupidly trumping her winning tricks; Grace was giving Dick the silent treatment for spilling coffee on the table; Alice and Osmond finished their fjord and started working on a famous glacier before it melted; Nana had developed hotel empires on Park Place and Boardwalk; and Bernice, Margi, and Lucille were at each others' throats in a dispute over Liechtenstein that was threatening to throw the country into civil war, destabilize the neighboring regions, and force them into a conflict to preserve civilization as we know it.

"That turned out well," I mused when Jackie and I returned to our cabin. "Have you noticed how much more tolerant they are of each other than they used to be?"

Jackie pulled a face as she detached her phone from its charger. "Yeah. The only thing that could have made the evening more enjoyable is if we'd hit an iceberg and been forced to run around in our carrot suits."

"C'mon, Jack. That couldn't have happened."

"How do you know?"

"Because Norway doesn't have icebergs. It has glaciers."

"Whatever." She sat on her bed, fiddling with her phone. "Emily? Can I ask you something?"

Uh-oh. "You know you can always ask me anything, Jack."

She heaved a pathetic sigh. "Do you think I'll ever be a successful novelist?"

"Of course you'll be successful!" I sat down next

to her and gave her a sympathetic hug. "It could just take a little time for your name to become a household word."

"How much time?"

"You want me to make an actual calculation?"

"Go ahead. Give it a stab."

"I can't do that. I don't have any inside information. Don't you have an easier question?"

Her shoulders sagged, as if she were bearing the weight of the world. "Mona refuses to return my calls. The company president won't answer my emails. My name's not on any bestseller lists. Amazon readers hate me. I got less rejection when I was an unemployed actor. Why am I doing this?"

I patted her back. "Because you won a contest?"

"I wish I'd never entered. I wish—" Her voice trembled with emotion. "Why do people think they have the right to treat other people so badly?"

"I don't think they're personal attacks, Jack. It's just business. Hey, I wrote Mom's number down for you. Do you want to call her to talk about the wedding? That might cheer you up." Or induce a complete mental breakdown.

"What'll I do if my book bombs?" she sniffed. "I'll be humiliated. Disgraced. What'll happen to me?"

"Nothing will happen to you unless you let it. You'll shine no matter what you do. You've been blessed with some wonderful gifts."

"Like what?"

Why did *I* always get stuck with the hard questions? "Well, you get along great with people. You even get along with Bernice. That could earn you a position in the diplomatic corps."

She nodded apathetically. "She really likes me, doesn't she? What else?"

"You have wonderful insights into the male psyche."

"I think it's making me schizophrenic. What else?"

I regarded her, at a complete loss. "You . . . you're really tall."

"*Mesdames et Monsieurs,*" announced a hushed voice over the cabin intercom. Four translations later, we learned we were about to make a fifteen-minute stopover in Berlevag.

"A port!" I encouraged. "Cell towers. I bet you'll get through to Tom this time."

Jackie nodded like a wounded puppy. "Do you need to use the phone while we're here?"

"If we're still in port when you finish your conversation, I'll try Mom and Etienne."

She exhaled a weary breath. "Maybe I should forget about writing. Maybe I should just stay home and have babies."

"You could do that. International adoption has really taken off. You and Tom could adopt a Chinese baby, or a Romanian baby."

"But I want to have my own."

"I'm sure you know this already, Jack, but that would require a uterus."

"Could I use yours?"

"No!" I pulled her off the bed and aimed her for the door.

"But surrogacy is done all the time, Emily."

"Not with my uterus."

"I've probably caught you at a bad time. We'll talk about it later, okay?"

"No!"

"What if I promised to name it Emily if it's a girl?"

I shoved her into the corridor, where passengers were already ambling toward the disembarkation point. "Say hi to Tom for me."

"Etienne if it's a boy?"

I shut the door and returned to my sofa to flip it into a duplicate of Jackie's bed. I closed the porthole curtains, punched my pillow, kicked off my shoes, and stretched out on the duvet, my jetlag and sleepless nights hitting me like one of Nana's flying drop kicks.

When I opened my eyes again and squinted at my travel clock, the time read 8:11, which caused me to realize two things: I'd just enjoyed my first good night's sleep since arriving in Scandinavia, and Jackie wasn't in her bed.

From the looks of things, it hadn't even been slept in.

CHAPTER 15

"Has anyone seen Jackie?"

My Iowans were seated at the good tables by the window in the dining salon, and they were happily snapping pictures of each other as they drank their morning coffee.

"Last time I seen her was last night," said Nana.

"Here's Emily," said Dick Stolee, focusing his camcorder on me. "Doesn't look like she bothered to comb her hair this morning."

"At least she's got hair," mocked Bernice.

"Her bed wasn't slept in last night," I said in a breathless rush. "She went to call Tom when we arrived in Berlevag, and she never came back. I'm really worried."

"Have you checked the rest of the dining room?" asked Tilly.

I cast a long look from starboard to port. "I made one pass, but I'll make another one."

"A little late to start looking for her, isn't it?" asked Dick Teig.

"I only realized she was missing about ten minutes ago! I fell asleep after she left and slept right through the night."

Mouths fell open. Eyes widened. "You hear that, Dick?" Helen thwacked his arm. "Not everyone has to be up all night going potty."

"That's 'cause Emily don't got a prostate," said Nana.

"Have you asked Annika or the Hamlets people if they've seen her?" asked Tilly.

"I haven't run into any of them yet this morning, but that'll be my next move."

"I bet she got off the ship at Berlevag and got left behind," said George.

"She was terribly depressed about her Amazon reviews yesterday," said Tilly. "I hope her depression didn't cause her to do something—" Her voice faded into silence. She cleared her throat. "Never mind. I've never known anyone to adore themselves as much as Jackie. I'm sure that's not the case."

"I bet one of those wackos from Florida offed her," charged Bernice. "If you're getting away with murder, why stop at two?"

"Show of hands," said Osmond, rising to his feet. "How many folks think—"

Nana grabbed his elbow and wrenched him down into his seat. "You don't wanna go there, on account a if you do, I'll take Tilly's cane and wrap it around your neck."

"We need to form search teams to look for Jackie," said George. "How do you want us to split up, Emily?"

Bless his little heart. It was wonderful having responsible adults around in moments of personal panic. "We have access to six decks, so let's divide up into six two-person teams, one team for each deck."

"I hosey anyone except Bernice," Margi called out.

"Could I be paired with someone other than Dick?" asked Grace Stolee. "We're still not speaking."

"I don't want to be paired with anyone," said Bernice.

"You have to pair up with someone," complained Lucille. "If you don't, we'll have an uneven number of people and everything'll get thrown off."

Bernice smiled archly and continued to drink her coffee.

Dick Stolee panned his camcorder in her direction. "Here's Bernice, acting like a pain in the ass."

I flashed a time-out sign. "No cherry-picking partners. We'll do it alphabetically." Mom would be so proud of me. I drew imaginary lines in the air, coupling people. "Osmond and George, Tilly and Lucille, Nana and Dick Stolee."

Margi looked confused. "M comes before O. Shouldn't my name come before Osmond's?"

"Alphabetical by last name," I explained. "Grace and Margi, Dick and Helen." I narrowed my gaze at Helen. "Are you speaking to Dick today?"

"Yeah. I forgot I was mad at him."

"And Alice and Bernice. If the twelve of you will search the indoor areas of your deck, I'll search all the outdoor areas."

"Do we get to choose what deck we want?" asked Margi.

"No!" If they did that, we wouldn't get out of here until we reached Bergen. I pulled a pad of sticky notes from my shoulder bag, wrote a number on each sheet, and handed them out. "That's the deck you're responsible for."

"Can I be a team leader?" asked Dick Teig.

"No leaders! You're all co-captains."

"If we don't want to be co-captains, can we be cheerleaders?" asked Margi.

"How long do you want us to search?" George asked me.

"Until you find Jackie," I said. "If you can't find her, head to the library. We'll regroup in there and assess what to do next."

They stared at me, immobilized by what appeared to be a sudden onset of communal paralysis. I stared back. "What?"

"You'd best give us a time to meet in the library," said Osmond. "We gotta have a deadline."

"It's easier on our nerves if we know we can avoid being late," said Alice.

"Sorry. I wasn't thinking. It's eight-thirty now, so let's plan to meet in the library in an hour and a half. Any more questions?"

"I been thinkin', dear," Nana said a little hesitantly.

"Could be another reason why Jackie's not here no more."

My breath lodged in my throat at the thought of a fate even more horrible than suicide or murder. "What's that?"

"Could be she got raptured."

No way had she been raptured.

I wrestled with the scenario as I made a second pass of the dining salon.

I didn't care if she *was* the only person on earth who liked Bernice. When our marriage fell apart, I'd had to take a job in phone solicitations to support myself. Phone solicitations! Shouldn't that earn her some time splitting rocks in Purgatory before she got admitted to the Pearly Gates?

I finished my search of the dining area, quickly consulted my tour notes, headed for the deck below, and knocked on the door of cabin number three-ninety-two. "We have a problem," I said when Annika answered. "Jackie's missing."

She waved me into the cabin. "Come in, come in. I would be dishonest if I told you I wasn't expecting news like this."

"You knew Jackie was going to disappear?"

"We had avoided a major incident in over fifteen hours. I somehow knew we were overdue. Tell me what happened."

When I finished filling her in, she riffled through a stack of papers in her briefcase and handed me one. "This is a printout of our groups' cabin numbers.

I suggest you knock on doors to see if anyone has seen Jackie." She paused meaningfully. "Perhaps Mrs. Thum decided to spend the night with another guest and was seduced into sleeping late. It wouldn't be the first time a wife has cheated on her husband on one of my tours."

My mouth fell open. "Jackie wouldn't do that!" Of course, she'd done it to me, but she wouldn't be stupid enough to do it again, would she? "She loves her husband. She's even talking about having a baby. Besides, she'd never sleep with anyone shorter than she is—which eliminates all the men on the tour except Jimbob, and I don't think he's her type."

"Just a warning. Do not be surprised at anything you find. However, I will notify the captain and have him radio back an inquiry to see if we have left behind someone other than the German passenger. I suspect that is our most likely scenario."

"So you don't think she's been murdered?" I needed to hear it from someone else's lips.

"I think it would take a great deal of effort to overpower Mrs. Thum. She's quite large-boned for a woman."

I guess that was a small comfort.

"While you're here, Emily, I spoke with Officer Vitikkohuhta a couple of hours ago. He has given me permission to share new details with you. Concerning Mr. Manning's sister—"

"Is her name May?" I asked eagerly.

"Her name is Sister Christine Marie."

I stared at her, nonplussed. "She's a nun?"

"A cloistered nun, which is why it was so difficult to contact her. But the wheels are now in motion, so Mr. Manning's body will soon be making its way back to America."

So there was no connection between Gus and someone named May? Shoot. This was so frustrating.

"Also, the crime lab has finished testing the rope used to strangle Mr. Manning."

"Did they find the killer's fingerprints on it?"

"Probably the killer's and every Midnight Sun Adventures guest who ever tried to lasso Emppu's reindeer. There were countless prints smeared up and down the rope, but none that could be identified, so the police are unable to draw any conclusions."

"Damn." I studied the list of cabin numbers. "Not to state the obvious, but when I do my door-to-door canvassing, I'm a little concerned that I might be walking in on our killer."

"You don't have to go inside. Ask them to hold the door open, and you can observe the room from the passageway."

I winced at the suggestion. "It's just that— I've had a few close calls in hotel rooms over the last couple of years, so barreling into them Hell bent for election is at the top of my 'Things to Avoid' list."

"Hell bent for election? What does that mean?"

"Umm . . . damn the torpedoes, full speed ahead?"

"Ah, full speed ahead. I understand that. You Americans have far too many idioms."

"My fiancé tells me there's a new dictionary of American slang. You can probably order it on Amazon."

She escorted me to the door. "We arrive in Hammerfest at eleven o'clock. If you haven't found Jackie by then, please remain on the ship, because the captain will probably want to talk to you. If he receives confirmation that we've left her behind, I'll have you paged over the intercom."

"What happens if *I* disappear while I'm searching?"

"Has your grandmother taught you her flying drop kick?"

"No."

She tsked her disappointment. "That's too bad."

Halfway through my list and batting zero, I decided that all the Floridians must have gone up to breakfast while I'd been talking with Annika.

When I finished with not one response, I checked the dining salon again, finding no familiar faces at any of the tables. This was so weird. Where was everyone?

I ran into Tilly and Lucille along the starboard arcade. "Find anything?"

"Some passengers sleeping in the bar area," said Tilly, "none of whom are Jackie."

"We checked the two conference rooms and both ladies' rooms," said Lucille. "They're all empty. We'll need to drag the fellas down here to check out the men's rooms."

"We're going to explore the ship's store next," Tilly informed me. "There's a Norwegian sweater in the window that's speaking to Lucille."

We cut through the café to the opposite side of

the ship, and while Tilly and Lucille slipped into the store, I eyed the passengers who were seated at tables in the public area, drinking coffee and watching some international version of CNN on the ship's only television.

"In business news from America," announced the female commentator in a crisp British accent, "as we reported earlier, publishing powerhouse Hightower Books, which has seen flagging sales since its corporate reshuffling last year, has filed for bankruptcy and is immediately closing its doors. This will affect over one hundred fifty employees who were given pink slips yesterday, with no promise of future pensions. Hightower is best known for publishing such popular classics as *Nucular: You Don't Get To Use It Until You Can Pronounce It*, which was a former Oprah selection. In other business news—"

I stared at the television screen, not hearing another word. Hightower Books was filing for bankruptcy? Hightower was Jackie's publisher! Oh, my God. She was going to be devastated. All the work she'd put into that book, all her hopes and expectations—

I blinked at the woman on the TV screen. "*As we reported earlier . . .*" Oh, no. Had Jackie heard the report earlier in the morning when she'd been trying to call Tom? If she'd been depressed before, this could have been the clincher, especially with her hormones the way they were. Oh, God, what if—

I peered at the choppy sea, fearful that a size fourteen stiletto heel might be floating in our wake.

The thought took my breath away.

She can't be dead.

I raced up the main staircase and pushed open the bulkhead door, my hair flying around my head as a blast of wind whipped across the promenade deck. The mainland might have been sizzling at a hot ninety degrees, but on the open sea it felt more like Iowa in January. People in sensible coats and hoods stood at the rail, taking pictures of the granite headlands, while I brushed past them, hugging my arms to myself and shivering.

I circled around to the bow and looked down on the foredeck to find an orderly clutter of capstans, chains, cables, and black metal cylinders that resembled oversized spools of thread. I leaned far over the rail, darting looks left and right, but there was nothing out of order. No shoes. No phones. No Jackie.

I continued my search down the starboard side, running into only a couple of shutterbugs who were willing to brave the cold for a shot of the open sea. I paused at the stern to look back at the aquamarine water churned up in our wake, then followed the port rail back to midships, where I scooted inside, teeth chattering and goose bumps wearing goose bumps.

"I hope you're having better luck than we are," said Margi Swanson as she walked by with Grace. "We're heading down to the library." She tapped her watch. "Fifteen minutes until showtime, Emily. Are you going to make it?"

"You bet." I took the stairs two at a time and, finding no bulkhead door on deck six, raced up to deck seven. I hurried through the lounge and bar area and pushed open the aft door, stepping out onto the sun-deck, where a score of passengers in matching navy blue hooded windbreakers reclined in deck chairs, apparently impervious to the cold. Damn. Who were these guys? Eskimos?

"Ahoy there!" called Joleen, waving enthusiastically.

Good Lord, they were Floridians! I glanced at the jumble of deck chairs, spying Vern and Reno, Jimbob, April and June, Lauretta and Curtis. They must have eaten breakfast really early so they could claim the best chairs on the sundeck.

I tapped the arm of April's chair as I walked by. "A little cold up here, isn't it?"

She lowered her sunglasses so she could look me in the eye. "Doesn't matter what the temperature is. Once a sun worshipper, always a sun worshipper."

"Have any of you seen Jackie this morning?" I asked, raising my voice to be heard above the wind.

Heads shook. Shoulders shrugged. Reno looked up from the miniature Scrabble board in his lap, his windbreaker embroidered with the word *Hamlets* in bright gold lettering. "I saw her last night as we were about to dock in that place that starts with a B, but I haven't seen her since."

The Klicks came to attention like bird dogs on the scent. "Is she missing?" asked Curtis, holding onto his video camera.

"Yes, she is," I said, watching all of their faces for a reaction.

"I *told* you we should have come up here earlier," Lauretta scolded, whacking her husband with a tube of sunblock. "She was probably up here at the crack of dawn and got raptured before us."

"Lighten up on the poor guy," chided April. "In case you hadn't noticed, it's crack of dawn all the time around here."

"You need some help looking for her?" asked Vern.

"Thanks, but—" I gave them a stony look, not trusting a single one of them. "We have everything under control."

"We'll tell her you're looking for her if she walks by," said Jimbob.

"Triple word score," said Reno, handing the board to Vern. "Add fifty-seven points to my score, ole buddy. And do it before your hand freezes up."

I marked the time as I wended my way around the chairs. I had six minutes to make it down to the library with one last outdoor area to check.

I descended the metal stairs of the aft companionway, aware of the kind of *hrrrm*ing you'd hear in a sewage treatment plant or a kitchen with a really big refrigerator. The Jacuzzi at the base of the stairs was still covered with a tarp, but when I turned to the port side, I saw that the cover had been removed and—

"OH, MY GOD!"

CHAPTER 16

"Put a sock in it, would ya?" Bernice griped as she adjusted her bathing cap. "It's called old age. Deal with it." She lowered herself into the Jacuzzi, the water bubbling over her black thong bikini and Tyson chicken flesh like a steaming witches' brew. "And close your mouth before drool starts running down your chin."

I snapped my mouth shut, but I wasn't sure what to do about my eyes. I might have to pluck them out.

"Five-ninety-nine at Wal-Mart," she boasted, lifting the shoulder strap of her bikini top. "Though it's not even worth that much, since they only sell you half the suit these days."

I nodded like an Emily Andrew bobble head.

"What's wrong with you? Cat got your tongue?"

I shook my head no.

She flicked water at me. "My Harold would have loved seeing me in this suit. Did you know I used to be a model?"

I nodded again.

"Those were the days when women were shaped like hourglasses instead of number two pencils." She angled her head coquettishly. "My Harold was a butt man. Some men like legs, others like chests, but my Harold liked butts. Especially mine. You know what he used to call me?"

Euw boy. Way too much information. "We have a group meeting in five minutes, Bernice."

"Not for me. I'm playing hooky."

I gave her an exasperated look. "Did you even bother looking for Jackie?"

"Deck two. It's only half as long as the other ones, so we finished fast. That lower level is really creepy."

"Aren't you even curious to find out if someone else found her?"

"Alice said she'd take notes at the meeting. Don't worry; I won't get left out of the loop. Alice takes good notes."

I locked my jaw, too irritated to speak.

"There you go, giving me that 'I'm put out' look of yours. Here's the deal. My son paid a whole lot of money for me to take this trip, so if I'm given a choice between attending a boring meeting or taking advantage of an unoccupied hot tub, guess which one I'm gonna choose?"

"Jackie really likes you," I spluttered, unable to contain my anger. "If you were missing, she'd be the first one out looking for you. And she'd attend all the meetings!"

"Sure, sure. If I went missing, *no one* would look for me. I'm old, but I'm not stupid."

"Oh, yeah? Well, whose fault is that?"

She gave me a squinty look from beneath the rubber flowers on her bathing cap. "Whose fault is what? That I'm old, or that I'm not stupid?"

"Whose fault is it that none of your friends would look for you?"

"Shoot, they might call themselves my friends, but they don't really like me. If *you* disappeared, they'd tear the boat apart to find you, but not for me. They're your friends, not mine." She shrugged a bony shoulder. "I don't really have any friends."

It was Bernice—crotchety, irascible, pain-in-the-neck Bernice. She made all our lives miserable. I shouldn't feel sorry for her, but I did. "So . . . did you ever have friends?"

"Harold was my friend. Can't say I've had one since he passed on. Money got tight, and when money's tight, it leaves a sour taste in your mouth. It's hard to like yourself or anyone else when you're just scraping by. I almost had to declare bankruptcy once. That was a real low point. If I'd had to appear in front of a judge and admit to the world that I didn't have a pot to piddle in, it would have been all over. I've got pride, you know."

I came to attention as if electrified. "Bankruptcy—that's it. *That's* the motive! What is wrong with me? I am *so* blind." I hopped onto the Jacuzzi platform, grabbed Bernice's face, and kissed her on the mouth with a loud smack. "Thank you, Bernice! You are absolutely brilliant!"

"*Euuuuuuw!*" she sputtered as I wrenched open the bulkhead door. "Hey! I'm not that way!" The echo of her voice followed me down the passageway. "Not that there's anything wrong with it!"

I ran down four interior staircases, my feet in a footrace with my brain. I needed to call Mom. With any luck she'd be able to verify—

I checked my watch. 10:01. It was the middle of the night in Windsor City. Waking people up from a sound sleep was so jarring, but—

I collapsed against the reception counter on the gangway deck, gasping for breath. Man, I really needed more cardio in my daily routine. "Is there a phone I can use to make a call to the United States?" I asked, wheezing pathetically.

The crewman behind the desk eyed me curiously. "The public phone is behind you."

I swung around. The wall opposite me was hung with large-scale maps, brochures in wooden pockets, and a solitary phone framed by a privacy cubicle. "That's a real public phone? I can dial the States on it?"

The crewman nodded. "If you have the proper phone card."

"I don't *have* a phone card."

He pointed upward. "Ship's store. Deck four."

"It costs *how* much?" I asked the store clerk when she rang it up.

"Six hundred kroner."

"How much is that in American dollars?"

"Approximately one hundred U.S. dollars. It is not profitable for us to sell the cards in smaller units. My apologies."

I checked my cash reserves and sighed. "Do you accept credit cards?"

I plugged the card into the phone and dialed, flinching at the ship's clock. 10:16. I was really late for the meeting. They were going to kill me. "Mom!" I said when she answered. "*Pleeease* forgive me for bothering you and Dad at this hour of the morning, but it's really important."

"My goodness, Emily," she said in a froggy voice, pausing to yawn. "You're never a bother. Why, it's— Just a second, I can't see the clock. It's quarter past three here. I was just about to get up."

She was so sweet, and such a bad liar. "Mom, did you have time to check out those names I gave you?"

"Yes, I did, but can I run something by you first?"

The second hand on the ship's clock kept eating up precious time. "Real fast, okay?"

"Accordions."

"Excuse me?"

"For the wedding. The synagogue doesn't have an organ, so I found four accordion players from the Myron Floren Institute who'll play music for the service and the reception. Do you remember Myron Floren, Emily? He was on Lawrence Welk with the Lennon Sisters, and Jo Ann Castle, and Wayne Newton when he was just a little nipper singing 'Danke Schoen.' Do you remember Lawrence Welk? A one-uh and a two-uh. Such a nice man."

"Accordions?"

"I've asked them to play lots of polkas."

"AT THE SERVICE?"

"At the reception. Your grandmother loves a spirited polka." A thoughtful pause. "We'll have to remind George to strap his leg on extra tight."

Oh, God. "Accordions sound wonderful, Mom. Are you anywhere near the information you have for me?"

"It's in the office. Hold on. I'll pick the phone up in there."

I watched the second hand on the ship's clock tick away more time. I also noted that it was 9:20 in Rome, 8:20 in London, and 5:50 in Newfoundland. *Huh?*

"Who do you want me to start with?" Mom asked when she picked up again.

"Portia."

"I found a lot of archived material about her from the *Boston Herald* web pages. Did you know she was a debutante? Van Cleef was her married name, but Pingree was her maiden name. I think she's one of those Eastern blue bloods. She married a fella who spent a lot of time playing polo and sailing in his yacht, but he died some years back when he fell off a horse. They owned several vacation homes, but she put them on the market after she was widowed. They were both on the board of directors for a bunch of charitable organizations. Can you imagine the commitment of time, Emily? Sitting in all those boring meetings and attending all those fancy benefits? We don't give rich folks near enough credit."

"Did Portia and her husband own a home in Las Vegas?"

"Yes, they did! How did you know that?"

"Lucky guess."

"Do you suppose they ever got to see Wayne Newton perform? After he left Lawrence Welk, he grew a mustache and became the King of Las Vegas."

"What about August Manning? Did he have a Vegas connection?"

"Not that I remember. Let me see. He won a Pulitzer Prize for journalism and spent most of his life in Washington, D.C. He was a member of various professional societies and organizations and served as president of the Atlantic Journalists Foundation for almost a decade. He was involved in an accident some years back and was laid up for a long time. No mention what the accident was, but I'm thinking vehicular. He isn't married, doesn't have kids, and never seems to do anything except work. On paper, he looks pretty dull. Maybe he should play polo or bowl, or something like that."

"No Vegas connection that you can see? Are you sure?"

"Do you think he has a gambling habit? I wouldn't have any way of checking, but maybe his idea of the perfect vacation is to fly out to Vegas to hit the casinos."

That prompted a burst of inspiration. "What about

his Atlantic Journalists Foundation? Organizations have conferences and conventions. Is your computer on? Can you check to see if they ever meet in Vegas?"

Tick . . . tick . . . tick . . .

"They don't sometimes meet in Vegas, Emily. They *always* meet in Vegas. It's an annual event held at a different hotel each year."

"Yes!" I did the jump-around and would have started the wave if there'd been other people around.

"Do you want to hear about May Peabody now?"

"Don't need to. You've given me all the information I need. Thank you *so* much, Mom. Love you!"

I ran up the main staircase to the dining deck. It was ten thirty, and I was screwed. I burst into the library—to find it empty.

"Aw, come on, guys. Where are you? Why is everyone disappearing?"

I stood outside the library door, looking both ways, relieved when I spied them shuffling around the corner in a tightly packed clump.

"Where've you been?" Dick Teig huffed, looking happy to see me despite his indignant bluster. "We've been all over this tub looking for you."

"Did you know there's an infirmary on deck two?" asked Margi, waving a Polaroid snapshot. "Your grandmother let me borrow her camera because my battery died."

Nana gave me a hug. "When you didn't show up on time it gave us a fright, so the Dicks said we oughta form a search party."

"No kidding?" I smiled at the Dicks. Bernice had

been right. Despite their sometimes gruff facades, these guys really liked me. I blushed at their adulation.

"We'd be up a creek without you," admitted Dick Stolee.

"Aw, that's so sweet."

"It's because you're carrying our plane tickets," Helen spoke up.

"Did you find Jackie?" Nana asked me.

"No. Did you?"

Her mouth drooped woefully. "None of us seen no sign a her. She's got swallowed up like a golf ball on the last green a one a them miniature golf courses."

"We did, however, find all the Floridians on the sundeck," said Tilly, "so they're all present and accounted for, and if the world ends in the next few hours, they won't have to worry about being diagnosed with skin cancer. One tube of sunblock among them. Ridiculous."

"I have pictures," enthused Margi, waving more snapshots.

"I'm happy to find all of you in one place," Annika said as she joined us. "I have just received word on Mrs. Thum, so please"—she opened the library door and held it wide—"it will be more quiet in here."

We filed in and took seats at the room's many tables, my heart ready to burst from my chest in expected dread.

"The purser has just informed me that the captain radioed every port where Mrs. Thum might have been left behind, and no one reports having seen a six-foot brunette in a miniskirt and stiletto heels."

"That's not exactly the right description," George objected. "She's a lot taller when she's wearing those spike heels."

Nods. Rumbles of assent.

"George is right," said Osmond. "She's at least six-feet-four in heels. Maybe six-feet-five."

"I bet everyone was looking for the wrong person," Margi concluded. "Do you think they'd mind looking again?"

Annika regarded us with a blankness that was probably borne from guiding one too many tours with American guests. "She was not left behind. She has not made her presence known at the ship offices in Berlevag, Mehamn, Kjollefjord, Honningsvag, or Havoysund."

"When did we visit all those places?" snorted Dick Teig.

"In the early morning hours," said Annika.

"How come I didn't hear the ship stop?"

"Because you were snoring," said Helen. "You wouldn't have heard your own head explode."

"So what are the captain and them folks gonna do about findin' Jackie?" Nana called out.

"They're beginning a systematic search of the ship," Annika announced crisply.

"We already did that," said Tilly. "She's not here."

"Did you alert the captain about the two deaths on our tour?" I asked Annika.

"The captain has no jurisdiction over what transpired on Finnish soil," she said in defensive mode.

I stared at her, thunderstruck. "You didn't think it

would be good policy to tell him he was transporting a killer?"

"Of *course* I wanted to tell him! But the head office told me if I wanted to keep my job, I had better keep our problems under my hat. Do you know how much money the company would lose if it was forced to fly us to Bergen because we were refused passage on this ship? Only one word can describe such a calamity."

"Bummer?" threw out Dick Teig.

"*Uff-da!*" sobbed Annika. She sank into an uphol-stered armchair, throwing her hands up in defeat. "I will tender my resignation when we return to Hel-sinki. I have failed you as a tour guide. Two guests dead. One missing. I look at you, knowing one of you is guilty of heinous crimes, and I cannot even guess who it is!"

"I know," I said, rising to my feet. "It's the Klicks."

Gasps. Jaw dropping. Looks of disbelief.

"I thought we decided the Klicks couldn't a done it 'cause they don't got no motive," Nana reminded me.

I lifted my brows triumphantly. "We were wrong."

"Gee." Dick Teig sniggered. "That's a first."

I glared at him. "We had the right people but the wrong motive, and the right motive makes everything fall into place. Since the Klicks weren't shy about tell-ing people their secret, there had to be another reason why—"

"What secret?" asked Lucille.

George let out a frustrated sigh. "Curtis owned a girlie joint and Lauretta worked for him."

"*Euuw.*" Helen curled her lips in disgust.

"I knew there had to be another reason why they'd kill two people in cold blood," I continued breathlessly, "and it all boiled down to—"

"I know, I know," burbled Margi. "They didn't want anyone to find out their secret!"

We fired collective stares at her. She looked confused. "Has someone already guessed that?"

"Revenge!" I said, thrusting my finger into the air.

"Why'd they want revenge?" asked Osmond.

"Because," I announced in my best theatrical voice, "August Manning was the reason Curtis had to declare bankruptcy."

More gasps. Clueless stares.

"Bless my stars," said Nana. "You mean Gus was the fella what slipped on that girlie feather and sued 'im?"

"What's a girlie feather?" asked Alice as she frantically scratched out notes on a writing pad.

"She's talking about a feather boa," explained Tilly.

"Boas have feathers?" puzzled Margi. "Seriously?"

I let out one of my signature whistles, which widened eyes and closed mouths simultaneously. "Hear me out." I began ticking off points on the tips of my fingers. "Curtis's strip club was in Las Vegas; Gus visited Las Vegas every year for a conference. Curtis was sued by a patron who ended up in traction; Gus was involved in an accident that laid him up for a long time. Both Curtis and Gus end up in the same retirement community, and Curtis bides his time until he can get even. It fits! Because of Gus and his lawsuit, Curtis lost everything. Think how devastating that must have been."

Nana nodded sagely. "Durin' the Great Depression, folks didn't fret about bankruptcy; they just jumped out windows."

My confidence faltered as I eyed the wary expressions on everyone's face. "Don't you think it fits?"

"I think it fits, dear," offered Nana.

"Me, too," said George.

"I don't think the little guy is tall enough to commit a crime," argued Dick Stolee.

Lucille fluttered her hand for attention. "If Curtis and Lauretta were working together, they'd almost be as tall as a real person, wouldn't they?"

"Show of hands," prompted Osmond. "How many people agree with Emily that—"

"I don't understand what connection this has to Mrs. Van Cleef," Annika protested. "Did Mr. and Mrs. Klick kill her as well?"

"Yes!" I squealed. "Portia and her husband owned a vacation home in Las Vegas. I don't know all the details yet, but I'll bet you anything her husband was involved in that lawsuit of Gus's."

"Do you suppose Mr. Van Cleef might have witnessed the incident?" asked Tilly.

"And testified at the trial?" said Nana.

"And been the deciding factor that turned the judgment against Curtis?" offered George.

"*Ooo*," cooed Helen. "Did the two of them kill Portia's husband, too?"

"He fell off a horse," I said.

Dick Teig grew thoughtful. "They couldn't kill the husband so they knocked off the wife." He stuck out his bottom lip and shrugged. "I like it. All those in favor of throwing the book at the Klicks, raise your hand."

Horrified gasps. Horrified stares.

"No one calls for votes except Osmond," Alice wheezed, staring at Dick's upraised hand as if it had been five hundred pounds of goat intestines.

He dropped his arm like a plummet. "Oops. I got so caught up, I forgot myself."

"All those in favor of throwing the book at the Klicks, raise your hand," repeated Osmond.

Every hand in the room shot into the air.

"Opposed?" he followed up, waiting a beat. "There's no one opposed. The motion carries."

"Wait a minute," Lucille said suspiciously. "We never have unanimous votes." She scanned the room. "Where's Bernice?"

Heads swiveled in confusion. "I could have sworn she was with us when we were searching for Emily," said Grace.

"She's in the hot tub," said Alice, switching to a fresh sheet of paper.

"What hot tub?" asked Helen.

"There are two of them on deck six," said Alice. "Some fella coming out of the fitness room told us about them when we were looking for Jackie."

Helen stared at me accusingly. "You never told us there were hot tubs."

"Well, I—"

"Show of hands," said Osmond. "How many folks would rather soak in a hot tub than do the port walk in Hammerfest and get left behind like Jackie?"

A bunch of hands shot enthusiastically into the air.

"It's not unanimous," he declared, "but close enough. Last one into the tub is a rotten egg!"

They scrambled out of their seats like passengers on a downed plane, leaving all their valuables behind. They funneled through the doorway with curses and grunts and a painful entangling of limbs. "Tell me honestly," Margi cried as the door swung shut behind her. "Have you ever seen a snake with feathers?"

"Osmond's slippin'," Nana announced to the near empty library. "He didn't ask if no one was opposed."

Annika stood up, jaw squared, eyes determined. "Emily, do you honestly think the Klicks are responsible for Mrs. Thum's disappearance?"

"I think there's a good chance they are. I don't know why they would harm Jackie, or what they did to her, but if someone doesn't make them talk, I'm not sure we'll ever find her. Can't you do something?"

She checked the time. "Yes, there is definitely something I can do. Please wait here for me. I'll be back in a moment."

"Where do you s'pose she's goin'?" Nana asked when she'd gone.

"Maybe she's going back to her cabin for a weapon," George said, the color suddenly draining from his face. "I hope it's not a gun. A bullet ricocheting off steel plating is not a pretty sight. Pepper spray would be okay, though."

"Maybe she's gonna fetch duct tape," suggested Nana.

"That's an interesting concept," mused Tilly. "Duct tape as a weapon?"

"A weapon of restraint," Nana explained. "It works real good. A couple a strips around the ankles and wrists, and your captive's not goin' nowhere."

I gave her a measured look. "How would you know that?"

George cleared his throat and stared at his shoe lacings. Nana looked sheepish. "Court TV?"

I struggled not to smile. "I'll bet."

Tilly clucked at the disorder on the tables and set about tidying things, pausing to study Alice's forgotten notepad. "Does anyone know why Alice was writing the minutes of our meeting?"

"She was doing it as a favor to Bernice," I said, pitching in with the cleanup. "She didn't want Bernice to be left out of the loop."

She considered the notes thoughtfully. "It defies logic, doesn't it, that no one's handwriting matched the handwriting on the killer's note?"

"You don't think it was Alice what wrote the note, do you?" asked Nana.

"No, no," said Tilly. "It's just perplexing."

I gathered up discarded pamphlets of Hammerfest and Bergen and stacked them next to Joleen's Hamlets brochures, then collected odd scraps of paper, a couple of paper clips, and Margi's photos. "Don't forget your camera," I said to Nana, handing it back to her. "Margi obviously did."

"That's all right, dear. Margi's got other things on her mind."

"Like what?" asked George.

"I dunno," said Nana. "Walkin'. Rememberin' to breathe. Stuff like that."

The door flew open and Annika appeared, her face flushed with emotion. "I'm taking them off the ship," she said, fighting for breath. "I've just phoned Jukka-Pekka and he instructed me to—"

"Who's Jewka-Pecka?" asked Nana.

"Officer Vitikkohuhta." Annika flashed a shy smile. "We're on a first-name basis. He's instructed me to escort Mr. and Mrs. Klick off the ship at Hammerfest and to deliver them to the police station. That seems the best solution for everyone involved. We walk directly past it on our port walk, so I hope it won't enter their minds where I'm taking them. Jukka is calling ahead to explain the situation to the local authorities, but it falls upon my shoulders to make sure the Klicks accompany the rest of the group off the ship. So first, I need to find them."

"We seen 'em on the sundeck just a little while ago," said Nana. "You want me to show you where they're at?"

"I would very much appreciate that, Mrs. Sippel."

"I'm going with you," said George. "You might need backup."

"And a weapon," said Tilly, making a sword out of her cane and stabbing it into the air.

Nana grabbed Annika's arm. "But we better hurry on account a—"

"*MESDAMES ET MONSIEURS,*" the familiar voice rang out over the speaker system, deafening us.

"We're almost there," Nana said as she whisked Annika out the door. "Come on."

They were gone before I had a chance to ask Annika if the captain still wanted to speak to me. So what was I supposed to do? Stay here? Go down to my cabin? Go up to the bridge?

By the time the announcement that we were arriving in Hammerfest was repeated in all its various incantations, I'd decided the surest way to track down the captain was to show up on the bridge. However, the main staircase was clogged with so many passengers streaming down from the upper decks that I returned to the library to wait for the crowd to clear. Antsy with nervous energy, I straightened books on the shelves, pushed in chairs, resisted the urge to alphabetize the fiction collection by author, and finally forced myself to sit down at a table, where I leafed mindlessly through the pile of stuff the group had left behind.

Margi's photos weren't exactly ready for *National Geographic,* but they showed potential. She'd taken one close-up of bold black lettering that read *Sykestu,* which I assumed was the infirmary on deck two, and the rest were candid shots of the Floridians. April Peabody scowling at the camera beneath her sunglasses and hood. Vern and Reno, dressed in their matching navy blue windbreakers, concentrating on their Scrabble game. Joleen proudly showing the Hamlets insignia on her jacket. Vern catching a tube of sunblock midair. Wow. That was quite a comeback from a guy who hadn't been able to hold onto his cup last night.

Curtis, with his expensive video equipment in his lap, waiting for the heavens to open up so he could—

"I'm going to sue their tight little Norwegian butts right off them!" Jackie raged as she burst into the room. "I'm going to sue the shipping line, the designer, the captain, the country of Norway, the . . . the—"

"The crew," suggested Bernice, trailing behind in her flip-flops and chenille coverup. "Negligence on their part might be worth a few hundred thousand extra kroner."

"Jack!" I leaped out of my chair and threw my arms around her, gushing little sounds of happy surprise and blinking away tears. "You're safe! I didn't know if I'd ever see you again. I thought you might be dead! What a relief. I'm so glad you're okay!" I stepped back and clasped my hands in breathless gratitude. "So where the hell have you been?"

"I'll tell you where I *haven't* been," she blustered. "Berlevag, Mehamn, Kjollefjord, Honningsvag, or Havoysund. Are you surprised I can recite them in order? I can even spell them." She braced her fist on her hip and lengthened her eyes to slits. "I can spell them *backwards.*"

"You were studying the ship's schedule all night?"

"No, no. I had other reading material." She fished inside her shoulder bag and slapped a Hamlets brochure on the table. "For what it's worth, I have memorized every freaking word in this freaking brochure and could offer my services as a human website for the freaking place. What would you like to know about the Hamlets, Emily? Ask me anything. Average age of resident? Average number of golf carts per household? Average number of clubs the average resident belongs to?"

"WHERE WERE YOU?"

"In an emergency supply room, dammit!"

"Where?"

"On the car deck!"

"All night?"

"Well, I'm sorry I didn't phone you to come get me out, but it's hard to pick up a signal when you're locked inside a steel-plated room!"

"I was really worried, Jack!"

"Hey, I had to spend the night in a janitor's closet with gunked-up engine parts and motor oil. How do you think I felt?" She seized the hem of her miniskirt. "Do you know how impossible it is to get grease stains off delicate fabric?"

Bernice pulled her bathing cap off her head with a noisy snap. "Can you skip over all this emotional crap and get to the part where I come to the rescue?"

I regarded her in disbelief. "*You* went to the rescue?"

"She most certainly did," Jackie said proudly, hanging an arm around Bernice's shoulders. "I yelled until I was hoarse for someone to let me out, but there's so much reverberation and rattling on that car deck, not one person heard me—until Bernice arrived. Yo, Bernice," she hooted, squeezing tightly.

"It was nothing," Bernice demurred.

Bernice to the rescue? Bernice Zwerg? The Klicks were right: the world really *was* ending. "How did you happen to be on the car deck, Bernice?"

She looked at me grudgingly. "I—uh, I remembered looking through that partition door when Alice and I were searching deck two, but we didn't go in because of the fumes. All that was in there was cars, anyway. But I got to thinking after I talked to you that Jackie might have ended up in there somehow, so I went back to check it out."

"And I'm ever so grateful you did," Jackie cooed, bending over to plant a big sloppy kiss on her mouth.

"What *is* it with you two?" Bernice squirmed out of her embrace, scrubbing her lips with the back of her hand. "Get this into your heads: I only bat right handed! You understand what I'm saying? Oh, never mind. I'm leaving. I've had colonoscopies more comfortable than this damn thong."

"Thong?" asked Jackie when she'd left.

"Don't ask. So how in the world did you get locked in an emergency supply room?"

"Faulty hinge or something. The door opened easily enough, but when I went inside to look around, it locked behind me. They had to use a blowtorch to get me out."

"What were you doing on the car deck in the first place?"

"Exploring. After I got hold of Tom, I went back to the cabin and you were sawing logs, so what else was I supposed to do? Talk to myself? I thought I'd look around to see if I could find a really cool place to hide a dead body."

"Excuse me?"

"I'm so excited, Emily." She jiggled from head to toe. "Tom said we always lose so many guests on your trips that for my next project, I should write a murder mystery! Isn't that fun? So I was officially doing research. See?" She dragged a travel journal out of her bag and flipped it open. "I even took notes."

Uh-oh. "Jack, about your writing career."

"Do you want to write it with me? Ooo, we could be writing partners! Come on, Emily. The fame. The fortune. And think of the fun we'd have picking out a pen name!"

"I hate to have to tell you this, Jack, but you're going to learn it eventually. I heard on TV a little while ago that Hightower Books has just declared bankruptcy. They've closed up shop and let go all their employees."

Her eyes glazed over. She appeared to stop breathing.

"Jack? I know. It really sucks."

She staggered to the nearest chair and fell into it. "Closed up shop? You mean, no one's there to handle orders? To add sales numbers into the computer? To answer my freaking phone calls?"

Her voice became a wail. I kneaded her shoulder in sympathy. "I bet there are plenty of other houses who'd love to publish a Jackie Thum novel. Don't let this discourage you."

"Discourage me?" She whooped with laughter. "Emily, this is the best news I've had in days! Don't you see? It's not me, it's them. They don't hate me. They're not deliberately ignoring me. They've closed up shop! They're not *there*! It's not about me; it's about them. I'm *so* relieved."

There was one conclusion I could draw about Jack with some authority: She was either the most resilient or the most delusional person I'd ever met. "But . . . what about your book? Your career?"

"Screw the career. I hate deadlines." She unfolded her Hamlets brochure and poked her finger at a glossy picture. "See this building? It's the Hamlets clubhouse. I've decided I want to work there."

"Won't you have to wait about thirty years to meet the age requirement?"

"I don't want to *live* there; I want to work there. A clubhouse like that has to have a director. Don't you think I'd make a crackerjack social director?"

I felt an almost imperceptible jolt as the ship bumped against the quay. "Welcome to Hammerfest," I said, glancing out the window.

"Thanks for the vote of confidence." She flipped the brochure over. "Did you see these pictures of the board of directors? The mini-interviews are very insightful."

"Is there anything about Lauretta Klick?"

"Yup. It lists all the clubs she belongs to, how long she's been on the board, and her proudest accomplishment. She's president of the fox-trot club because she's their best dancer, and vice president of the dominoes club because she's their second-best player. It looks like they have a rule that if you're the best, you get to be president, and if you're second best, you get to be vice president. Portia and Gus were president and vice-president of just about every club, so I predict a major reshuffling of power when everyone gets back."

I scanned the text over her shoulder, curiosity turning to alarm when I reached the end. "Holy crap."

"What?"

"Why didn't Joleen hand these things out sooner!" I grabbed Margi's photos and spread them out over the table. "It was so obvious, nobody picked up on it."

"Picked up on what? Ooo, pictures." She spun one around. "Nice one of Curtis and his camera."

I studied another of the photos, plucking it off the table as I realized what was wrong with it. "Damn! Bernice isn't the only one who bats right-handed. They're going to arrest the wrong people."

I ran from the library and charged around the corner to the main staircase. The stairs were clear, but the lower deck was gridlocked with passengers waiting to exit.

Changing direction, I sprinted up to the promenade deck and pushed through the bulkhead door to the rail that overlooked the gangway. Forklifts were already *hrrrm*ing. Car engines were idling. Passengers were pouring onto the quay in endless numbers.

I spied Nana's white hair in the crowd and George's green-and-white Pioneer Seed cap. They were stepping off the gangway, directly in front of Annika, and behind them was—

"Stop him!" I shouted. "The man in the navy blue jacket! He's a killer!"

Passengers glanced up at me. I heard a rumble of

unease. Footsteps slowing. Heads turning. "Grab him before he gets away!"

A tall man on the perimeter of the crowd caught Curtis by the scruff of his neck. "Not him!" I shouted, doing a double take. *Etienne?* How had he gotten here so fast? "The other guy!" I yelled, pointing frenetically. "Him!"

Etienne tackled Reno and brought him down like a felled tree amid screams and shouts. *Oh, dear.*

"Nana!" I shouted, making a megaphone of my hands. "Vern! It's Vern! He's behind you!"

She pitched her pocketbook to George, dropped into a predatory stance, made a wavy gesture with her hands, and with a banshee cry of "Eeeeyaaaa!" jumped straight up in the air and spun around like a top, smacking her foot into Vern's face. He swayed precariously for a half second before falling flat on his face.

Ouch. That had to hurt.

Jackie came up behind me. "What was that? Another flying drop kick?"

"Spinning roundhouse," I said. "She likes to mix it up."

CHAPTER 17

Two days later, at nine-fifteen in the morning, the atmosphere aboard ship was bubbling over with festivity. Neptune, costumed in flowing robes and wielding a rubber trident, dumped ice cubes down our backs, after which we toasted him with shots of strong liquor and much laughter.

We'd just crossed the Arctic Circle.

Nana handed me a couple of Polaroids of the metal sphere that marked the imaginary latitudinal line. "I seen a globe exactly like this back in sixty-four when your grampa and me took your mother to the world's fair. Only it wasn't perched on no rock in the middle a the ocean. It was in Queens. They called it a unisphere."

We were sitting in the panoramic lounge, with the signs of the zodiac painted like a giant *Wheel of Fortune* on the ceiling above us and ice cubes melting at our feet. "I hope you never part with your camera, Nana. It saved the day."

"You was the one what saved the day, dear. Don't know if I ever woulda noticed Vern catchin' that tube a sunblock with his right hand."

"Everyone made such a big deal about his being a lefty. No one ever noticed he became a righty after he took his pain meds."

"Hard to imagine them pills made his left hand shake so much that he had to learn to write with the other one. I guess that's why his handwritin' never matched up with them samples the police took."

I nodded. "He must have written the note before he took his meds, and given the writing sample *after* taking them. But the pills eased his knee pain, which allowed him to maneuver pain-free for the length of time it took to kill Portia and Gus."

"You s'pose we'll ever know how he done it exactly?"

"Annika says he was extremely uncooperative with the police. He wouldn't give them any details because he said his methods are a military secret that would jeopardize national security if revealed. The only thing he admitted was that if Portia hadn't knocked on his door that night in Helsinki and asked him to escort her to the sauna, none of this would have happened." I shook my head. "Sounds like his defense is going to be that it was all Portia's fault."

"Has anyone figured out how come he didn't leave no fingerprints on that note?"

"Gloves. It came in handy that he'd packed for cold weather."

"You think he was wearin' them gloves when he killed Gus? Is that why there wasn't no marks on his hands?"

"I doubt he needed gloves. Vern's knees were bad, but there was nothing wrong with his upper-body strength. Gus had pretty much gone to seed, so Vern just overpowered him."

"I still can't believe a fella would kill anyone over Scrabble."

"It's all he had left. His knees kept him from cycling, kayaking, horseback riding, and being the cha-cha king. He couldn't even beat the Peabody sisters in a speed drinking contest."

"He lassoed that reindeer real good."

"Yeah, but how many reindeer herders live in Florida? He was accustomed to being the best at everything he did. So when his body started to fail him and he had to become more sedentary, he set his sights on being the Scrabble king."

"But Portia and Gus was better players than him."

"President and vice president of the Scrabble club, according to the brochure, so he needed to take them out so he could be first at something again."

"Knee replacements woulda been smarter."

"He *had* both knees replaced, but he had such a horrible experience, he swore he'd never go through it a second time."

Nana stuffed her photos back into her pocketbook. "He was probably wishin' the world would end so he wouldn't get caught."

"I'm not so sure. I think he was arrogant enough

to assume that if he disappeared in one of the larger ports, like Trondheim, he might never get caught. So it's a good thing we stopped him when we did." I glanced around the lounge. "Have you seen Etienne? Or Jackie?" I frowned. "Or anyone?"

"How 'bout your young man?" Nana continued. "Charterin' a jet instead a flyin' commercial. Isn't that romantic?"

"Expensive," I whispered. "Especially when we have a wedding to pay for."

Nana made eye contact with someone behind me and popped out of her chair, tittering breathlessly. "You gotta come with me," she said, hauling me to my feet.

"Where are we going?"

"You can't ask questions. You just gotta follow me."

She tugged on my hand, guiding me through the upper deck bar area, where Curtis and Lauretta sat side by side on a sofa, studying a sheet of handwritten notes.

"What about August twenty-fourth?" asked Curtis. "It could happen then, right?"

Lauretta shook her head. "I'm leaning more toward October tenth."

"You thought it was going to happen on October tenth *last* year. Or November fifth, or December first, or—"

"Are you fussing at me for being wrong, Curtis Klick? Do you want to be reminded how many times you've been wrong?" She snapped the paper with a flourish. "July twenty-second, nineteen-eighty-two. April twelfth, nineteen-eighty-five. December twenty-fifth, nineteen-eighty-six. Remember that Christmas? We didn't even bother to put up a tree!"

George was waiting for us just inside the door to the sundeck. "All set," he said, handing me a nosegay of daisies and yellow sweetheart roses.

"Why George Farkas, how sweet!" I sniffed the flowers and smiled. "What's the occasion?"

"Can't say. It's a surprise." He cracked the bulkhead door, signaled with his cap, then held the door wide for us as the strains of chamber music floated throughout the stern.

I listened with delight. "Is that the Pachelbel Canon in D?"

"It's four Germans in monkey suits playing violins," said Nana. "There isn't no organ on board, so it was either the Germans or an old guy with a kazoo."

"This is the song I want played at the wedding." I dipped and bobbed my head to the flow of the music. "How do you think it'll sound on an accordion?"

She ushered me past unoccupied chairs along the rail, and when the deck opened up to its full width, I stopped . . . and gasped.

The whole group was here, standing excitedly on both sides of a makeshift aisle, grinning like Cheshire cats. The captain stood at the aft rail in full uniform, flanked by Jackie and Tilly, who wore surprisingly well-coordinated outfits and held nosegays that looked like the centerpieces from the dining salon. Etienne stood off to the side, elegantly European in a black sport coat and turtleneck, his blue eyes locked onto mine with heartstopping intensity.

"Oh, my God, Nana, when did?— How did?—"

"We can make things happen when we gotta. Even Bernice. She bought your flowers, and she didn't even fuss about havin' to pay full price."

"But what about Mom and Dad? My church wedding? My—"

"You can have your church weddin' after Holy Redeemer gets rebuilt. And your mom and dad aren't gonna miss a thing." She nodded to an impressive-looking phone that was propped on a table beside Tilly. "Satellite phone. Compliments of the captain."

"But what about blood tests? A marriage license? International laws governing—"

"Your young man seen to all that," Nana assured me. "He said somethin' about a cousin." She squeezed my hand, tears welling in her eyes. "Ready?"

I brushed a tear from her cheek and hugged her close. "Ready."

To the melodious strains of Johann Pachelbel, Nana escorted me down the aisle. She delivered me onto the arm of Etienne Miceli, who cupped his hands around my face and, in front of all who had gathered to witness this happy occasion, kissed me long and thoroughly.

"The kiss comes *after* the ceremony," I laughed when I came up for air. "You're supposed to wait."

He gave me a steamy look. "On the contrary, *bella*. I've waited long enough." Then to the enthusiastic applause of all on deck, he kissed me again.

Turn the page to enter into the world of

Maddy Hunter

Pasta Imperfect
Hula Done It?
G'Day to Die

Now available
from Pocket Books

PASTA IMPERFECT

"They're gone!" I cried in a semipanic. "How can they be gone? They were here a minute ago. I *saw* them!" The street dead-ended to my right, but to my left, it intersected with a noisy artery of traffic about a block away. I ran to the opposite sidewalk and peered down a long pedestrian walkway that tunneled beneath the main road and emerged on the other side.

Empty.

"Where's the bus?" Jackie called out to me.

Fifty-three people could *not* disappear into thin air! I squinted toward the street, where small, angry cars chased after each other. That had to be where the bus was picking us up. I gestured wildly in that direction and took off at a dead run.

Click click click click. Jackie pulled abreast of me halfway down the street, a throwback to her high school track days when she'd laced herself into running shoes instead of satin corsets. "Emily . . ." she gasped out beside me, "why are we running like this?"

We skidded to a halt at the traffic-jammed street running perpendicular to us. I looked left. I looked right.

No bus. No group. No nothing.

"They've disappeared," I choked out, numb with disbelief. "They were here a minute ago; now they're gone. How is that possible? HOW CAN THEY HAVE VANISHED?"

Jackie dug a tissue out of her bag and mopped her throat, looking curiously left and right. "Gotta be alien abduction. I bet it happens a lot more than people realize."

"I *knew* something like this was going to happen. I *knew*

someone was going to get left behind. But it was supposed to happen to someone else! It wasn't supposed to happen to me!"

Jackie's face lit up. "Female intuition! That is *so* cool. I'm dying to have my first flash of female intuition, but it hasn't kicked in yet. I hope I don't have to wait too long though. I have zero intuition at the moment. It's like being a guy again." She balled her tissue into her fist and regarded me hopefully. "So, now what?"

I was racking my brain to recall what my *Escort's Manual* said about getting lost when I suddenly realized why I couldn't remember. There *was* no section on getting lost. The topic was considered unnecessary because, unlike directionally challenged people in the rest of the civilized world, Iowans didn't *get* lost! Ever!

"Should we call someone or something?" Jackie prodded.

"We should, but . . ." I took a deep breath and spoke in a rush of words. "My address book and phone are in my shoulder bag."

Jackie lowered her head and stared at me over the top of her sunglasses. "Good one, Emily. What about a public phone? Call your cell and when your mom picks up, she can tell you where the group is."

I bobbed my head a little sheepishly. "I uh . . . I didn't memorize the number."

"You WHAT?"

"I said, I DIDN'T MEMORIZE THE NUMBER! Why should I? I wasn't planning on calling myself!"

"Oh, this is lovely. Just *lovely*." Her hand flitted to her face where she massaged her temple with long-suffering fingertips. "Good timing. My female intuition just kicked in, and you know what it's saying? It's warning me that we're going to be wandering around here forever. Like . . . like the Robinson family in outer space!"

"Didn't they eventually get back to earth?"

"Did they? I must have missed that episode."

I checked my watch. "Okay, wherever everyone is, this

was the last stop of the day, so I suggest we just hop into a taxi and meet the bus back at the hotel."

Jackie straightened up, seemingly electrified. "Meet them back at the hotel? Take a taxi? Right. I . . . I hadn't thought of that yet." She opened her arms and crushed me to her chest. "I knew you'd think of something! You're so clever, Emily."

That's what I've always loved about Jack. Consistency. I wiggled out of her embrace and straightened the bodice of the Laura Ashley sundress that fell modestly to my ankles and buttoned up the front—not my usual style, but it had been perfect for traveling eight hours on a plane yesterday. I glanced down the street, wincing at the roar of car engines, the buzz of scooters, the screams of irate drivers. Ireland had been chaotic. Rome was insane. "We need to find a taxi stand."

"We can't just flag one down?"

"Duncan mentioned it's almost impossible to wave down a cab in Rome."

"Why?"

"He didn't say why. He simply said it was."

"We'll see about that." Hips swiveling, chest out, she sashayed toward the street, scanned the lanes of traffic, then without warning, raised her arm in a kind of *Heil Hitler* salute and stepped off the curb into the path of an oncoming car.

"JACK!" I covered my eyes with my hands.

Tires squealed. Rubber burned. Horns blared. Terrified, I inched my fingers apart and took a peek.

Jackie stood before a miniature white car, a sultry smile on her lips, her stilettoed foot perched on the front bumper. But this wasn't just any car. It had a little sign on the roof. It was a taxi!

The driver laid on his horn and yelled something out the window. Jackie motioned me toward the car. "Emily! Will you get *in* before he decides to run me down!"

I opened the door and jumped into the backseat. "*Mal-educato!*" the driver screamed at me, followed by a string of Italian that didn't sound too flattering. A cigarette hung from the corner of his mouth, a half inch of ash threatening to fall off. He wore a slouch cap that sat low on his forehead and a stained white shirt with sleeves rolled to the elbows. His forearms were dark, hairy, and bulged like sacks of seed corn.

"Hi," I countered, offering him a two-fingered wave. "You don't happen to speak English, do you?"

He projected his right fist in the air and slapped his elbow with his left hand—a rather subtle gesture that I took to mean, NO! I caught his eye in the rearview mirror and flashed a conciliatory smile. He glared at me, using his forefinger to slash an imaginary line across his throat from ear to ear. Oh, this was nice. All the taxis in Rome, and we had to get the one driven by Vlad the Impaler.

Jackie scrambled into the backseat and collapsed beside me. "There," she said breathlessly. "That wasn't so hard, was it?"

Not if you were a six-foot transsexual in stiletto heels. The rest of us could have a slight problem.

I gave the driver the name of our hotel in my most precise Italian, then fell backward as he gunned the engine and charged across two lanes of traffic. He drove with one hand on the wheel, one arm out the window, and one eye ogling Jackie in the rearview mirror. He wove left. He wove right. He thrust his head out the window to yell at a passing bus, then outraced a pack of scooters in a competition to be first across a bridge. The G force pinned me to my seat. Scenery sped by in a blur. I realized everything I'd heard about Italian drivers was true. They were rude. They were short-tempered. They ignored speed limits and signs. And considering the lunatic way they maneuvered through the raging disorder in the city streets, they had to be the most skilled drivers in the world.

Jackie angled her head away from the glare of the rearview mirror and whispered behind her hand, "Why is he leering at me like that?"

"He's Italian. I think they're all programmed that way."

"How come he's not leering at you?"

"I'm not wearing white spray paint."

We took a corner on two wheels and shrieked to a stop in front of a building with curved ironwork fronting the second-story balconies and lots of black window shutters. "Albergo Villa Bandoccio Maccio D'Angelo," the driver announced with an emphatic wave of his hand.

I peeked at the building through the car window. I sidled an uneasy look at Jackie. "Do you remember balconies on our hotel?"

"Nope."

"This is the wrong hotel, isn't it?"

"Yup."

EH! "Excuse me." I tapped the driver politely on the arm and enunciated slowly so he could understand me. "Is there another hotel by this name somewhere else in Rome? This isn't where we're staying."

"Albergo Villa Bandoccio Maccio D'Angelo," he repeated, pounding a hand on the meter to indicate the fare owed him.

"I can *see* what the name of the hotel is," I fired back. "The problem is, WE DON'T HAVE A RESERVATION HERE!"

HULA DONE IT?

The *Aloha Princess* boasted thirteen decks, three swimming pools, two five-star restaurants, a miniature golf course, a climbing wall, a world-class fitness center, an exotic spa, and thirty-two kinds of ice cream—but nowhere within its luxurious chrome-and-glass interior was there a blue M&M to be found. Striking out at the Coconut Palms Cafe, we ventured to the casino on deck six, where we ran into the rest of the scavenger-hunting Iowa contingent, their voices raised in complaint as they brandished their lists.

"They don't have vending machines on this boat," whined Bernice Zwerg in a voice that scratched like coarse-grade steel wool. "How are we supposed to get our hands on those over-priced packets of M&M's without vending machines?" Bernice had undergone emergency bunion surgery on both feet last June, but she'd bounced back in time to book a last-minute reservation on our cruise. Lucky me.

We were gathered near the front of the casino, opposite the glassed-in cashiers' windows, where a coin-counting machine rattled like a faulty race-car engine. Reflective disco balls hung from the ceiling. Slot machines hunkered in military formation on the floor. Gaming tables flanked the perimeter. Digital sound effects rang out like a chorus of off-key kazoos, joined by the hoots, hollers, screams, and laughter of the casino's patrons.

"Did anyone try the General Store on deck five?" asked Dick Teig, hitching up the belt of his size 52 waist Italian knit trousers. I'd discovered a killer in Italy; Dick had discovered couture. "They should have M&M's in the candy section."

"Osmond and I checked," announced Alice Tjarks in her KORN radio voice. "All they have is Skittles." She waved into the lens of Osmond Chelsvig's camcorder, then gave him a big 'I'm on vacation' smile.

"Skittles?" crowed Helen Teig, Dick's wife. "I love Skittles. Did you buy any?"

"At three dollars a bag?" Alice shot back. "Who's got money like that?"

"I do," said Nana. Nana had won millions in the Minnesota lottery, so she had money to burn. "But I'd rather spend it on them midget Tootsie Rolls. The fresh ones don't even stick to my dentures."

Ding ding ding ding ding. A victorious shriek echoed out from the depths of the casino.

Helen Teig rubbed her eye, accidentally wiping her left eyebrow off her face. "So what else are we missing besides M&M's?"

Lucille Rassmuson raised her hand. "I can't find a balloon. I even checked the florist shop. They don't do balloons, only flowers."

"I found a balloon!" enthused Margi Swanson. This was Margi's first trip with us. She worked part-time as an RN at the medical clinic in Windsor City, but she said she was reaching the age where she needed to start spending some of the money she'd spent a lifetime earning. She'd recently lost seventy-five pounds on the "Eat Everything in Sight and Still Lose Weight" diet, so as a reward to herself, she'd signed up for the cruise.

"Did anyone find a rock?" asked Osmond as he adjusted one of his double hearing aids.

"I did," said Bernice, pulling it out of her *Aloha Princess* tote. "In the spa. There was a whole bunch in one of the rooms I toured, so I borrowed one."

A cocktail waitress with a tray of tall, icy beverages skirted around us, offering free drinks to the people camped before the dollar slots.

"Which way is the spa?" asked Lucille.

"That way," said Bernice, pointing right.

"That way," said Dick Teig, pointing left.

"Three decks up," attested Alice.

"One deck down," corrected Margi.

Uff da. What was happening here? Iowans never got lost. Ever. Since the beginning of time, no Iowan had even taken a wrong turn! The fact that no one knew how to get anywhere revealed an incredible phenomenon: Everyone's natural directional system apparently stopped functioning near large bodies of water. Either that, or the new souped-up metal detectors at the Des Moines airport had caused the first incidence of group dementia ever recorded.

"Show of hands," Osmond shouted. When there was a vote to be taken, eighty-eight-year-old Osmond always did the honors. "How many of you found a paper clip?" All hands went up. "A map without advertising?" Five hands went up. "An eraser?" Nine hands went up.

"Mine's attached to a number two pencil," confessed Margi. "That won't get me disqualified, will it?"

Ding ding ding ding ding.

Seated on a high stool before a shiny one-armed bandit behind us, Grace Stolee let out a scream and pointed to the circular white light atop her machine. If the *dings* and flashing indicated a winning jackpot, Grace had just hit it big.

"Don't move!" instructed her husband as he leaped off an adjacent stool and aimed his camcorder at her. "This is Grace winning a big jackpot aboard the *Aloha Princess.*" He shot a close-up of the coins pouring into her tray. "Quarters." He panned higher. "Flashing light." Then lower. "Three winning sevens." Dick Stolee kind of had a thing for stating the obvious.

"What's the payout, Grace?" he asked, zeroing in on the payoff chart below the window.

Osmond Chelsvig abandoned the group to film Dick Stolee filming Grace. Alice Tjarks dug her camcorder out of her tote and positioned herself to film Osmond, filming

Dick, filming Grace. What *was* it with these guys and the infinity shots?

Grace stabbed her finger at the payoff chart. "Three sevens, three quarters, that's—" She screamed again. "TWENTY THOUSAND QUARTERS!"

"How much is that in real money?" asked Dick Teig.

Inhaling a calming breath, I headed out the door, with Nana and Tilly hot on my heels. "Where to, ladies?" I asked, digging a floor plan of the ship out of my shoulder bag. "A spin around the Promenade deck, which is . . . let's see . . . one deck down? Or would you prefer a round of miniature golf on the putting green on deck thirteen?"

"I've never played miniature golf," Tilly admitted. "The closest I've come to it is playing croquet with a tribe of Pygmies in the Andaman Islands."

"I'd like to hit the spa and borrow a rock like Bernice done," Nana said. "And while I'm there, I'm gonna sign up for one a them Ionithermie treatments. It costs a hundred and twenty dollars, but the flyer promises you can lose up to eight inches a ugly cellulite in the first session. And it's not real complicated. They plaster you in seaweed and wire you up like the Frankenstein monster, and that detoxifies your fat cells and firms you up real good."

"I underwent a similar ritual in New Guinea," Tilly recalled, as we approached the elevator. "Only they plastered me in jungle foliage instead of sea vegetation, and I wasn't sure if their goal was to cleanse me or eat me. Cannibals are oftentimes quite hard to read."

When the door to the elevator slid open, we stepped into a cylindrical glass tube that overlooked the atrium at the center of the ship—a huge column of open space between decks four and eleven that was rimmed by tiers of balconies and overhung by a crystal chandelier that looked like a giant upside-down sno-cone. I punched the button for deck eleven then clung to the safety rail as we glided upward on the barest whisper of air.

"I'll be," Nana marveled, her nose pressed to the elevator glass. "This is like bein' inside a hypodermic needle."

I looked down at the elegant champagne bar on deck four, where a staircase of illuminated acrylic risers spiraled toward the next floor. That would be the perfect place to have the group pose for pictures on Halloween night, when we were all expected to dress in costume for the masquerade gala. I hadn't decided on a costume yet, but I figured I could rent one at the clothing shop on deck five. They were supposed to have a good selection in a variety of sizes.

"It's breathtaking, isn't it?" mused Tilly, as we peered outward through the ship's glass walls. The gleaming waters of the Pacific Ocean appeared calm as bathwater. There was no land in sight, only blue sky and open sea. "Balboa first named this ocean the South Sea, but Magellan changed the name to the Pacific, no doubt for the calm waters that greeted him after a harrowing passage around the tip of South America. Can you feel the stillness, ladies? The wonderful calm? This must be the same calm that Magellan felt."

A bell *pinged*. The elevator door *shushed* open.

"MAN OVERBOARD!" shrieked a woman as she banged through the door from the outside deck. "Man overboard! Help me! Somebody help me! PLEASE!"

G'DAY TO DIE

A gust of wind whistled through the room as our guide banged through the main entrance, his navy blue uniform putting him in danger of being mistaken for a United States Postal Service worker. His name was Henry, and in addition to narrating our travelogue, he drove the bus, prepared and served midmorning tea and cakes, directed us to the restrooms, counted heads, snapped guest photos, maintained our vehicle, treated minor injuries, exchanged currency, and could belt out a rendition of "Waltzing Matilda" that made your teeth vibrate. I was dying to see what he'd do for an encore.

"If I can trouble you for your attintion!" he called out. "I apologize to those of you waiting to board the Aussie Advintures bus, but one of our tires has blown, so I'm waiting on a mechanic from Port Campbell for assistance. No worries, though; we'll only be delayed an hour or two. Sorry for the inconvenience."

Groans. Hissing. "What are we supposed to do for two hours?" a disgruntled guest yelled.

"Introduce yoursilf to your mates!" Henry suggested. "You're in this for two weeks togither. Give it a go."

Battening my hair down with a bandanna, I signaled Etienne and Duncan that I had to leave, then exited the building, bracing myself against the brutal force of the wind.

Interrupted by the sudden clatter of footsteps behind me, I turned to find Guy Madelyn hiking my way. "The wind's a pain," he called out, his shirttails flapping around him, "but at least it keeps the flies from tunneling up your nose." He paused beside me and nodded seaward. "Did you know that if you leaped off this cliff and started swimming south, you wouldn't run into another landmass until you reached Antarctica?"

"Assuming you leaped at high tide."

He raised his forefinger in a "Eureka!" kind of gesture. "Timing is everything. I'm sorry, I didn't catch your name in the visitor's center."

"Emily Andrew. You want to hire my grandmother as your new crack photographer."

"Mrs. Sippel is your grandmother? She has some fine photographic genes. Did she pass them on to you?"

"I got the shoe and makeup genes." I regarded him soberly as he opened the lens of his camera. "Were you serious about wanting to hire Nana?"

"I'll say! And I'd like to sign her up before the competition finds out about her." He scanned the horizon through his viewfinder before motioning me toward the guardrail. "Could I get a shot of you with the great Southern Ocean as a backdrop? I don't charge for my services when I'm on holiday."

Was I about to be discovered? Oh, wow. I might not have made it as an actress, but could Guy Madelyn transform me into a cover model?

I struck a pose against the guardrail and emoted like a *Sports Illustrated* swimsuit model. Sexy. Sultry. Windblown.

"Can you open your eyes?"

I tried again. Sexy. Surprised. Windblown.

"Maybe we should try this from one of the lookout points. We're getting too much light here."

Which I interpreted to mean, it was a good thing I was otherwise employed, because I had no future as a cover model.

"So you're not here to shoot a wedding?" I asked as I walked double time to keep up with his long strides.

"Family reunion. It seems the Madelyn side of my family played as important a role in Australian history as the *Mayflower* passengers played in American history, so when my wife and kids fly out from Vancouver in a couple of weeks, we're planning to meet all the Aussie relatives for the first time. The kids are really fired up, which is remarkable since they're at the age where nothing impresses them. But I think they're finding the idea of celebrity status for a few days 'way cool.'"

"Because they're related to a famous photographer?"

He laughed. "Because the town is planning to honor us with an award to recognize the contribution my ancestors made toward populating this part of Victoria. We've dubbed it the Breeder's Cup. The kids figure we'll be the only family in British Columbia with a commemorative plaque for inveterate shagging, so that gives them bragging rights. Kids, eh?"

Noticing a discarded candy wrapper littering the wayside, I ducked beneath the guardrail to pick it up, frowning when I realized what I was holding. "This is one of Nana's photos. What's it doing out here?" It was bent, and a little scratched, but in good shape otherwise. I showed it to Guy, who threw a curious look around us.

"I was positive all your grandmother's photos found their way back to her. People can be so damned careless. I hope this is the only one she's missing."

"Dumb luck that I found it." I slipped it into my shoulder bag for safekeeping. "So, where did your ancestors emigrate from? England?" I knew everyone in Australia was an import, except for the Aborigines, who'd been roaming the continent for either four centuries or sixty thousand years, depending upon which scholarly study you wanted to believe. Yup. The scientific community had really nailed that one.

"Portsmouth. They set sail in the early eighteen hundreds on a ship called the *Meridia,* and fifteen thousand miles later wrecked on a submerged reef along this very coast. My relatives were among the lucky few who survived." He bobbed his head toward the open sea. "Look at all that water. If you took it away, do you know what you'd find? Sunken vessels. Over twelve hundred of them. More than anywhere else on earth. This whole place is a graveyard, which hammers home a very salient point."

"What's that?"

"Air travel is a wonderful thing."

We followed the walkway through a stand of trees that were as stunted and gnarled as Halloween ghouls, then descended a short flight of stairs to a lower level with sweeping views of the deeply scalloped coastline and the thundering—

Guy suddenly ducked beneath the guardrail and charged through the underbrush, heading straight for the cliff's edge. Eh! Were Iowans the only people who ever observed the rules?

"What are you doing?" I screamed after him. "Didn't you read the signs? You're supposed to stay on the walkway!"

He dropped to his knees twenty feet away and rolled something over.

Oh, God. It was a body.